To my oldest friend
Dean Long.

A truly gentle man, who was taken from us far
too early.

Minos Rising

Contents

Chapter 1

"Why the fuck are you making me do this?"

Barry's face, scarlet with rage, was only a few inches from Rachel's.

She froze.

As he bellowed at her, she could feel his breath, thick with the sickeningly familiar peaty odour of expensive whisky.

"I just want things to be right when I get home! Is that too much to ask?"

Standing a little under five foot six, Barry had a stocky well-muscled physique, sharply toned by many hours spent in the local gym. His neatly trimmed black beard and hair had been recently dyed to erase those first hints of grey.

You would have been forgiven for thinking that Rachel was shorter than her fiancé, not two inches taller. A hunched posture, lowered head and unkempt long blonde hair pulled across her pale features obscured her height advantage.

As he sneered down at her, the muffled sound of seventies disco music began to pound out from the flat directly above.

In response, Barry bellowed up at the ceiling: "Old bitch, if you don't turn that down I'll come up there and do you one." A chill worked its way down Rachel's spine. In that moment, as he yelled up at the yellowing plaster ceiling, Barry looked like a feral animal. He was the predatory beast howling at the sky, letting his prey know trouble was coming and that he intended to rip it apart.

Barry lowered his gaze from the ceiling and menacingly muttered, "One day she's gonna get hers." With a violent motion he snapped his head back towards Rachel, his saliva splattering against his cheek as he bellowed, "What the fuck are you looking at? I haven't forgotten about you!"

In a well-practiced act of subservience, Rachel dropped her gaze down towards the apartment's cheap, brown carpet. As her fiancé continued to rage, she focused her attention on a mottled patch at her feet.

Beneath the tired nylon weave, black mould grew relentlessly. It would already be eating away at the carpet's rubber backing. Soon its spores would appear on the surface. Rachel pondered that if she stood here long enough perhaps those spores would begin to spread up her own feet, perhaps work their way...

The pain... the pain of the slap was familiar to her but the brutal force behind the attack, driving her to her knees, that was a new and terrifyingly unexpected experience.

Rachel clasped her face reflexively against the intense pain and let out a stifled sob. Barry hesitated; for a moment, she thought he would lash out at her again. Finally, he stepped forward, placed a gentle hand on her shoulder, bent down beside her and whispered, "Look, baby, you know I don't like to do this, but it's for your own good. You got to learn to be better and all will be good for us."

He paused.

Rachel could feel the hand that still rested on her shoulder begin to tense. "Look Rach, I see you're trying. I won't hit you again, I promise, Babs."

The placating words had been delivered with his usual half-hearted soothing tones. This time there was the addition of cold contempt to his voice. The delivery of the nickname Babs that had been so endearing when they started going out together now felt like he was addressing his pet dog.

"Listen Babs, I'm gonna head over to the Bucks Head and grab a couple of pints with Max. You be good and get dinner ready. We won't mention what you did wrong, that's a good girl." He stood up and patted her on the head, as if she was an obedient Labrador.

Still on her knees, Rachel nodded mutely in response.

She worked her jaw left and right, carefully checking for lasting damage from Barry's strike. Apart from the lingering pain of the slap, she was relieved to have suffered no serious consequences.

"Laters," he cheerfully called out as he closed the front door, his voice now all but devoid of the previous malice and fury.

The familiar sound of two sturdy deadlocks engaging as he double locked the door were barely audible over Katherine's disco music tracks.

Rachel was alone.

A little voice within her urged her to stand. She had better get a move on and get dinner ready. She did not want to make him angry again. She didn't want to make him lose his temper again. She didn't want to be punished again.

The resurgent stinging pain in her face interrupted what she had come to call her inner voice of anxiety. Rachel recalled, with concern, the force of the blow Barry had landed. A little stronger and he might have broken her jaw. Would that be the punishment to be dished out next time?

Her anxiety chipped in. 'If we behave, if we keep him happy, there won't be a next time!'

Rachel knew that wasn't true.

She had spent the last four years of their five years together convincing herself that she could change him. That she could change for him. That things would get better.

Instead, they steadily deteriorated.

She needed to escape, she needed to be free. 'Where can we go? We do not have any friends, we don't have any money and the door is locked!' cried out her anxiety voice.

That was all true.

Rachel had been in London a little over six months when she had gone to a party thrown by her work colleague, Hannah. Barry came along as a friend of a friend. They met in the kitchen and she felt an immediate spark. He listened intently to every word, laughed at her jokes, and appeared fascinated when she talked about her high-powered work.

As they drank wine, conversed and danced, Rachel felt a real connection with this mysterious man. At the party's end, they had exchanged mobile numbers. Five days then passed without a word from him, so Rachel sent a text suggesting they meet up for a drink.

How could she have known that she had stepped onto the edge of his carefully spun web of entrapment?

After several months of dating, Barry broke the news that he would have to move back home to Brighton. His lease had expired on his flat in Clapham and he had not found anywhere else he could afford. His plan? To go back to his parents' place and commute daily into London. Obviously, he would see a lot less of her, but he hoped they could make a distance relationship work. Rachel gave it some thought and decided to invite him to move into her garden flat in Maida Vale.

During the next few months, their love blossomed. It eventually peaked when he proposed to her on a rowboat as they drifted through Little Venice. She said yes, and they were engaged.

Little did she realise how firmly she was entangled in his web.

Barry had already begun to isolate Rachel from her friends and family. He meticulously engineered situations of conflict, arguments and issues. On each occasion, she would find herself having to side either with them or her beloved fiancé.

She always sided with the man she loved.

They tried to warn her about him: how he manipulated her, cut her off. But each time, Barry had been so happy with her choice and the love he showered on her vindicated and reinforced her decisions.

Next, he convinced her to give up her career. They would soon want to think about a starting a family together, he explained. Rachel hesitated. She had uprooted from Manchester and came to London to pursue her dream job. Rachel had prospered and proved to be - as her boss called her - a rising star. Promotion had already been discussed, so did she want to lose that dream?

After a few months of careful manipulation, Barry finally convinced her that it was the logical development of their relationship. If Rachel absolutely loved him as much as he did her, she would see it was the right thing to do.

The following week she quit.

A month later, Barry arrived home from work early. He explained that, since they could not afford to live in Maida Vale anymore, he had rented them a fifth-floor apartment on the eastern edge of Camden Town. Within two days, they moved out. He ensured that they did not leave a forwarding address.

One year after she met Barry, Rachel realised that all of her friends, her family, her work, her money, her independence - in fact, everything that was not directly controlled by Barry - had been taken from her.

She was alone, trapped in the centre of his web.

The thumping music from the flat above stopped. When Rachel and Barry had first moved into their cramped flat, Katherine invited them upstairs for a cup of tea and a chat. In her late sixties, she kept her modest apartment in good condition.

Katherine told them how she met her late husband Ron on the dance floor of a Soho night club. According to her, it had been "love at first dance". They continued dancing from the 1970s up until his tragic death six years ago. A speeding driver struck Ron as he crossed a pedestrian crossing outside Kings Cross Station, the impact hurling him over twenty feet across the road. They never caught the driver. There had been tears in the old lady's eyes as she sighed, "My favourite memories of Ron are of us disco dancing."

Secretly, when Barry went out, Katherine would come down and knock on the secured door, checking if she needed anything from the shops. That tenuous lifeline of human kindness proved to be a godsend.

Last year, as punishment for walking in front of the TV during a darts game, Barry had forbidden her food for four days. Each evening he brought home a takeaway meal and forced her to watch him finish it off. He would have been incandescent with rage had he known that each day Katherine lowered a bag of desperately needed supplies from her living room window into Rachel's grateful arms.

Her anxiety voice began to plead, 'Get up. Start cooking. Let us not get him angry.' She ignored it, stood up and walked to the living room window.

The rush hour cars, taxis and buses were slowly transporting their occupants along Camden Road towards various destinations. To her left, a train clattered over the railway bridge having disgorged its passengers into Camden Road Station. Soon they would appear on the pavement to join other commuters, shoppers, children, buskers, dog walkers, joggers; each of them fighting for their own bit of space, each of them trying to move forward a little quicker.

Rachel felt gripped by the desire to be one of those pedestrians. To enjoy the freedom of being swept along by the crowd. To be free to stop and go as she desired. To be able to look in a shop window, admire the fancy clothes, perhaps go in and waste some money on a pair of red stilettos.

'Oh, really,' her anxiety voice scolded her. 'You know that Barry thinks those things are slutty; you know what he likes you to wear and anyway you don't have any money, so stop fooling yourself. Now let us start dinner before it's too late.' Rachel continued to ignore the pleading voice and watched the street below.

The commuters now emerged from the railway station entrance and Rachel mused about how wonderful it would be if one of them were to look up at the apartment window. Perhaps it would be a bored child waiting for its mother to finish her telephone call. Rachel would wave at the young kid; they would enthusiastically wave back. They would exchange smiles. It would be an innocent moment of connection with another living soul.

No one looked up.

No one ever looked up.

She was alone.

The force of the slap that Barry had inflicted on her was a rude wake-up call. How long would it be before he hit her that hard again? Next time would he show less restraint? Would he break something or perhaps worse?

In that moment Rachel resolved that she had to escape the hell that she was trapped in.

Once again, her little voice pointed out the flaw in her reasoning. 'Escape? Are you a master locksmith or an accomplished cat burglar? How are you going to get out through the apartment's double-locked front door without a key?'

Ignoring the voice, Rachel walked over to the window and recovered the spare widow key she had carefully secreted under the wilted Busy Lizzie plant pot. Unlocking the window, she swung it open allowing the noise of the road below to flood into the apartment.

It was five storeys down to the pavement. She thought it would be all over pretty much instantaneously. A quick end to her worthless existence. A final acknowledgement that she had failed to live up to Barry's expectations. Her anxiety voice fell silent, perhaps stunned by the revelation of Rachel's terminal escape plan.

Her dark thoughts were interrupted as a large bag, suspended on a piece of string, dropped into view. An unexpected gift from Katherine? Rachel leaned forward and pulled it into the living room. For a moment she considered climbing out of the window and completing her final escape plan but curiosity as to the contents of the bag won out for now.

To her surprise, the bag contained a crowbar. Painted with shiny black enamel and nearly three feet long, it felt sturdy and remarkably heavy. Attached to the bar by a piece of string, a simple, brown cardboard label. Upon this had been penned the message 'Use Me!'

Turning her back on the street below, Rachel ran the short distance to the apartment's front door. Her pulse began to race. It had been more than two years since she last passed through this portal. Two years of hiding away. Two years of being under the complete control of Barry.

"No more!" she shouted out.

Her anxiety voice chimed in, 'Better be quick about this, Barry will not be happy if he finds us breaking out through his precious door.'

She grunted and drove the wedge end of the crowbar into the gap beneath a door hinge. With increasing ferocity Rachel began to heave on the bar.

The wood gave a satisfying creak. Encouraged, she channelled her growing rage through that black enamelled bar. With each heave on the bar, she yelled out another heart-rending regret, to be rewarded with the sound of splintering wood.

"Five years of my life lost."

"Friends and family lost."

"Freedom surrendered."

"My dignity removed."

"And...all...done...by...that...bastard... Barry!"

In her final pull, she focussed all of her pent-up frustrations and disappointments and wrenched the door from its hinges with a thunderous crash. It toppled forward revealing the bare concrete hallway beyond. A single light illuminated the barren corridor and the stairway down that led to freedom.

Like a warrior of old after slaying a terrible beast, Rachel panted, triumphantly brandishing the crowbar over her head as she stood astride the now-fallen obstacle.

The door to flat 52 momentarily opened and an indistinguishable face peered out at the unusual scene. The door quickly slammed shut. Probably to make a call to the police.

Dropping the crowbar, Rachel ran towards the stairs and gingerly started down the concrete steps. It had, of course, been years since she walked down a staircase. Fearing that the police might soon arrive to deliver her back into the fateful grasp of Barry, she picked up her pace, bounding down two steps at a time.

As she reached the final flight of steps, her enthusiasm and rusty co-ordination proved too much to handle. Rachel missed her footing and tumbled head over heels down the final seven steps, her left ankle buckling beneath her as she slammed face first into the unforgiving concrete floor.

She was once again her six-year-old self, living in the town of Chadderton, to the northeast of Manchester. Rachel, a precocious young girl, had been desperate to learn to ride a proper bike, constantly pestering her mum and dad to teach her.

At her mother's insistence, her father agreed to do so and, on a hot Sunday afternoon, he took her to Chadderton Hall Park. As he taught her to ride, he constantly urged her to take it slowly, to be careful.

Rachel hadn't been interested in slow progression; as soon as she mastered the rudimentary skills, the young girl had been off, racing along the park's narrow pathways, embracing her newfound ability.

Unfortunately, her understanding of the use of bicycle brakes proved less comprehensive than that of pedalling furiously. This imbalance in her skill set eventually resulted in her going over the handlebars and crashing face first into the path.

Her father, a man born and bred in Chadderton, strode up to the young girl, who now sat sobbing at her unfortunate turn of fortune, and exclaimed, "That'll teach you for not doing what you're told!" He picked both her and the bike up and carried them home.

Her mum had fussed over her baby girl and quickly treated the cuts and bruises with copious amounts of ointment and plasters, whilst berating her father for not taking proper care of her. As the childhood memory receded, Rachel flicked open her eyes and stared along the concrete floor towards the flats' main entrance. Through the glass-fronted door, she could again see the outside world.

She had no idea how long she had lain unconscious on the concrete. She considered herself lucky that no one had stumbled upon her lying there.

Rachel gathered her resolve and fought the tears of pain back down: no-one here to pick her up whilst she sobbed, no-one to tend to her wounds as she cried in pain. If she were going to escape, it would have to be done on her own.

Having satisfied herself that apart from a bleeding lip and probable black eye there were no other substantial injuries, she grabbed the metal banister and carefully hauled herself up onto her feet.

Her attention was caught by the sudden sound of the door buzzer. She peered along the corridor. Through the glass pane she could see two police officers, leaning forward and talking into the flats' intercom box.

The police would help her - of that she had no doubt. But they would contact Barry. He would carefully spin his web of lies. Weaving his charms on the police, the doctors and social workers, beguiling them into believing that all was well. His silken untruths would relentlessly drag her back into that smothering prison on the fifth floor.

With Rachel once again trapped in his web, he would wait, biding his time. Only when all the furore she had caused had calmed down, only when no one was watching, only then would Barry punish her for this disobedience.

She could not risk it, she had to evade the officers.

Desperately, Rachel looked for somewhere to hide, but there was no cover to be found in the spartanly furnished corridor. Only the dimly lit open space beside the stairwell provided scant refuge. With little choice, Rachel hobbled into the stairwell, leant against the wall and tried to make herself look as small and inconspicuous as possible.

The jarring sound of the front door being buzzed open echoed menacingly down the corridor. Grumbling voices could be heard as the officers approached. "Typical. It would be the fifth floor. Why don't these places have lifts?" They walked along the corridor to the foot of the staircase and began to climb upwards.

Rachel held her breath and did not move. Despite being less than six feet away, the policemen failed to see her. They continued their laborious climb up the stairs whilst discussing the spate of violent burglaries that had been plaguing the Camden area, one of them wondering if this new incident was related.

As soon as Rachel thought they were out of earshot she allowed herself to breathe and emerged from her position of limited, yet surprisingly effective, cover. Using the wall for support, she hobbled along the corridor towards the front door.

At the threshold of freedom, she paused and peered through the glass pane. Outside, pedestrians, cars and buses were going about their usual business, unaware of the drama that had unfolded within this nondescript building.

Feebly, her anxiety voice attempted one last pitiful plea, 'Go back,' it begged. 'Tell Barry you're sorry. Beg Barry's forgiveness. Barry will understand. Barry will protect us. Barry might not punish us too severely if...' The voice in her head faded away as she flung open the door and stepped out onto the pavement of Camden Road.

For the first time in an exceedingly long time, she felt like herself again. Rachel Minos, ready to face whatever life was going to throw at her.

She could never have suspected the reality of the journey she was about to embark upon.

Chapter 2

The dress was a magnificent black waterfall of elegant beauty. It cascaded down from the mannequin's shoulders, parting across the chest to reveal a daring, plunging neckline. The perfect location to display a piece of eye-catching bling. Rachel's eye was drawn further downwards, following the contours of exaggerated curves that the dress sensually hugged. Finally, just below the hip, the black flow was sharply sliced open, falling loosely on each side of the provocatively posed plastic leg.

Her wardrobe had boasted similar sartorial masterpieces, capable of turning any head when she entered a room. To Rachel they had been her silky suits of armour, providing a confidence boost that humdrum clothes never seemed able to. On top of that, she had looked just bloody amazing in them.

There were distant memories of preparing herself for extravagant work events. Much as a knight would prepare himself on the eve of battle, Rachel had much to do to ensure she was ready to make an entrance.

Top of the to do list had been the visit to the stylist who lavished care and attention on her blonde locks. As he worked his creative magic, she drank prosecco and read magazines trumpeting the exotic lifestyles of the rich and famous.

That stylist would have thrown his combs to the floor in despair and stormed off in search of a skinny latte if confronted by the long, lifeless mane that hung limply from her head.

Her eyes refocussed on the shop window and her own pitiful reflection. The hunched figure staring back was dressed in a plain brown tee-shirt, grey hoody and jeans. 'He' had allowed her to keep a couple of those magnificent dresses, securely locking them away, only to be worn when he wanted her to. Transforming them from liberating garments into symbols of her subservience.

Unconsciously she had stopped using Barry's name. Rachel realised instinctively that there was a power in names and perhaps refusing to acknowledge Barry was another step in exorcising his grip upon her.

Earlier, having escaped the apartment, Rachel had turned left and drifted along the pavement towards Camden Tube Station. She had no idea why she chose left, it just felt like the correct direction to go.

After so long in near isolation, she struggled with the waves of humanity that streamed around her. Dressed in heavy winter outfits, they drove forward with the determination and bloody-mindedness that all big city commuters rapidly develop. Push in or be pushed out. Cut in or be cut out. Hesitate and be left standing. It is a cutthroat environment and those without the mettle to seize the day will be getting home late tonight.

Struggling onwards, she reached Bayham Street, which thankfully had fewer walking warriors surging along it. Choosing the path of least resistance, she decided to follow it south. There was no destination. There was no plan. The only driving force was to put as much distance as possible between herself and that hellish apartment.

The drizzle of a winter rain had begun to fill the air. Her anxiety voice, silent since leaving the apartment, sulkily piped up. 'You clearly haven't thought this through. We are hardly dressed for a sojourn through London in winter. Let's go back. We can say there was a burglary. The police said there had been a spate in the area. We ran away from the burglars but returned when they had gone. He will see we are a good little Babs. He will see that we were well behaved. Perhaps he won't...'

"Shut the fuck up!" shouted Rachel.

Her sudden, violent outburst drew nothing more than a few disapproving head shakes and tuts from jaded passers-by. She pulled the grey hood over her head and pressed on.

The bright light of the clothing shop front on the corner of Greenland

Street had caught her attention. Like a moth drawn to a flame she moved towards it. Crossing the road, dodging between the heavy traffic, Rachel soon found herself staring longingly through the shop window, lusting after the exquisite black dress and the lost life that it represented.

A movement inside the shop drew her attention. Two bored-looking assistants were standing by the counter, waiting for seven o'clock to arrive so they could shut up for the day.

The younger was in her late teens, perhaps early twenties. Dressed in designer jeans laced with rhinestones, she wore an expensive-looking matching tee-shirt; short, spikey peroxide blonde hair framed a face plastered with generous amounts of make-up. Her gaze was fixated on a mobile phone, as she binged on the never-ending feed of social media posts.

The second assistant was older, probably early forties. She wore a plain white silk blouse and a classic black pencil skirt. Rachel - somewhat cattily - thought that the jet-black hair, clinically cut into a perfect bob, was probably a wig.

Wig Lady's eyes were rigidly fixed on Rachel. She bore the concerned look of a gardener watching the stray dog that had wandered into the centre of her pristine lawn and looked about ready take a dump.

She stepped forward and ineffectually waved her left hand several times in a shooing motion. When Rachel didn't immediately respond, the shop assistant employed both hands in a broader waving motion and shouted, "Go away, you junkie, or I'll call the police."

Rachel backed away from the window. She took one last, longing look at the black dress, the melancholy reminder of much better times, then resumed her journey south along Bayham Street.

The drizzle began to thicken into light rain. The cold droplets soaked into the hoody's thin material. From her right, obscured from view by houses, came the deep rumbling and squealing of metal wheels on steel rails. It was the sound of trains arriving and departing Euston Station. Those long metal beasts would be whisking people to destinations afar or bringing others into the beating heart of the city.

Rachel's thoughts drifted back to the time she had first arrived at Euston. Annoyingly, the train on that day had been fifteen minutes late. Desperate not miss her interview, Rachel splashed out on a black cab to whisk her across London to Saint James's Square.

In her best tailored business suit, she confidently strode across the threshold of Sheol Publicity. Rachel had been taken aback when, without a word being uttered, the receptionist had known who she was. A concierge then escorted Rachel to the plush waiting room and, after enquiring about her journey from Manchester, provided Rachel with a richly aromatic cup of Black Ivory coffee.

The office's décor, the staff, the general ambience: all had been carefully crafted to provide the observer with the image of power. It was an impression that Sheol Publicity certainly lived up to, given its enviable performance record and remarkable roster of A-List clients.

It was a week ago to the day that the head-hunter had called her. Rachel had been surprised that Sheol wanted to interview someone like her. Sure, she had done good work at the small Manchester PR firm where she worked. But had that really been enough to get her noticed by the grandee of PR companies?

Deep down, she still expected someone to appear and apologise for the confusion. They would explain that there had been a mix-up and that she was the wrong candidate, but they would graciously allow her to apply for the cleaner's role instead.

Proudly displayed on the wall opposite her seat was a pastiche of Da Vinci's 'The Last Supper'. The figure of Jesus had been replaced by the company founder and Chairman, John Viath, and each of the apostles were substituted with the company's senior executives. In the foreground, the artist had cheekily replaced the supper with bottles of Boërl & Kroff Brut and cans of Strottarga Bianco caviar.

Rachel couldn't help but smile at the absurdly self-indulgent pomposity of it all.

The interview with John Viath proceeded far better than she could have dreamed. She had spent weeks preparing, memorising all the key achievements that might help sway their decision. It had certainly gone well, as Mr Viath was brimming with enthusiasm about getting her on board. He had been relentless on selling her the idea of becoming part of the Sheol Publicity family.

As the interview concluded, he stunned Rachel by making her the immediate offer of a role. She would be a Senior Creative Executive, taking on a portfolio of influential clients. Rachel, perhaps intoxicated by the emotion of the moment, had surprised herself by immediately accepting.

"Oi luv, hang on!" The coarse voice shouting at her snapped Rachel back to the present as a large black Mercedes pulled up next to her. In the passenger seat, a young man - pale skinned with a number one haircut and a prominent scar on his left cheek - was leaning out and flashing an unpleasantly salacious smile in Rachel's direction.

"You look cold and miserable; bet you'd love the Cobain seat." asked the passenger. Rachel, having no idea what she was being asked, could only respond with a dumfounded 'what?'.

The driver, a similarly aged Asian man, sported a neat, short-cropped beard and thick hair pulled into a man bun. Unlike his passenger, he barely glanced in Rachel's direction.

With impatience creeping into his voice, the young man continued, "You a bit slow or summat? You not comprehending the English, luv?" Rachel could only dumbly shake her head and continue to walk.

The Mercedes kept pace as the young man continued to pester her, "It's raining, luv, why don't you jump in the back. It's dry and warm in here. We'll look after you, all good and proper like."

The rear passenger door, its windows blacked out, cracked open an inch with a menacing click. Rachel recognised the sound of a trap arming, unseen jaws preparing to snap closed around her. She had no intention of going anywhere near it.

She kept walking at the same measured pace, kept facing forward and continued to ignore the vehicle as it stalked her. A taxi-driver angrily sounded his horn, having finally managed to squeeze past the slow-moving Mercedes and sped onwards towards Euston Station with his fare.

This spurred the young man into more aggressive dialogue. "Are you fuckin' deaf, bitch? Get in the bloody car now." It wasn't said, but she recognised the threatened 'or else' at the end of the statement. It was sickeningly familiar as 'he' had begun to use the same implied threats not long after they moved into the Camden apartment.

Rachel desperately looked for an escape route, a path that could deliver her to safety, whilst maintaining her façade of a calm outward appearance. If they thought she was about to bolt, there was no telling what these creeps would choose to do.

A cascade of blue flashes lit up the buildings around her, throwing crazy shadows and patterns against the brick walls. The occupants of the Mercedes looked around in surprise, the driver muttering an involuntary, "Oh shit!"

A police car, unimpressed with the Mercedes blocking the road whilst it slowly menaced Rachel, had lit up its Blues and Twos.

"You idiots, drive. We will pick her up later," came the firm order from the back seat. The voice of the unseen occupant was calm and yet commanding.

With a look of frustration, the front passenger snarled his parting warning: "We'll catch you soon, luv!" and the vehicle sped off south along Eversholt Street.

The police car, its lights extinguished, now pulled level. Rachel continued walking at the same measured pace. The next few seconds felt like an eternity as she worried that they might be looking for her. The weaselly anxiety voice took its opportunity to chip in. 'You see, I told you this was pointless. They are going to pick you up. Now you are going to be for it. What will Barry do when they take us back?'

"Excuse me, ma'am, are you ok?"

The enquiry had come from the policewoman who was now watching Rachel intently from her passenger seat. The rain was increasing in intensity as Rachel fought to keep her voice level and calm. "Yes, thanks. No problem here. Just want to get home before this gets heavier."

There followed a muffled conversation with her partner before the policewoman called out, "Ok, have a good evening," and, to Rachel's relief, the police vehicle also moved off.

Heavy raindrops had begun to pour from the sky. They splattered noisily on the pavement and quickly soaked through her hoodie.

Rachel was weary, having not stopped since her escape, and cold, since she was ill dressed for the weather. As an icy gust of wind howled down the street, it slowly dawned on her that she had no idea what she was going to do next.

Approaching a disused shop entrance, Rachel decided her priority was to find shelter from the downpour, a place to sit and perhaps work out a coherent plan of action.

The glass in the long-abandoned tailor's shop had been covered with unpainted sheets of plywood, transforming the entranceway into a discreet tunnel that the rain could not access.

The right side of this tunnel had been blocked with a large, jumbled pile of discarded cardboard. Rachel carefully worked her way up the left side until she reached the old shop door.

At last, in this dark corner, she felt momentarily secure.

Time passed as she stood motionless in the dark, scrutinising the passing pedestrians and cars, trying to convince herself that no-one could see her in this bolthole.

Across the road, behind a high wall, a two-tone horn announced that another train was leaving Euston Station, commencing its journey northwards, perhaps to her home city of Manchester.

Rachel recalled her own triumphant return home after securing the role at Sheol Publicity. As she had turned into Partridge Way, it struck her that this would soon no longer be her home. She had always assumed she would move somewhere near to her parents when she left. She had never even considered the possibility of relocating all the way down to London.

Upon hearing the news, Rachel's mother had been ecstatic. Her father had been equally dismayed. Over the two weeks that remained before she boarded the train back south to London, they had become involved in numerous bitter rows. He would complain 'You're not old enough to go', 'You don't know what these people are really like', 'They are after you for something else' and many other irrational arguments, originating from what Rachel assumed were the fears of an over-protective father.

During her final night at home, as they sat eating her favourite childhood meal of Lancashire Hotpot, there had been a palpable air of tension. Her father slammed his knife and fork down, turned to face Rachel and, with a trembling voice, shouted, "No, I cannot allow this!" He raised his right arm and pointed at his bemused daughter. "By all my power, I command you to stay. By all that I control, I forbid you to…"

"No. Be silent. It is her choice to make and it is not for us to interfere." Rachel sat in stunned silence, as her normally tranquil and easy-going mother suddenly leapt up from her chair and, with a thunderous face and an air of unquestionable authority, scolded her husband into complete silence.

After a stunned pause, he opened his mouth to protest only to remain silent as she ominously raised her left index finger. Rachel fancied that at that very moment she could hear the far-away rolling of thunder.

The next day, her father was nowhere to be seen and only her mother had escorted her to Manchester Piccadilly railway station. "Don't think too poorly of him, my dear. He does mean well. It is hard for him to accept that it is your life, that these are your decisions, that it is, after all, your destiny."

The platform for the Euston-bound train was announced and immediately tears began to well up in both of their eyes. "Look at me, getting all silly and emotional," her mother complained. As Rachel gathered up the bags that contained all her possessions, she had continued, "He's not wrong, you know. They are not like us down there, so please, please, please be careful."

She gave her daughter a sloppy kiss on the cheek followed by a bone-crunching hug before concluding, "Right then, go and make us proud and don't forget to come back and visit."

She had never returned home since that day; she had been too busy and then 'he' had writhed his way into her life.

Those happy memories of her mother faded, along with the sound of the departing northbound train.

Shivering and tired, Rachel slowly slid down the door and slumped onto the faded, red mosaic tile floor. She gathered her knees under her chin and pulled herself into a tight ball, then rocked slightly forwards and back, trying to recall the long-forgotten feel of her mother's loving embrace.

The pile of cardboard stirred and began to move.

Rachel immediately thought it might be rats. Her anxiety voice chuckled nastily at her, 'Well, that would top off the perfect day, wouldn't it? Eaten alive by a pack of starving rats!'

A shape slowly emerged, as if the haphazard pile of cardboard were giving birth. First a large head in a thick woolly hat. A pair of eyes followed, then a dark-skinned Afro-Caribbean face and finally a rotund upper torso.

In the gloomy light reflected from the street, Rachel thought that he looked like a nightmarish human/caterpillar hybrid, the upper half of a man, the lower thorax and abdomen formed from the large heaps of cardboard. She couldn't decide if that would make him a Manpillar or a Caterman. She eventually decided that Manpillar sounded more appropriate.

"I do apologise, my dear. As you can see, I wasn't anticipating guests." The Manpillar spoke with a cultured Jamaican accent. "I am afraid the place is quite a mess. If you had forewarned me of your intention to visit, I would have made up the spare bedroom."

"I'm really so sorry. I didn't realise that there was anybody here. I'll move on," apologised Rachel.

The Manpillar laughed heartily, then countered, "Oh, don't be a silly ass! There is plenty of space on the pull-out sofa. What kind of host would I be if I turned a lady out of my palatial abode into a tempestuous night such as this? No, please stay."

Rachel apprehensively looked out into the soaking wet street. A bus passed by, rainwater streaming from its side in great waves. A shiver involuntarily passed through her damp and chilled body. The Manpillar didn't seem hostile or dangerous, so she decided it was worth the risk to remain in shelter, at least for a little longer.

"How dreadfully rude of me. We haven't been formally introduced. My name is Abso - and you are...?"

Rachel hesitated. There was no logical reason to lie to the Manpillar. Yet, after the tumultuous evening she had endured, Rachel didn't feel comfortable supplying anyone with her real name. Instead, she gave the first name that popped into her head. "Nice to meet you, Abso, I'm... Alice." The Manpillar nodded slowly. "Of course you are." An uncomfortable silence descended between them.

"Chocolate?"

Rachel was bemused by the Manpillar's question, unsure how to answer. Abso, picking up on her confusion, eventually added, "You look hungry, my dear. Would you like a chocolate bar?" From deep within his cardboard thorax, he extracted a chocolate bar and proffered it to Rachel.

'He' had been restricting her to a single meal a day for some weeks, so Rachel hadn't eaten since yesterday evening. On seeing the bar, her stomach immediately growled in hunger, whilst she began to salivate in anticipation. It had been many months since Katherine sent a bag down to the living room window containing a chocolate bar as well as the usual essentials.

"I don't think it's too far out of date," mused Abso. "I am sure it's edible; if not, I can rouse the staff and see if they can rustle us up something from the pantry."

Rachel had to restrain herself from wolfing down the chocolate. It would have been easy to gobble it down like a frog swallowing a fly. No, she wanted to savour the luxurious taste. She wanted to enjoy her first meal not provided by 'Him'. She wanted to embrace the sweet taste of newly won freedom.

The chocolate bar was a little crumbly and dry, but to Rachel it tasted exquisite. At that moment, a meal at the Savoy Grill could not have provided her with any greater culinary satisfaction.

"I do apologise, but I have unfortunately mislaid the key to the wine cellar. The best I can offer you as a refreshment is this almost-in-date can of Coke." The can was proffered, and Rachel gratefully accepted.

An ambulance sped by, its lights flashing as it raced to the scene of an unfolding drama. The blue light reflected off the heavy raindrops, momentarily transforming them into brilliantly sparkling sapphires. Then, as quickly as the sapphires had appeared, they lost their fabulous lustre and crashed onto the road - nothing more than rain after all.

Abso took off his woolly hat and removed a pre-rolled doobie before carefully replacing the hat upon his balding head. Somewhat gingerly, given the surfeit of combustible material encasing his lower half, he lit the joint and inhaled deeply. He flashed a wide grin at Rachel and offered it to her. Her anxiety voice sneered, 'Sharing drugs with a junkie. Wouldn't mother and father be sooo proud'.

Rachel politely refused the offer.

"So... Alice, may I enquire how you have come to be in this most exclusive London establishment?" There seemed no harm in recounting her tale, though she continued to weave her cloak of deception by altering the names of those involved and the location of her long-served incarceration.

The act of putting her recent adventure into a narrative allowed Rachel to form some structure around the chaotic events that had befallen her. Though, at the end, she remained no wiser as to what course of action to take.

The Manpillar sat in a haze of intoxicating smoke, his gaze having never wandering from Rachel during her telling of the tale.

Her story complete, he dramatically cleared his throat, as if about to address an auditorium of waiting patrons and began. "Alice, it seems to me that people put things in cages for two reasons. In the first instance, it is done to possess something. Be that an item of beauty, a work of art, a beautiful person or an artefact of power. It is a driven desire to keep that thing solely for themselves.

The songbird, its voice so sweet, is stolen from nature and secreted away in a cage by the collector. He is pleased that only he can listen to those natural chords of beauty. It is by the act of possession that he draws false self-worth. However, this selfish act ultimately fails to quell the true desires that haunt his empty life."

A figure huddling under an umbrella appeared, silhouetted in the doorway. "Just checking you're are in there, Abso?" The Manpillar laughed heartily. "Indeed I am, young Arthur, and I have a visitor in my drawing room." The silhouette laughed in return. "Do you indeed!" Rachel remained silent, hoping to avoid being observed as Abso was offered of a cup of hot soup. The Manpillar turned down the offer and the silhouette moved on, promising, "I'll check in on you tomorrow."

"Au revoir, sir. Now… where were we?" The Manpillar took a drag of the joint before his face lit up and he continued. "Ah, yes. In the second instance, the cage is used to hold the thing that is feared or cannot be controlled.

The collector keeps a tiger in a cage. They feel they have it under control, a wild killing machine subdued to their will. But they know that to enter the tiger's cage will lead to their assured demise. It is the tiger that controls its domain, no matter how cramped its jailor may make it.

Some may think to break the tiger's spirit, to transform it into a performing beast that answers their commands and does demeaning tricks at their bidding. It is a most foolishly deluded notion. The tiger bides its time, patiently waiting for its moment."

The rain was beginning to ease, though waterfalls continued to noisily cascade from overflowing guttering onto the pavement below.

"There is, of course, the rarest of situations: that which incorporates both of the above. A prison designed to hold something that is both beautiful and wrathful, delicate yet indomitable. Should the occupant of that cage escape its confinement, well, it would be best to stand well back and let it rampage along its own path." Abso took another long pull from his joint and closed his eyes.

As the rain outside had reduced to barely a light shower, Rachel decided it was an opportune moment to move on. The occupants of the black Mercedes were still out there and 'he' might be searching for her. She wouldn't want harm to come to this gentle Manpillar after the generosity he had shown her. "Thank you for your hospitality and... I guess... the sage words, Abso, but I think it's time for me to head off."

As she stood, the Manpillar's eyes flicked open and he exclaimed, "My dear, you are hardly appropriately dressed for a rampage through the wintery streets of London. Now, let me see..."

From within his cardboard thorax was drawn a long burgundy leather coat. He unfolded it and offered the garment up to Rachel. "Now this, I believe, will be more appropriate." The coat still had the original sales label attached to the cuff, with the manufacturer's logo, 'Wear Me', clearly displayed.

Shrugging off the wet hoody and slipping on the coat, Rachel immediately found it to be a remarkably good fit. The cut of the shoulders and the arm length matched her body shape snugly. Its length dropped down to just above her knees giving some protection against the inclement weather. And, oh yes, it was infused with that intoxicating smell of fresh leather.

Doing up the four large buttons at the front, she was impressed that the coat fitted like a second skin. She immediately felt protected, once again enclosed within a metaphorical suit of armour.

She looked down at Abso and asked, "What do you think?" and did a twirl for him. He let out a feeble wolf whistle and chortled. "My dear, I think you and that coat were clearly made for one another."

"But I can't accept it," Rachel protested. "You could sell this. Perhaps you could get yourself a comfortable room for a couple of nights. Please take it back." She began to unbutton the coat.

The Manpillar smiled. "My dear, what need have I for a fancy hotel room when I am blessed with this magnificent abode? No, I will hear no more. That coat is yours. See how it fits you; it was clearly destined to be yours and no others." The Manpillar defiantly folded his arms and concluded, "I shall hear no more protests on this subject."

Rachel buttoned the coat back up and worked her way past the Manpillar's cardboard bulk. As she emerged onto the street, Rachel paused. "Thank you again, Abso, for the hospitality of your most comfortable abode and, again, thank you for this generous gift." He smiled and waved good-bye to her.

"Oh, and one last thing: my real name is not Alice, it's Rachel." With that she turned south and disappeared from his sight.

As the Manpillar shuffled back down into his cardboard cocoon he muttered, "Au revoir, Rachel Minos."

Chapter 3

"And then I threw his pint in his face and left him standing there like a right tosser!"

Four young women were clustered around the wooden table, loudly sharing their recent dating mishaps with each other. Dressed in their partying finest, they were all armed with cans of energy drink. Fighting to bolster wavering constitutions, they took great gulps of the sugar-laden liquid, hoping to undo the evening's liberal drinking.

At night, you can smell the plaza outside Euston Station long before you can see it. The wafting aroma of strong black coffee mingled with the aromatic delights of deep-fried food is a sign that a resting place for weary drunks, exhausted dancers and suited theatregoers lies just ahead. The junk food stalls, coffee vendors, wooden benches and tables provide an opportunity for them to gather their stamina before catching the bus, taxi, tube, or train to their next entertainment venue or to their home.

Two men passed close by the young ladies' table, heading for the railway station entrance. Dressed in the classic lines of pin-striped, double-breasted business suits with matching bowler hats, these two immaculately groomed gentlemen would not have looked out of place a hundred years ago - though the fact that their arms were linked in a tight embrace might have raised more than a few eyebrows.

The oldest of the four women called out as the men purposefully strode past their table, "Awww, shame. Two nice stallions all gone to waste. Why don't you come home with me and I'll teach you to be proper men!" The accompanying mock thrusting of the woman's hips in the direction of the retreating men caused her companions to burst into raucous laughter.

The men didn't break their perfectly synchronised strides as the shorter one called back, "Honey, you aren't butch enough to handle this tightly packaged love machine," and provocatively patted his partner's pert posterior. As they slipped out of view through the station door, his perfectly choreographed reply raised a roar of exuberant howls and wolf whistles from the ladies.

Rachel surreptitiously turned her head as two policemen moved through the Plaza: a physical presence to persuade people to curb their unintentional or even intentional antisocial behaviour.

She had taken advantage of an empty bench to sit down. Her legs were already cramping; after years of being restricted to that confined apartment, they were unaccustomed to the walking she had just undertaken. 'His' cast-off trainers didn't help as they were a distinctly ill fit.

The passing policemen barely even glanced at her as they strode purposely past her table. Perhaps the expensive-looking coat that now cocooned her projected a different, less negative image than the urban hoody she had discarded. Regardless, she was glad to be ignored.

One of the exuberant young women had left the table and precariously wobbled her way to a kebab vendor, the aroma of indeterminate meat turning slowly upon the rotisserie drawing the weaving woman forwards. Her companions enthusiastically shouted helpful, if sexually explicit, advice on how to get a free meal from the vendor.

Rachel's mind drifted, recalling a similar group of women that she had called friends. Their exploits had earned them the nickname 'The Sheol Posse'.

It had been around six months after arriving in London that Rachel had heard the office gossip that Hannah Bates, a peer of Rachel's at Sheol Publicity, had landed a huge new contract with the Italian client, Decem Fossas. It would take some months to finalise but landing a whale like that would cement her place as a rising star in the company. Hannah was going places.

It was a little after 8.00 pm on a Wednesday evening and Rachel had been sitting at her office desk, surrounded by scribbled notes of paper. The last four hours had been spent reading and digesting a particularly tortuous contract. The senior exec, Conrad Paymon, had tasked her with finding a way to legally break their contract with a client. Conrad had not wanted to involve the firm's legal department, complaining that their hourly rate was outrageous.

Leon Bay's career as a successful footballer had taken off a couple of years ago. Highly sought after on the pitch by teams and off the pitch by companies desperate for his endorsement, he was targeted by Sheol Publicity as a prime client.

In an earlier age, before the advent of the eternally alert and instantly judgemental lens of social media, his trajectory to join the superstars would have continued uninterrupted.

Instead, it came crashing down to earth in a spectacular fireball of public loathing when Leon, in a drunken night of online posting, had expressed his extremely controversial views on politics, women and LGBTQ+ rights.

In the aftermath of the online meltdown, Leon's agent had constantly badgered Conrad for a meeting. He wanted to discuss the joint approach to resurrecting the train wreck of his client's career.

"I want this toxic son of a bitch off our books. Find us a way to dump his sorry arse right now," had been Conrad's instructions. Leon's agent probably didn't realise that Conrad and his husband were approaching their third wedding anniversary.

The agent had done a thorough job with the contract: plenty of boiler plate coverage and exceptional activity clauses appeared to make it watertight. But Rachel had focussed on the minor sub clause that - Sheol would be notified fourteen days in advance of any club transfers. They had only received the news of Leon's latest transfer eight days in advance. Given the explicit wording and associated penalty clauses, the contract had been breached and Leon Bay could be dispensed with.

"Hey Rachel, you got a moment?"

Hannah was probably two inches shorter than Rachel, with a curvaceous physique that she deliberately exaggerated with her choices of outfit. Her soft, oval face was topped by an unruly mop of permed fire-red hair. She enthusiastically bounced across the half-empty office and enquired, "Rachel, what are you doing on Friday night that you can't cancel?"

Before she had time to reply, Hannah forged on, "Viath has approved a girl's night celebration, all to be charged on the corporate card." She made no attempt to contain the almost childlike bubbling excitement in her voice as she continued in a passable John Wayne accent, "What you say liddle lady? Ready to ride with the Sheol Posse and cause a bit of mayhem?"

Since arriving in London Rachel had felt out of her depth as she plunged headlong into this corporate powerhouse. During those initial months she had been desperately keeping her head above the ocean of information she had to absorb. Working long into the night had become her normal office routine. The distinction between weekdays and weekends blurred into a relentless seven-day slog.

What little time she had managed to take off had been spent relaxing on her sofa, wrapped in a duvet. Isolated from the outside world she indulged in a procession of chick flicks, the more mindlessly romantic, with tear-jerking, happy endings, the better. Especially when accompanied by an extra-large tub of wine gums.

Wine gums!

She hadn't eaten a wine gum in years. Her mother had always loved wine gums and passed that craving onto Rachel. Her empty stomach groaned in distress as she attempted to recall the texture and flavour of black and red gums. She would munch her way through the tub, eating all the other colours, until all that remained were the precious black and reds.

These final gems would not be munched down but allowed to slowly dissolve in her mouth, savoured with the respect they deserved. A rare smile came to Rachel's face as she recalled her mother saying 'if a person doesn't like wine gums, you better keep a wary eye on them, because they are probably a monster'. In hindsight, she shouldn't have been surprised that 'he' didn't like wine gums.

A crash of metal falling to the ground shattered Rachel's recollections. Her heart pounding and her body shuddering uncontrollably, she glanced fearfully around for the source of the noise.

The young woman from the party of four had knocked over the kebab vendor's condiments tray, sending it and assorted sauces clattering onto the plaza floor. In a state of mild hysterics, the girl drunkenly attempted to pick them up whilst maintaining her decidedly precarious balance. The kebab man, a long-suffering look on his face, repeatedly told her that he would clean it up.

Despite there being no immediate danger, the trembling in Rachel's body and the pounding in her chest didn't subside.

That simple crashing noise had released four years of pent-up agony and torment from the murky depths of her memory. All that she had endured: the constant humiliations, the relentless verbal abuse, the degrading punishments, the painful physical attacks - they all crashed over her in a tsunami of emotions.

Rachel panicked as she struggled to draw a breath.

That wave of pain submerged her; cutting her off from life-giving air; pulling her down into the darkest depths of her memories.

Try as she might to block out those excruciating experiences, they relentlessly flooded through her mind.

Desperately gasping at the cold night air, she lurched to her feet and staggered aimlessly from the bench. Her head swimming, her heart threatened to burst out of her chest as she stumbled out of the plaza and through the bus station.

The driver of the number 18 bus to Sudbury barely had time to slam on the brakes. Rachel, now oblivious to her surroundings, had blindly staggered out in front of him. She didn't register the angry squeal of tyres on damp tarmac and never heard him shouting at her about bloody drunks.

Four years of 'his' derogatory words were spinning through her head.

She had endured a never-ending tirade of spite and derision, each one of them a precisely administered blow, carefully aimed to break down and destroy her self-worth.

Feeling faint, Rachel fell clumsily onto her knees at the foot of the Euston war memorial. The stone monolith loomed high above, bronze statues solemnly standing guard at each of its corners. Those young men who had fought for their lives in the trenches and battlefields of one hundred years past stared down upon her with pity in their metal eyes.

The pedestrians chose to carefully avoid the stricken woman and studiously averted their eyes, apart from two young tourists. They gleefully filmed her distress on their phones whilst providing a running commentary before scampering off to find a Wi-Fi hotspot to post their latest creative masterpiece onto the internet.

Finally, the smothering sea of confusion began to retreat. Her rapid breathing gradually slowed as she began to regain control. At last, calm breaths of London night air were drawn into her lungs, punctuated only by her pitiful sobbing.

Her anxiety voice pitilessly mocked Rachel. 'A panic attack? How pathetic. Maybe you should have stopped breathing and given everyone a break from your relentless mewling!'

It took a few minutes to regain sufficient strength to stand and prop herself against the memorial. Her right knee throbbed in pain – a trickle of ruby red blood ran from a jagged slice in her jeans. The residual tremors haunting her hands hindered the attempt to dab the gash clean with a ragged tissue.

She felt physically and emotionally spent. She wanted to lie down and sleep. She was tempted to curl up at the base of the memorial, trusting that the bronze soldiers would stand guard over her, to surrender herself to the night and trust to fortune's blind decisions.

"Are you ok?"

A lady, dressed in a bulky red quilted winter coat and wearing a light grey, furry Cossack-style hat, looked at Rachel with concern etched in her face. Between laboured breaths she replied, "I'm fine… just a panic attack… that's all."

"You don't look fine," the woman countered. "Here, take this." She offered a bottle of water which Rachel gratefully took and swigged. The cold water washed away the bitter taste in her mouth and immediately revived her flagging spirits.

"Do you want me to call anyone? Can I get you a taxi to take you home?" Rachel shook her head. After all, who could Rachel call? 'He' had ensured that Rachel stood alone on a secluded island, surrounded by the charred remains of bridges that had been burned down a long time ago.

"No, I'm fine, thank you and thanks for the water." She proffered the bottle back, but good Samaritan declined. "Don't be silly, you need it more than I do. Are you sure you are ok? I can always catch a later train if you need some company?"

Rachel wanted to ask this kind stranger to embrace her. To engulf her in those quilted arms and to deliver a bone-crushing hug. A moment of comforting physical contact not driven by fear of mental or physical torture. Instead, Rachel insisted that she run and catch her train and again thanked her for the help.

Watching her saviour disappear into the station, Rachel felt a renewed rising tide of bitter emotions. How had she let 'him' do what he did to her? Why had she meekly endured 'his' relentless abuse?

'At least with him you had a soft, warm bed to sleep in. Now look at us,' chastised her anxiety voice. Perhaps it was right. Was she ready to face the uncertainty that lay ahead, or would it be better to seek the comfort of the familiar and return to the Camden flat?

No. she was stronger than this. Yes, she had been beaten down and yes, she had been wounded. But she had never been broken and she could still stand and walk tall.

Like a flying beast unfurling long-unused wings, she slowly uncurled her shoulders and drew up to her full height of five foot eight inches. Muscles that had become accustomed to being cramped rewarded her new upright posture with a sharp stabbing sensation in her neck. Rachel mentally added this to the growing list of accumulated aches and pains.

Once again, she was on the move. Walking without a destination, she allowed her legs and whimsy to take her where they may. Leaving Euston behind, she walked along Grafton Way, passing a drunken couple who were futilely attempting to flag down every black cab that sped past them. After crossing an eerily quiet Tottenham Court Road, Rachel entered Maple Street. Heralding the arrival of the next day, the nearby tolling of a church bell proclaimed midnight.

High above, in the night sky, loomed the dark outline of the BT Tower. The iconic structure had towered over London since its completion in 1964, its rotating restaurant - now closed to the public - providing unrivalled panoramic views across the city. The signing party for the Decem Fossas contract had been Rachel's opportunity to experience that exclusive tower and enjoy the view.

Rachel recalled how, on the day before the expected contract signing, she had been making herself a cup of green tea when she overheard a gaggle of Sheol PAs, huddled in one of their conspiratorial groups. They were gossiping about the problems that had beset the Decem Fossas deal. 'I've heard senior management is livid'. 'Unforeseen contractual complications, that's what I've heard.' 'The client has threatened to walk away from the entire project!'

Rachel had already noted that Hannah had been showing signs of stress, though that wasn't unexpected when closing a deal of this magnitude. She was snapping and shouting at her team as she desperately struggled to resolve what she had claimed to be a few minor issues.

After returning to her desk, Rachel became engrossed in crafting a letter of condolence to the family of a client who had recently died. It took her a little while to realise that Mr Viath had appeared beside her.

"Good morning, sir. I didn't see you there. Can I help you?"

Dressed in his Savile Row finest, Mr Viath never looked anything other than perfectly presented. It had occurred to Rachel that she had never seen him in anything but a sharply tailored suit. For a moment she imagined him standing there in floral swimming shorts, a white sun vest and a straw beach hat. A strangely disturbing image that she immediately attempted to forget.

"Minos, come with me. I have a task for you." He immediately set off at his customary rapid pace. Rachel gathered up a pen and daybook and quickly trotted along behind him.

They entered a small office in which had been placed a chair, a table with a lamp, three bottles of water, a glass and a contract document.

Mr Viath pointed at the substantial bundle of paper. "Ok, Minos, that's the Decem Fossas contract. The known issues are highlighted; you have until tomorrow morning to try and fix them."

Rachel began to protest: "Doesn't this belong to Hannah and wouldn't Legal be better placed to..." Mr Viath impatiently cut her off. "The contract belongs to Sheol Publicity. Others have failed to resolve the issue and I don't intend to lose billions by doubling down on incompetence. It's survival of the fittest. Prove to me that you have what it takes and fix it."

With that, he closed the door and left a stunned Rachel alone.

Twenty-one hours later, Mr Viath re-entered the room, finding a sleep-deprived and dishevelled woman who bore the satisfied grin of a Cheshire Cat across her face.

"Well?" he enquired.

Rachel leaned back in the chair, pushed her notes forward and with some considerable pride in her voice explained how she had resolved the problems and two more that hadn't been previously exposed. She handed over the handwritten contractual wording changes that would allow them to close the deal.

Mr Viath read through the suggested changes, his handsomely rugged face betraying no emotion as his eyes darted along the written words and digested their content. At last, his face cracked into a smile. "Outstanding work, Rachel. Truly outstanding. I can see that we will be adding your name to the Rising Stars list after this Houdini act."

With a wry smile he added, "Now, go home and clean yourself up. We can hardly have you at tonight's contract signing event in the BT Tower looking like you haven't slept all night."

Tired but satisfied with the night's work, she took the lift down to the office lobby and waved to Madeline on the reception desk.

The company chauffeur stood waiting and said, "Ms Minos, I have your car ready for you." Surprised, Rachel had checked: "For me, are you sure?" Madeline chuckled. "Oh yes, Mr Viath has asked William here to take you home. You are obviously in his good books today."

Ensconced in the luxury of leather and wood, she had immediately drifted into a slumber, that was all too quickly rudely interrupted by their arrival at her Maida Vale apartment. "I'll be back at 6pm to take you to the event, if that works for you, Ms Minos?" Rachel had agreed.

Entering the garden flat, she thought about making a cup of strong coffee, but instead flopped onto the bed to momentarily catch her breath before doing anything else.

Buzzz, Buzzzz, Buzzzzzzzzzzz.

Rachel cracked open an eye as the bedroom filled with the sound of an electric buzzer.

Buzzzzzzzzzz, Buzzzzzzzzzzzz, Buzzzzzzzzzzz

Emerging from the realm of sleep it took a moment to recognise that someone was at the door.

Buzz, Buzz, Buzz, Buzz, Buzz.

"Yes, I'm bloody coming," she yelled as she sat up on the bed and cleared the encrusted sleep from her eyes. She sighed as the realisation sunk in that she still wore yesterday's business suit. Now creased and crumpled, it would need a trip to the dry cleaners to recover its normal sharp lines.

BUZZZZZZZZZZZZZZZZZZZZZZZZZZZZZZZZZZZZZZZZZZZZZZZZZZZZZZZZZZ

Rachel opened the door to find a tall, lean man with black, curly hair and immaculately applied make-up carrying a large metallic case. "You must be Rachel? I'm Serge. Dearest John has asked me to come and get you ready for tonight."

He critically looked Rachel up and down before humming quietly and continuing. "I think we have our work cut out for us, sister. Let's get cracking. Chop, chop."

He barged his way into the flat. "Now, you get a shower, I'll put the kettle on - you clearly need coffee. Hmm, strong coffee and lots of it."

Fifteen minutes later, she emerged from the shower and found the mug of coffee waiting for her in the hall. Serge was already in her bedroom, rummaging through her wardrobe. "No... Definitely no... Oh my dear god, throw this in the fire right now... Ah! Here we are. This will do."

He extracted her classic black cocktail dress and placed it on the bed next to a pair of matching stilettos. "You're not going to make a dramatic entrance with this, but it's the best we can do with that horror show you call a wardrobe."

Feeling hurt that her style choices were viewed with disdain, she tried to object, only for him to interrupt. "Not to worry. Serge will pick you up next Thursday afternoon and together we will fill your wardrobe with appropriately fabulous outfits."

Serge was a force of nature that Rachel felt incapable of resisting. Not that she wanted to. She was warming to the wild ride he provided and feeding off his inexhaustible supply of self-confidence.

"Now your hair and makeup..." Rachel had begun to explain what she normally did for an event. Serge placed his finger to her lips "Shhh, Rachel, my sweet. Serge works with water colours, not emulsion wall paint. Serge knows what he is going to do, and you are going to look fabulous."

He did, and she did.

When the doorbell buzzed at 6 pm, she barely recognised the elegant woman staring back from the hallway mirror. Serge also appeared content with his work, "You will do!"

As she had wafted outside to the waiting car, the chauffeur dutifully swinging open the rear door for her, Rachel had hoped that the neighbours were watching.

The contract signing party was the usual razzmatazz affair: lots of speeches and self-congratulations being doled out and received, powerful people downing drinks with household celebrities, whilst businessmen hatched the embryos of new ideas over cocktails with exotic garnishes.

Hannah had looked weary when Mr Viath called her up to the stage. Rachel overheard whispered comments from an adjoining group of junior employees: 'Oh dear, that silver sequin evening gown is just so last year', 'It's looking a little tight in places, I do hope nothing bursts out', 'Do you think she will spend some of her bonus on a gym membership to lose all those extra kilos?'

Hannah managed to maintain her smile as Viath half-heartedly congratulated her on setting up the deal and putting, as he disingenuously described it, the little details in place.

Her smile grew thinner as he took a little extra time to highlight the issues that had beset them and how, with a little foresight, they could have avoided those pitfalls. She looked relieved when he concluded and the audience finally began to applaud.

Rachel had been enthusiastically clapping with the rest of the guests when Mr Viath called out, "Now. Before I finish tonight, I must commend a spectacular talent that saved the day. The hero that went the extra mile and got this deal over the finish line. Come on up here, Rachel."

To thunderous applause, Rachel had sheepishly joined them on the stage. Hannah was unceremoniously pushed into the shadows of the stage's left side as Mr Viath vigorously shook Rachel's hand, before turning to face the audience with it held high as if she had been awarded a unanimous point win at a boxing match.

His pronouncement that, "Yes folks, I think we got a champion here," was greeted with rapturous applause.

It took Rachel over an hour to manoeuvre herself away from the stage. With John Viath's endorsement, she was in demand. All twelve senior execs had personally introduced themselves, talking as if they were old friends. There were offers of visits to their country estates or to enjoy weekends away on private yachts. Conrad wanted her to meet his husband and have dinner at their Kensington apartment.

Numerous other people, few of whom she recognised, were keen to shake her hand and make unsolicited offers. "If you need Centre Court Wimbledon tickets, call". "Want to be on the starting grid at the British Grand Prix, let me know, I'll make it happen." "You look like you enjoy live music. Name the event and I'll get you backstage passes. Want a one-on-one with the performers? That too can be arranged."

Finally disentangling herself from the mass of people, Rachel had sought out Hannah, eventually locating her hiding away from the centre of the party. She was standing reflectively staring out over the city panorama as it slowly rotated by, a half-drunk glass of red wine absent-mindedly tilting to one side in her hand.

As she approached, Hannah turned and recognised Rachel. "Oh, it's you," she muttered with a tone of contempt and an unpleasant facial expression to match.

Rachel, taken aback, apologised. "Hannah, I'm sorry, I had no idea that was going to happen. Please forgive me. I am really sorry."

Hannah's face mellowed and, with a more wistful tone in her voice, she turned back to stare out of the window at the tiny streets below. "No. No, it's me who should be apologising." She took a drink from the wine glass. "If you hadn't fixed the contract, I wouldn't have landed a big fat completion bonus. Instead, I would be polishing my CV and looking for a new employer."

She paused, watching the distant lights of an airliner slowly descending into Heathrow airport. "It's just..." her face was filled with undisguised disappointment, "It's just that there is only ever one rising star at Sheol Publicity and it's clear that it's no longer me."

She turned back to Rachel and with mock formality raised the glass in salute. "The rising star is dead. Long live the rising star." She drained her wine glass. "I guess I should take comfort that it's you and not Bothington-Smithe from accounts. He still hates me for dumping him after our one and only date."

An awkward silence descended between them, eventually broken as Hannah had loudly declared, "Fuck it, Rachel, let's get some hard liquor and let's kick this party into life..."

Braaaaaaap... Rachel's attention was abruptly drawn from the silhouette of the tower and the memories it contained back down to street level. On the opposite side of the road, a motorcyclist sitting astride a Yamaha XSR900 looked directly towards her. The female rider wore a Held-Ayana one-piece leather suit in white with black flashes and a matching helmet.

Braaaaaaap, Braaaaaaap, Braaaaaaap

Menacingly, the rider blipped her bike's throttle three times in quick succession, each blast of the engine echoing off the surrounding buildings. It reminded her of the echoing roar of a predator about to strike.

Chapter 4

With training and dedication, the human body can be pushed to undertake previously impossible feats of physical endurance. There are many examples of sportspeople who have pushed back the limits in their chosen event and produced results once thought unachievable. However, after four years of incarceration, Rachel's body screamed for rest before jogging more than a few hundred meters.

The motorcyclist persistently toyed with her. Riding close behind, blipping the bike's throttle, the revving of the engine acting like the crack of the cattle driver's whip. If Rachel slowed her pace, the biker would accelerate forward, getting dangerously close before slamming on the brakes at the last moment. The screeching of the tortured front tyre on drying tarmac pierced through Rachel's weary head adding to her confusion.

During her time at university, Rachel had become a motorbike rider herself. After being convinced by her parents to remain local to them, she had accepted a place at Manchester University. Rachel then argued that a motorbike would prove to be the quickest way to commute between campus and home. Grudgingly her parents eventually agreed to pay for a motorbike and lessons. Her father had not been keen on the idea, perhaps recalling her early exploits learning to ride a bicycle. For Rachel, it was a taste of rebellious freedom.

At the time she had found it puzzling how people would react so differently to a young woman arriving on a large lime green Kawasaki. They could be fascinated, others would be hostile and a small group even intimidated. Now, being harassed by one herself, Rachel could understand the intimidation.

Even for such an early hour, the streets were suspiciously quiet. London, like many large cities across the world, never sleeps. There is normally a taxi, a drunk, a dog walker, a delivery van or even a sleepless jogger taking advantage of the quiet pause in the city's relentless daily cycle.

Tonight, there was not a single soul to observe Rachel being herded onwards. No bedroom curtains twitched to peek at the events unfolding in the street below. The ever-present CCTV cameras that blanket London, tracking and logging individuals as they go about their business, seemed ignorant of the activity on Clipstone Street.

Standing in the road ahead were two motorcyclists ominously garbed in one-piece black leather suits, each with matching matte black helmets. Arms on hips, they patiently waited for Rachel to be herded to them. With a final blast of the engine, the motorbike came to a halt behind her, trapping Rachel between the three of them.

"What do you want?" she rasped, trying to recover some composure after her enforced run. Concealed behind their crash helmets and dark tinted visors, the three bikers betrayed no sign that they had heard her question. "I've got no money. I'm nobody. Please, please let me go," she pleaded.

The taller biker gave a single nod of his helmet, spurring the figure to his left to walk forward, producing a pair of silver handcuffs from his belt. Rachel yelled in desperation, "No, no, what have I done to you? Get the fuck away from me. Help, somebody please help, HELP!"

Her desperate pleas went unanswered.

As Rachel backed away from the advancing assailant, the white-clad motorcyclist noisily revved her engine. A reminder that there could be no escape.

The black-clad biker had stopped directly before her, held up the silver handcuffs and deftly clicked them open with a snap.

Rachel's memory released a deluge of flashbacks. Each one a hauntingly similar scene she had endured with 'him'. Each replayed in excruciatingly painful detail. "If you were less disobedient, I wouldn't have to use these on you so much," he had often purred into her ear. "But you just want it, don't you!" came his familiar taunt.

It wasn't fair. It wasn't bloody fair. She had thrown off one set of shackles, she wouldn't be imprisoned once more!

Her anxiety voice sniggered, 'Isn't this what you want? Don't you crave the freedom of surrender? You did it for four years.' Aping Barry's voice, it laughed, 'you just want it, don't you!'

Rachel watched helplessly as the biker provocatively displayed the open handcuffs, showing that they were ready to be slammed closed on her wrists, then as he reached out and roughly grabbed her left wrist.

Deep within Rachel, the tiniest spark ignited as she whispered, "No!"

The tiny flame grew, fed by the abundance of combustible emotions, for too long bottled up tightly within her, as she said, "No!"

A chain reaction had commenced. Four long years of frustrations tearing free from their confinement, fanning the inferno that now raged within her as she cried out, "No!"

The emotional firestorm, born from all that she had endured, at last welled up through her body. Those pent-up forces could no longer be contained and exploded outwards as she screamed out, "NO!"

Far out in space there are monsters that defy humanity's understanding of science. At the centre of a Black Hole, a titanic mass is crushed by its own gravity into a single miniscule point, a stupefyingly dense object that tortuously twists the fabric of space-time. In that singularity, the passage of time stands still and the fundamental laws of physics themselves break down. It is an environment beyond mankind's current comprehension. Perhaps something similar had been inadvertently unleashed on that London street, distorting space-time as Rachel released her pent-up fury.

She stood dumbfounded as the three bikers and their motorcycles slowly tumbled away from her, driven majestically through the air as if propelled by an invisible yet irresistible fist.

In fascination, she watched as the lazily cartwheeling motorcycles gracefully twisted and tore themselves apart in a symphony of destruction that slowly shattered them into a thousand fragments.

The riders lethargically flexed and writhed as the invisible storm front ponderously propelled them away, arms and legs helplessly flailing in the grip of the tempest, reminding Rachel of children's rag dolls being thrown through the air.

It is pointless to speculate how long she stood and watched the unfolding scene of carnage. Time had been bent into submission and, for Rachel, for a while, the rest of the world now proceeded at a lazy snail's pace.

Like a cinema film slowly accelerating up to its proper frame speed, the street scene finally regained its momentum. Time, at least as Rachel experienced it, had returned to normal.

The city air echoed with a howling cacophony of electronic wailings. Car alarms, building alarms, fire alarms: they had all been spurred into life by the impact of the reality-bending forces that had been unleashed.

The visibility across the street had become obscured by a cloak of dust. Rachel walked through it towards the nearest ragdoll motorcyclist, the twisted form having come to rest over thirty meters away.

The biker's leather suit had been burst, torn and shredded. The crash helmet was badly battered and dented. Rachel's anxiety voice summed up her own thoughts best as it uttered a breathless, 'What the fuck did you do?'

This moment of triumphant wonderment and horror ended quickly. Rachel held her breath as the biker's left hand moved. Slowly the chest heaved up with a slow deliberate intake of a breath as the left leg began to violently twitch.

Rachel fled. She managed to jog for nearly five minutes before seeking shelter in a dark restaurant doorway. Here, she bent over to regain her breath.

She couldn't understand how any normal person could have survived that terrible impact. Rachel carefully avoided thinking about the actual explosive event itself. She wasn't ready to attempt to process that particular bit of insanity.

Who were they? Why did they want her? How could they be so resilient? There were, of course, no answers to these questions. Her fellow Sheol Posse member, Bethany, when confronted with such an odd situation would have laughingly said, "Aliens. It's got to be."

It had been a long time since she had thought about the Sheol Posse. Hannah, Lucy, Bethany and Rachel had formed that elite group. Their self-appointed mission: to meet up once a week after work, to party hard and have a lot of gratuitous fun. The four members of the Posse were amongst Sheol Publicity's brightest performers. Each one had been touted as an exceptional talent and each of them had been groomed for the possibility of a future senior executive position or perhaps even higher.

One Friday night on a rainy October day, the Posse had descended on Louis Champagne Bar. On these nights, the ladies donned their best glad rags; after all, they were never sure where the evening would lead, or where they would wake up in the morning.

Bethany could be described by some as painfully thin. Rachel often worried that she might be borderline anorexic. That night Rachel noticed, with concern, that Bethany's tiny leopard-skin halter top and skinny vinyl jeans were hanging baggily off her diminutive five-foot-two frame. Over her narrow shoulder hung her obligatory oversized designer bag, its bulk further exaggerating her slight build.

Lucy towered over the rest of the Posse. She loved to deliberately exaggerate her natural six-foot vertical dominance, adding a few extra inches by piling up her auburn hair and pinning it in place. The black and white, vertical-striped mini dress ended near the top of her thigh, daringly revealing long, muscular, toned legs supported on white four-inch heeled pumps.

Hannah had struggled with her weight since the BT Tower event. She had dabbled with expensive pre-packaged diet shake courses. After a week of imbibing these wonder cocktails, she would lose two kilograms of weight only to frustratingly put four back on during the following seven days.

That Friday, she was dressed in a baggy black silk blouse, loose-fitting black jeans and low-heeled ankle boots. Her curly red hair was left to hang naturally around her shoulders. Rachel had gone for the simple look of a red lacy top and a dark brown skirt with black tights and flat calf boots.

As the suave and playfully charming sommelier cracked open the second bottle of bubbly, the four of them had been speculating about the upcoming corporate cull.

"Who do you think will be on the chopping block this time?" mused Lucy, her empty glass waving in the air, hinting that it required refilling. It hadn't escaped Rachel's notice that Lucy was spending a lot of time keeping one adoring eye on the sommelier.

"I overheard the admins at coffee time," confessed Rachel. "They think Rufus in Overseas is a certainty and also Karen down in Personnel."

Her glass recharged, Lucy nodded. "After that disastrous settlement they had to make with Henri I am not surprised about Karen. Shame about Rufus though. He's young and kind of cute." The rest rolled their eyes and made various derogatory cougar jokes at Lucy's expense.

Bethany, absentmindedly playing with the fringe of her short black hair, leaned forward in a conspiratorial manner. "But what about senior cuts? Do you think they will be creating any senior exec vacancies? Could this be the moment one of us gets the nod?"

To the Posse's collective disappointment, none of them had uncovered any rumours about potential vacancies in the upper echelon. "Even if a vacancy appears, we know I have no chance now," grumbled Hannah as she grabbed a large handful of bar snacks.

"You sealed the biggest deal in the last financial year. You have got to be a certainty for that step up," Rachel countered. Swallowing down the bar snacks, Hannah let out a half-hearted guffaw. "Not so much. The deal means I keep my job, but Viath has burned away the rungs of my corporate ladder, so I won't be going any higher." She grabbed another handful of snacks. "Anyhow, we all know who the current rising star is, don't we, ladies?"

Bethany, Lucy and Hannah all swivelled in their seats to face Rachel. In mock reverence, they bowed down and venerated her whilst chanting in comedically deep voices, "All hail the raising star; all hail the mighty Rachel." After allowing this mantra to be repeated three times she requested them to kindly all fuck off.

In a mock worshipful voice, Lucy asked, "Please, Magnificent Mistress Minos. When you are shamelessly topless sunbathing on Mr Viath's luxury yacht, anchored in Monaco bay, eating your peeled grapes, don't forget your old Posse. We could come and serve you drinks, maybe make your bed or clean your toilet." The three of them began to repeat in grovelling voices "Yes mistress, no mistress, as you so wish, mistress." Rachel sat back in the plush suede chair and gave the finger to each one of them.

"You know what, fellow peons," Lucy whispered in an exaggeratedly secretive voice. "The only way for one of us second rates to become an exec is to... do away with Rachel!"

Hannah added a dramatic, "Dah-Duh-Daaaah."

The three now cackled like witches gathered around a bubbling cauldron, discussing how they could remove Rachel from the picture and clear their own path to the Monaco yacht.

When Lucy volunteered that, "Unless, of course, you would get us another bottle of champoo," Rachel had sighed, "That's the first sensible thing any of you losers have said all evening," and had clicked her fingers at the sommelier.

They were happy memories, but it was time to return to the present.

Rachel had been massaging her bruised ankle, vainly attempting to ease the pain. After gingerly testing her weight on it, she broke cover from the restaurant entrance and turned south. At last Rachel had a plan, or at least a destination. She would head down into the West End; whatever the time, there were always people there. She could mingle and vanish amongst them, perhaps gain some anonymity.

Walking down Great Titchfield Street, passing a gaggle of restaurants all closed for the night, she stopped short as a shadowy figure appeared in the centre of the junction with Foley Street. It took only a second to recognise the dishevelled white leather-suited figure.

Any anger this biker had at having been violently assaulted remained concealed. With a slow, deliberate movement, her right arm was raised, and a large pistol was pointed in Rachel's direction. Rachel was no firearms expert, but the barrel looked disturbingly wide for a handgun.

The left arm beckoned her to come closer; Rachel held her ground. Inside, she attempted to summon forth the miraculous power that had previously struck her attackers low. Unfortunately, apart from her face contorting as if she were desperate for a pee, nothing else happened.

With a deafening crack of thunder, the biker fired a single shot from her pistol. The projectile whistled by Rachel's left ear, wafting a few strands of her hair as it passed perilously close. Now, with increased urgency, her left hand once again encouraged Rachel to come forward. With no viable escape route, she acquiesced and, with the laboured steps of the condemned woman approaching the gallows, advanced.

The biker produced the now slightly bent set of silver handcuffs with her left hand, throwing them on the floor at Rachel's feet. She pointed at the cuffs and motioned towards Rachel's hands, all while keeping the pistol firmly trained on her head. With a resigned sigh, Rachel leaned down and gathered them up.

From Rachel's left, in a blur of motion and with the roar of an engine, a black Mercedes sped into the junction. With a screech of tyres on damp tarmac, it slithered to a halt directly before her. The white leather-clad biker bounced off its bonnet, hurtling through the air before slamming with bone-crunching force into a red post box.

The Mercedes driver stepped out - an Asian man dressed in a black suit with an open-neck black shirt. Rachel recognised the driver from the Mercedes near Euston. "Shank, you get the woman, I'll deal with this one," he yelled.

Shank emerged from the passenger side, dressed in a denim jacket, a union flag tee-shirt and faded jeans. "'Ello luv, told you we'd see each other again soon." His voice thick with salacious suggestion, he added, "I bet you'll be up for party time before we hand you over to him."

Rachel began running, but those tired legs had already given their all this night. Instead, she staggered unevenly in her attempt to escape. Shank jogged along easily behind her, tauntingly calling out, "Where you going? Don't you get too tired. We wouldn't want you passing out when you get what's comin' to ya."

Closing her eyes, Rachel attempted to push through the excruciating pain of physical exertion. She was finally on the brink of giving up, of surrendering to the hand that fate seemed keen to deal her. Rachel had escaped from captivity to find herself immediately and inexplicably targeted. Why? What could these pursuers possibly want with her?

Perhaps her anxiety voice had been right. Perhaps she should have stayed in…

Rachel thought she had run into a brick wall as she came to an abrupt halt. It wasn't until the wall softly enquired, "Are you ok, Madam?" that she opened her eyes and realised that she had collided with a giant of a man.

At least six foot four in height, he looked even taller in his black felt top hat. The red frock coat with gold braids could barely contain his broad shoulders and muscular frame. Looking up at his wide, bearded face, Rachel thought he may have originated from the southern pacific area.

They were standing outside a row of white, freshly painted Georgian terrace houses merged into a large, state-of-the-art five-star hotel. The single entrance: a large rotary door of opaque mirror glass framed with copper trim. Above the doorway, brass lettering welcomed guests to the Vestibule Hotel.

"Get the fuck away from her," threatened Shank as he menacingly stepped forward. Drawing himself up to his full five foot ten, he pulled out a viciously serrated combat knife from its sheath and snarled, "Come with me, bitch, and I won't have to bleed Lord Snooty here."

"Do you have a reservation with the Vestibule, Madam?" enquired the doorman. His voice, thick with a Tongan accent, betrayed no hint of fear or concern at the deteriorating situation. Instinctively, Rachel nodded: she would gratefully embrace any lie that could temporarily get her off the street. "In which case you had better head on in, Madam," he calmly declared while pointing towards the slowly rotating door.

"No fuckin' way," yelled Shank. He lunged forward, pulling his knife back to drive it into the doorman. "That bitch is comin' with me."

Rachel barely registered that the doorman had moved his oversized fist before it slammed into Shank's stunned face. He would have taken less damage if struck with a sturdy iron bar. Shanks' nose immediately vanished with a sickening squelch, the cartilage smashed into a pulp whilst copious amounts of scarlet liquid sprayed across his pale face.

The fist continued its relentless forward motion, the denim-clad assailant being lifted clean off his feet and flung several meters backwards, eventually clattering down into the gutter.

"The safety of our patrons is our highest priority," the doorman calmly explained as if reading a tag line on a corporate brochure.

An enraged Shanks staggered back onto his feet and screamed, "Mew fuwkin bwoke my fuwkin dose, mew gomma pay mew wunt."

The doorman ushered Rachel past the splatters of crimson liquid that festooned the pavement and towards the hotel entrance. "I'll deal with this misunderstanding, Madam. The hotel reception is to the left of the entrance and please... do enjoy your stay with us at the Vestibule."

Chapter 5

"It must be such a great feeling to have achieved so much and at such a young age." Barry paused, handing Rachel a fresh glass of wine and checked, "A Sauv Blanc, wasn't it?"

"Yes, thank you," Rachel replied. Accepting the glass, she allowed her fingers to momentarily brush along Barry's hand. He flashed her a knowing smile as he offered up his own glass. "To new friends?" he suggested as they clinked their glasses together.

Hannah had cranked up the music's volume in the living room. As they had both been enjoying their conversation, they had retreated to an empty space near the sink in the crowded kitchen.

"Still, I imagine it must still be hard for a woman to reach such a position. I recently read an editorial piece on the glass ceiling and how it remains a substantial obstacle for working women's progress."

Arriving fashionably late to Hannah's party, Rachel had expected to spend most of the evening dancing and drinking. Having encountered many of the guests at work or similar events, she assumed they would be the usual shallow, narcissistic peacocks. Barry was new, a friend of a friend, and this stranger had immediately drawn her gaze.

He may have been under average height, but his attractive physique showed that he kept himself fit and healthy; remarkably fit, she thought with a naughty internal chuckle. Barry had dressed smartly and yet casually in a linen jacket, chinos and a loose light blue cotton shirt. Refreshingly, unlike several of the boors strutting around the party, Barry had no designer labels prominently on show.

Rachel, by contrast, had squeezed herself into her one-piece leather dress, her trim waist nipped in further with a wide waspie belt. Stockings and patent leather heels completed the wild ensemble.

When they'd been shopping, Rachel had been unconvinced when Serge handed her the burgundy leather outfit. He had pointed to the changing room. "Rachel, every woman must have something in their wardrobe that is daring, outrageous and drags them kicking and screaming out of their comfort zone. You will thank me when you build up the courage to wear it. You will see."

Inexplicably, Rachel had felt a sense of relief when Barry had complimented her. "May I say you look utterly amazing. I admit that I have barely been able to take my eyes off you since you made your entrance." Rachel blushed a little as he continued, "Added to the fact that you're an intelligent conversationalist, you have certainly brightened up my evening."

Rachel met Barry's adoring gaze. Perhaps it was due to the alcohol, perhaps it was his magnetic charm, perhaps it was caused by the long months of hard work without proper rest, but in that moment she desperately wanted him to engulf her in his arms and passionately kiss her.

The conversation had flowed easily between them for nearly an hour. In between the topics of music, films and books, he had wanted to know more about her and had confessed his admiration for the success that Rachel had achieved in her career.

Finally, Barry put down his glass. "Look, I was going to ask you, 'Is it difficult being a strong woman in the modern workplace'; instead, would you just like to have a dance?" She nodded enthusiastically.

As they returned to the living room, Hannah's latest dance mix boomed out louder than ever, the dry ice machine had gone into overdrive, the disco lights were in full strobe mode and the mass of writhing guests had built up an impressive sweat. Pressing forward and making themselves some dance space of their own, all Rachel could think about was how to subtly get Barry's telephone number.

"OH GOD, NO," Rachel shouted out as she violently sat up, sweat beading on her forehead. Languishing in that confusing twilight world between sleep and wakefulness, she momentarily struggled to recall where she was.

It took a few moments for her eyes to pierce the gloom of the room. Thick curtains hung over the windows, allowing only a sliver of daylight to illuminate the luxuriously furnished suite. Her eyes adjusted, revealing the furnishings: an elegant Victorian dressing table, an oak writing desk, soft leather chairs in a sitting area and a sixty-inch television. She flopped back down onto the bed thinking she must still be dreaming.

The stacked pillows and perfect mattress gently cushioned her fall before encompassing her in fresh-smelling linen. The mattress gently compressed beneath her form and she uttered a dreamily relaxed, "Oh my god, this is good."

If she wasn't dreaming, how on earth had she arrived here? The drowsiness of sleep slowly receded like the ebbing spring tide on a long, sandy beach, the sequence of events gradually returning to her.

Rachel had escaped from Shank, passing through the Vestibule's rotating door and entering the hotel's reception area. Simply decorated in a tasteful blend of dark wood and off-white marble, the black and white tiled floor led to a carved granite reception desk. Behind this Neolithic-looking structure stood a woman dressed in a charcoal grey suit and white blouse with a black neck scarf. She was shorter than Rachel, her face framed with wavy shoulder-length hair, chestnut brown in colour with red highlights.

If the sight of a dishevelled Rachel in torn jeans, a red leather coat and no obvious luggage was of concern, her subtly made-up face did not betray the fact. Smiling warmly, she enquired, "Welcome, Madam, to the Vestibule Hotel. How may I help you this morning?"

The receptionist tilted her head slightly to the left, the practiced smile continuing to mask any thoughts she might have. Rachel approached the desk. Her plan: to stall for as long as possible before being turned back onto the street. "Hi, yes. I have a reservation."

The receptionist, whose name badge identified her as Tina (Deputy Manager), nodded, looked down at the computer monitor carved into the stone desk and requested, "Madam, your name?"

For a moment she thought about using a pseudonym, but what would be the point? It wouldn't take this woman long to realise that Rachel had wasted her time and have her ejected back into the city streets. "Rachel Minos."

The receptionist typed in the name and waited. The screen flashed and the young women's eyebrows raised in mild surprise. "Hmm... One second please, Ms Minos," she apologised and walked through a door marked Private Office.

Rachel fantasised that a call would now be made to security. For a moment she considered running, but there was not an ounce of flight left in her. She could barely remain standing and doubted she could walk much further even if her life depended upon it - which it possibly did. Outside, the bikers and the two men from the Mercedes lurked, ready to sweep her up and carry out whatever nefarious plans they were intending to enact.

Tina reappeared, bearing a large, thick brown leather-bound book. The ancient tome was sealed with a broad strap and a polished copper clasp. She placed the curious book on the reception counter, took out a small key from her pocket and unlocked the clasp, "I do apologise, Madam, this won't take too much longer."

Bemused, Rachel watched her flick through yellow, aged pages of Latin text, before stopping around a third of the way through the book. Her index finger traced out the words of an entry and her eyebrows once again rose as she commented, "Oh... I see."

She again smiled at Rachel and picked up the internal hotel phone. "Mr

Typhon to hotel reception, please." After carefully returning the receiver, she politely explained, "The hotel manager will be here momentarily; he will want to deal with you personally." Rachel nodded. Whether that was good or bad, she didn't care.

Awaiting the manager's arrival, she leaned forward, supporting her weight on the hotel counter, giving her legs precious, much-needed moments of rest.

From the back office emerged a tall man - at least six foot one - wearing a light grey suit, with a bright vermillion folded handkerchief in his breast pocket and a matching necktie. He had the most intense dark brown eyes; they immediately focussed on Rachel as he joined Tina behind the granite desk.

"You see here, sir…" Tina explained as she pointed to the entry in the leather tome. He looked down, read the text, nodded and looked up, his eyes once again fixed on Rachel.

His voice boomed with an almost theatrical bass, "Thank you, Tina, I will take it from here." The woman gathered up the leather tome and returned through the back office door. "Welcome to the Vestibule Hotel, Ms Minos. It has been some time since we had a member of your family reside with us. Do you know how long you intend to stay?"

Rachel had been momentarily struck dumb. Of all the questions she had expected to answer, this one had never even occurred to her.

As he awaited her response, Mr Typhon tapped some more keys on the computer keyboard and, after reading the screen's output, added, "Your family does have a…" he paused as he double checked the figures, cryptically adding, "a substantial credit lodged with us."

He returned his gaze to Rachel who finally managed to overcome her fugue state to stammer out, "I'm not sure how long." Mr Typhon nodded in acknowledgement. "Not a problem, Madam, we shall make it an open reservation." Rachel nodded as he resumed typing on the keyboard.

Her mental and physical exhaustion had gradually pulled her under. Rachel made the decision to take the room and, after a night's rest, she would come clean with her deception and offer to pay for the accommodation somehow.

She had barely noticed when My Typhon mumbled to himself, "I assume that the address remains 13, Partridge Way," before looking up and addressing her with deep concern in his voice. "I must apologise, Ms Minos, but we currently have no master suites available. Would a junior suite suffice?"

Rachel felt too exhausted to burst out laughing at the absurdity of the question, managing instead to meekly nod in confirmation. Her legs had begun to give way and, like a shipwreck survivor clinging onto flotsam, she desperately clung on to the stone countertop.

Mr Typhon looked up and, with concern in his voice, had asked, "Do you have any luggage and... would you like someone to carry you to your room?" Finally losing her grip and slowly sliding down the stone and onto the floor, she had feebly replied, "No and yes."

Finally banishing the veil of sleep, Rachel lay on the bed, revelling in the luxurious comfort. Letting out a loud yawn and lazily stretching her arms over her head, a thought popped unbidden into her head. Who had undressed her? She checked under the duvet and felt partially relieved that she remained clothed in her tired-looking bra and panties. Rachel burst out into hysterical laughter. It seemed absurd, given all that she had endured, to now be concerned with her modesty.

Beside the bed, on a polished nightstand, stood a bottle of still spa water. Sitting up and drawing the duvet snugly around her, she opened the bottle and began to drink. She gulped the cool, refreshing liquid until the bottle was spent, putting it down with an exaggerated 'Ahhhhh'.

A loud growling noise filled the room.

Having been roused from its slumber, her stomach began to grumble, demanding immediate nourishment. Despite her best efforts to ignore it for several minutes, the requirement became more urgent and forced her to abandon the cosseting comfort of the bed and search the room.

As is traditional when staying in a hotel, she located the tea-making point and quickly opened and consumed the complimentary packs of biscuits.

Next, she hunted down the mini bar.

Sitting cross-legged on the deep pile carpet, she made short order of the obligatory chocolate bar, the jar of jellybeans and the box of dry roasted peanuts. Sadly, there were no wine gums.

Her hunger momentarily sated, given her still fragile mental state, she thought it best not to look at the price of the snacks.

Now her thoughts turned to what to do next. The Rachel of old was always meticulously organised and loved to have 'to do' lists. She found the act of crossing off completed actions to be immensely satisfying and rewarding. For the moment she had only one task. She wasn't a dishonest person but, given her predicament, she thought it best to beat a hasty retreat from the hotel. When she had got herself sorted and earned some money, she would settle the likely considerable bill with them.

Glancing up at the bed, Rachel sensed it summoning her back. It urged her to wallow once again amongst its luxurious high thread count Egyptian cotton sheets and lose herself amongst the mountain range of pillows. Resisting its allure, she instead stood up and entered the bathroom.

Flicking the light switch, she was stunned by the numerous lights reflecting off the copious surface area of marble, mirrors and chrome.

Having spent four years washing in a cramped bathroom fitted out with a drab olive-green bathroom suite, the palatial space that had been set aside for her bathing needs proved to be a wondrous sight.

The decision between the ocean-deep oval bath or walk-in rainforest shower proved difficult to resolve. The refreshing overhead downpour setting with turbo side jets edged the shower to victory.

Having exhausted every single one of the complimentary shower gels, shampoos, hair conditioners, body conditioners and facial scrubs, a much-refreshed Rachel stepped from the shower and wrapped herself in the oversized, fluffy bath towels.

Towelling herself dry, she caught a glimpse of her reflection in the giant, floor-length mirror. From beneath the four years of oppression that haunted her features, she thought she could see the merest hint of the Rachel that had been: a flash of colour in her cheeks; the tiniest spark in her eyes. Both hinted at the personality that had been submerged such a long time ago.

A desire to find scissors gripped her; half naked, with a towel wrapped around her chest, she ran out and searched through the suite's numerous cupboards before finding a sewing kit. The scissors were not the sharpest or largest, but she decided they would have to do and returned to the bathroom.

Standing before the mirror she grabbed a handful of long hair. Rachel had always liked her hair to be no longer than her shoulders. 'He', on the other hand, had preferred her to have exceptionally long hair. "All the better to grab you with," he would joke with little trace of mirth in his voice.

With a trembling hand she brought the scissors up to the first handful of hair. She hesitated, her anxiety voice meekly complaining, 'He won't like it. Stop, stop...' Snip, snip, snip, the blades closed and long strands of hair fell onto the bathroom tiles.

Staring down at the golden strands, Rachel's anxiety voice scolded her. 'Barry is going to be furious when he sees what you've done!' The confusing mixture of fear and elation that she experienced caused her hand to tremble for a full thirty seconds. Only once it had passed did Rachel feel a tiny weight lift from her shoulders.

Looking up into the mirror, she smiled at her handiwork before raising the scissors and cutting again, sending more hair tumbling down. This time there were no shakes; instead, a euphoric sense of liberation. She snipped again and again and was soon hacking away with abandon, those golden locks piling up around her.

It wasn't the most elegant haircut; Serge would likely have been horrified, but she was ecstatic with the results. She felt a sense of pride that a piece of 'him' had been excised from her body.

Admiring her off-shoulder hair, the euphoria of cutting her hair passed and deep down inside she could feel a painful knot begin to tighten within her stomach. She dropped the scissors into the sink as the knot began to spread up through her chest. The agonising pain rose to her throat and at last a loud, moaning sob burst free through Rachel's mouth.

Another followed, and another, until her body relentlessly convulsed with uncontrollable sobbing. She collapsed onto her knees, throwing her arms around herself in a desperate hug. As salty tears streamed down her cheeks and wave after wave of wailing cries broke free, she feared this raging torrent of long subdued emotions would never end.

It was perhaps half an hour before she regained her composure. Standing back up, she washed her face clean of the salty deposits and gave her reflection a hard look, warning it, "Get it together, Minos."

Returning to the bedroom, she resumed her search - this time for her clothes. In the closet, her red leather coat had been placed on a wooden hanger. A plastic laundry bag contained her old tee-shirt and jeans. Beside them, a neatly folded brand-new tee-shirt, bra, knickers and a pair of black jeans. On top of the fresh-smelling pile of clothes, a handwritten note: 'With the compliments of the Vestibule Hotel'. It had been signed 'Mr Typhon'.

Trying on the underwear, she felt surprised by the comfortable fit. These were not the ill-fitting, plain undergarments that 'he' normally allowed her to wear, but also not the skimpy and uncomfortably tight attire "he" had insisted she parade in when his desires required sating. They were simply nice to look at and comfortable.

Next, she pulled on the white tee-shirt and black jeans. They were a remarkably good fit. She looked in the mirror and admired how good they looked. She decided it best not to dwell on how they had managed to get her measurements so perfectly accurate.

Finally, she had a choice between her old trainers or a pair of new flat heel black ankle boots. Since the trainers had been too large, having been 'his' cast offs, there had, of course, been no contest as she slipped on the boots.

She stood up and walked around. Damn, they felt comfortable. Walking up and down the room with growing confidence in her stride, she savoured having footwear that actually fitted her feet. She had begun to realise that the ill-fitting shoes were one more of 'his' little controlling mind games that he had woven so expertly around her.

Rachel gathered up the bag of old clothes, added the trainers, strode confidently to the bedroom bin and tossed the lot in with a heartfelt, "Good Bloody Riddance."

Returning to the closet, she removed the red leather coat from its hanger and slipped it on. The mirror revealed the completed metamorphosis. Gone was the reflected image of a broken, desperate woman, replaced with that of a confident city woman dressed in her twenty-first century suit of armour.

"Damn, do I look good!" she declared out loud. She felt yet another tiny bit of 'him' had been successfully chipped away. Another tiny ray of Rachel that was now able to shine through.

Rachel smiled, yet she knew the scars and damage went deeper than clothes. 'He' had ground down and controlled her for four long years. There were memories that, for now, she must keep securely locked away. Things that 'he' had manipulated her into doing that she could not yet face.

It would take more than a fresh pair of jeans to repair the damage that 'he' had inflicted on her. It would be a long road to recovery, but today had been a good first step.

She took in a deep, calming breath and declared to her reflection, "Ok, Rachel Minos, it's time to go." She turned her back on the mirror, opened the door into the corridor and exited the hotel bedroom.

Chapter 6

Rachel had camouflaged herself behind the large potted fern. Through its verdant leaves she could see the whole of the hotel foyer and, most importantly, her intended route to the lazily gyrating hotel exit.

After watching people coming and going, she knew it would take less than ten seconds to cross the foyer, push her way through the reflective glass door and vanish into the city street beyond.

On her left, two people manned the reception desk: a young black man with spiky hair and an Indian woman, her hair drawn back in a magnificently long ponytail. They were focused on three guests wearing djellaba and keffiyeh who were going through a convoluted checking-in process that seemingly involved lots of loud exclamations and hands being thrown into the air.

Their mountainous heap of fourteen travelling trunks ensured that the two hotel porters were being kept busy as they struggled to stack the weighty luggage onto their trolleys.

To her right, the concierge was helping a Japanese couple, unusually dressed in what Rachel assumed were traditional silk kimonos. Conversing with them in fluent Japanese, he was pointing to various locations on a London tourist map, to which the two oriental guests were nodding enthusiastically.

With all the hotel staff thus engaged, Rachel had a clear path out of the hotel and onto the street outside.

She remained stationary. The nagging fear of the hostiles who could be lying in wait planted her feet as firmly as the fern's roots. 'You're pathetic!' her anxiety voice observed. "This is stupid," she agreed to herself. A quick check that the way remained clear and she resolved to go for it on a count of three.

"One, Two…"

"Good morning, Ms Minos, and how are you today?"

Rachel nearly jumped out of her skin as Mr Typhon greeted her. The elegantly dressed hotel manager had stealthily joined her in the shade of the potted fern. She mumbled out a surprised, "Errr…. Well, thank you."

He spoke in hushed tones, perhaps conscious of their hidden position. "Excellent. We were a trifle concerned, considering that you slept through the entirety of yesterday. I am heartily pleased that you are looking so much more refreshed than during our last encounter." Given her exhausted state, the fact that she had slept through a whole day didn't surprise her.

The manager leaned forward to peer conspiratorially through the leaves of the fern and continued, "I do hope that you did not mind our taking the liberty of supplying you with a fresh change of clothing."

Rachel thanked the manager for the items of clothing and offered to pay for them. He raised his hand, "It is an honour to once again welcome a member of the Minos family to our establishment. Please think nothing more of it."

Standing up straight, abandoning the cover of the fern, he gestured towards the dining room. "If you have finished your lurking for the morning, Madam, breakfast is still being served and I am sure that you must be famished."

Glancing wistfully through the fern at the rotating exit, she allowed the manager to escort her into the dining room. "I can heartily recommend our head chef, Antoine Careme's, new breakfast masterpiece: oyster and black pudding benedict."

A young waiter seated her at a small table near a cascading waterfall. The black slate water feature covering one wall of the room consisted of numerous small pools and chutes. The rhythmic falling water had been designed to provide the perfect relaxing ambience for the discerning diner. Or so the brass plaque at its base claimed.

Rachel passed her hand across the brilliant white tablecloth, enjoying the tactile experience of the material's smooth texture. Having escaped the smothering monotony of the apartment, she revelled in experiencing these new sensations.

Picking up and examining a spoon, she marvelled at the mirror finish of the cutlery, then leaned forward and smelled the single fragrant red rose which sat in a tall, thin porcelain holder at the centre of the table.

It was a far cry from her previous breakfasts: eating from the same discoloured bowl, perched on the edge of a sofa, constantly on alert in case 'he' had woken up.

The waiter arrived and took her breakfast order. Eschewing the chef's special, she instead opted for a Full English breakfast, with streaky bacon and white toast with New Zealand butter, accompanied by a pot of English breakfast tea. As the manager had surmised, she was remarkably hungry.

The waiter soon returned with a silver teapot and poured the amber liquid into her bone china cup. At her nod, he added milk and presented the cup with an exaggerated flourish. Thanking the young man, she took a sip and let out a sigh of contentment.

Her mother, being a good Lancastrian, had instilled in her the belief that the best cup of tea could only be brewed in a proper pot. A teabag in a cup made do for southerners and Americans: after all, they knew no better.

She finished the cup and poured another whilst, across the dining room, a man dressed in a classic pinstriped three-piece suit stood up from his breakfast table. A gold watch chain protruded from his waist-coat pocket and he wore an olive-green cravat rather than a tie. His face was clean shaven and what little hair remained on top of his head had been closely cropped.

He glanced around the room until his gaze fell upon Rachel. Pushing his chair neatly under the table, he walked over and enquired, "Pardon me for the intrusion, madam, but would I be addressing Rachel Minos?"

Rachel looked at him suspiciously, feeling justifiably wary given recent events. Yet she felt an aura of safety within the confines of the Vestibule Hotel, so nodded in confirmation and asked for his name.

"I had heard that you were a guest here." He smiled, his face showing lines that revealed his age. "You won't remember me. My name is Darius Long. The last time we met you would have been no more than two years old, at most three. I worked, on occasion, with your parents, before their retirement from the calling."

His mentioning her parents came as a mild shock. She had casually assumed this man had mistaken her for someone else or, perhaps, was attempting to gain her confidence for some nefarious purpose.

"Do they still live in...wasn't it Chadderton?" Rachel had no clue as to her parents' whereabouts. Since 'he' had successfully driven a wedge between them, she hadn't been able to keep in contact.

"I haven't spoken to them for a few years, but I would imagine so. Would you like to take a seat?" Rachel pointed at the vacant seat opposite. It felt good to have someone even vaguely connected to her family to talk to.

As Darius pulled out the seat and sat down, Rachel's substantial breakfast was placed on the table before her. The huge plate was piled high with a fried egg, scrambled egg, slices of both black and white pudding, sautéed mushrooms, hash browns, baked beans, fried tomato, two rashers of streaky bacon, two fat Cumberland sausages and two slices of lightly fried bread.

As Rachel tucked in, Darius enquired as to what had brought her to London. Piling her fork with a mixture of fried delights, she replied: "Well, I live here now, well I did. I am between jobs and places to live at the moment. It's kind of complicated to explain." She popped the overloaded fork into her mouth and savoured the delicious flavours.

"Really?" he remarked, his face visibly lighting up. "That could be fortuitous for us both. Would you be open to a short-term employment opportunity?" Darius leant forward and, in a hushed tone, added, "I know you didn't follow your parents into the calling, but you are, after all, of the Minos line."

Intriguingly, that had been the second time he had mentioned 'the calling'. Her parents had never spoken about their jobs before her birth. Throughout her childhood, her father had been employed as a night watchman at a local factory.

She was becoming increasingly curious about what Mr Long might know of her parents. As she loaded the fork with more bacon, she decided that more time with him might allow for the extraction of further information. "So, what would this job entail and how much would you pay me?"

As he explained, she continued to tuck into the rapidly shrinking breakfast. "It's very simple. We are delivering a final closure notice to a miscreant who has broken the terms of a contract. It should be trivial for the two of us. As for money: for a simple day's work, shall we say one thousand pounds?"

Rachel nearly choked on her mouthful of Cumberland sausage.

Back during her employment with Sheol Publicity, a sum of one thousand pounds would have seemed trivial. She had paid bar tabs that would dwarf such a figure. Four years further on and she now considered such a sum to be a mighty prize.

Finally swallowing the sausage, she cut off a piece of fried bread and began to soak up a pool of golden egg yolk. "OK, I'm still not sure what you want me to do to earn my money," she observed.

He smiled. "You shouldn't need to do anything. The process requires an additional person to be a witness. My usual companion, regretfully, is unavailable, but, as a Minos, you will be an admirable substitute." Rachel chewed on those words as she chewed on the final slice of black pudding. The money would be more than welcome and she might get the opportunity to shed some light upon her parents' emerging past.

Placing the cutlery on the plate, Rachel recalled one of the training courses she had attended at Sheol Publicity. Module 402, 'The Art of The Negotiation', had been run by one of the company's senior executives. Mrs Thomas had proven to be both exceptionally knowledgeable and skilled in the subject matter. During one roleplay session, Mrs Thomas had hilariously manoeuvred Bethany into agreeing to remove her underwear as part of the closure of the deal. After the embarrassment of that encounter, Bethany had vowed to never let someone get the better of her again and became her most ardent student.

An important lesson centred on pitching the right price during the bargaining phase. Not so high that you scare the opposition away, but sufficiently elevated that you drag them closer to their best and final offer. Reaching for the cup of tea she launched her counteroffer: "Make it three thousand, Mr Long."

Darius leaned back in his chair, rubbed his hands across his head and let out a small chuckle. "I see your mother's searing ambition has rubbed off on you." Crossing his arms, he added, "Two thousand, Ms Minos, and not a penny more." Rachel smiled and nodded. He held out his hand to seal the deal. "And I won't even ask you to sign anything," he added. A one hundred percent bump, thought Rachel, I still got it. Leaning forward, she shook his hand.

You can tell a lot about a person by their handshake. From the domineering hand cruncher to the limp lettuce embrace, you see a glimpse of what underpins them. Darius's had been firm and brief. Perhaps a little rushed, as if wanting to avoid prolonged physical contact.

Standing up, he whipped out his pocket watch and, after checking it, asked, "Shall we meet in the hotel foyer in, say, forty minutes?" Rachel, spreading a thick layer of butter on her first slice of toast, agreed to meet him then.

Having hoovered up the last morsel of food from the plate, she sat contentedly sipping her final cup of tea. 'You're mad! How can you trust him? He could be a psychopathic serial killer for all you know,' seethed her anxiety voice. Under her breath she quietly told it, "Fuck off." After sullenly muttering, 'Things were so much better with Barry; you used to listen to me,' it fell silent.

With the potential of becoming flush with money, Rachel decided to bite the bullet and find out how much her stay at the hotel had already cost.

Crossing the lobby, she dodged past three women standing gossiping. Rachel thought it curious that they were dressed in red ball gowns with long black gloves at eleven in the morning. She assumed they might be part of a corporate event or photo shoot.

The two receptionists were dealing with two elderly ladies, both wearing identical black chiffon dresses with matching grey fur coats and black berets. One was lambasting the other over losing her credit card whilst the receptionists looked on with endless patience.

Mr Typhon stepped up beside Rachel and asked, "Ms Minos, I trust you enjoyed your complimentary breakfast. How can we now be of assistance to you?" For the second time today, she was surprised by his arrival. The manager was certainly nimble on his feet.

"Thank you, Mr Typhon. I wanted to know how much my bill was so far." Fixing her with his deep brown eyes, he explained: "As I said yesterday, Madam, your family has a substantial non-refundable deposit with this establishment."

Her curiosity piqued, Rachel asked how much the deposit was. The manager deftly slipped behind the granite reception desk and quickly brought up the appropriate record on the computer. "Now let me see, taking inflation into account, that would be a little over... three point two million pounds."

Rachel could not help herself. Her jaw slackly dropped downwards as she exclaimed in bewilderment, "Sorry... how much?" The manager pressed more keys and in his calm voice stated, "That would be three million, two hundred and fifty-eight thousand, four hundred and ninety-five pounds and twenty-one pence exactly."

Looking up at Rachel's bewildered face, he offered, "Would you like me to write that down for you?"

Rachel said nothing.

She was desperately attempting to reconcile her parents' modest lifestyle - the comfortable but hardly flamboyant detached house in Chadderton, the ten-year-old Jaguar saloon car - with the astronomical figure the manager had casually provided.

"Are you sure?" she muttered. An amused smile spread across his face as fingers once again flew across the keyboard. "Madam, that it the correct figure. Were you perhaps expecting a more substantial sum? I could have Accounts check the historical expenditures?"

Her parents would go on coach trip holidays. Mother thought that flying was a frivolous waste of money. Father never threw anything out, as it might come in useful. How could she reconcile the parents she knew with the picture of her parents that had begun to emerge?

The manager continued to look on expectantly. "No, I'm sure that's correct," she finally replied.

It slowly dawned on Rachel that she could stay at the Vestibule Hotel for a good while longer. The thought of having somewhere safe to sleep and eat lifted a tremendous weight from her shoulders. Though she admitted to the manager that she didn't have a key and couldn't recall her room number.

"Not a problem, Madam," answered Mr Typhon. "You are in room 21 and you don't need a key; the door will recognise you." Having been isolated for four years Rachel assumed that technology had moved along. "Oh, a facial recognition system?" The manager smiled. "Yes... Something like that."

Darius stood patiently waiting for her as she left the reception desk. He must have picked up on Rachel's confusion. "Everything ok, Ms Minos? Is there a problem?" Rachel stopped and pointed towards the reception desk. "Yes... No, not a problem, just that..." she stopped mid-sentence, deciding not to expose her financial situation to this relative stranger. "Nothing at all. Ready to go?" He gave her a quizzical look before ushering her out through the hotel's rotating door.

Blinking they emerged into a clear, sunny morning. The azure blue sky was scarred by the contrails of planes going to and from faraway places. The hotel entrance faced north and was shaded from the low winter sun, so it remained bitterly cold. Rachel's breath left steamy patterns in the air even at this late hour of the morning.

She thrust cold hands into her leather coat's pockets to retain some warmth and mentally prioritised the acquisition of a warm hat and gloves.

The doorman remained as physically imposing in the cold light of day as he had in the shadows of night. He doffed his top hat to them both with, "Morning, Madam. Morning, Sir. The weather forecast today is for this cold snap to worsen, so please keep yourselves wrapped up warm."

Rachel stepped towards him. "Thank you again for the other night, Mr...?" His large face broke into a wide grin. "My name is Billy. It was my real pleasure to be of assistance. I know how bothersome the local vermin can be."

"Well, thank you, Billy. I can't tell you how grateful I am." It occurred to her that the obvious way to be grateful to a member of the hotel staff would take the form of a tip. When Darius had paid her for her services, she would ensure that Billy received a generous gratuity.

For now, she thanked him again and hopped into the taxi. Darius had already made himself comfortable as Billy closed the passenger door behind her. "Where to, mate?" asked the driver and was directed to 55, Montague Street.

Since breakfast, Darius had slipped on a light brown, camelhair overcoat as protection from the cold and now carried a thin leather briefcase. Rubbing his bare hands together to ward off the cold, he asked, "So, Ms Minos, did you experience a little trouble a couple of nights ago?"

Rachel stared out of the window, watching people and cars going about their business. She had spent countless hours staring down on similar street scenes from the Camden flat; it felt peculiar to view them at street level. "Nothing serious," Rachel lied. "Just some over-enthusiastic locals."

She resumed her people-watching as her anxiety voice added, 'Careful. I bet he's taking you to his murder flat!' Darius surprisingly responded, "Sorry, I didn't quite catch that."

Had he heard the anxiety voice as well? How could that even be possible? Her anxiety voice remained completely silent as the taxi driver replied, "Didn't say a word, mate." Darius shrugged his shoulders, opened his briefcase and pulled out a manilla envelope. He paused, considering the consequences of his next action, before handing it to Rachel.

"When I heard yesterday that you were in the hotel, I thought it best to let your father know. Since I couldn't locate a telephone number for him, I sent a Manchester contact of mine up to their house." He pointed to the manilla envelope "I received this in an email this morning."

Rachel peeled the flap open and removed a piece of A4 paper. A sales brochure for 13, Partridge Way. Describing it as a vacant property with no forward sales chain.

Her heart sank. Despite how things had been left when she had broken off contact with them, Rachel had secretly harboured the idea of turning up at the old house and begging for their forgiveness: her mother embracing her with a bone-crushing hug, her father grumpily calling her a stupid clot before joining in the group hug.

That precious dream had now been snatched away from her. "I've put out feelers with colleagues past and present, but as yet there is no news on your mother and father. If I do hear anything, I will let you know."

She sat, desperately fighting back another knot that had formed in her stomach. Breaking down in sobbing tears in the back of a black cab might not be considered suitable witness behaviour. Fighting back the tears, she thanked Darius but kept her eyes focused on the shops and pedestrians.

Curiously, her anxiety voice remained quiet. Normally it would have taken such an opportunity to undermine her self-confidence; perhaps with a barbed remark about having no one left but 'him' in the world.

By the time the taxi pulled up on Montague Street, Rachel had wrestled the knot into submission and regained her composure. As Darius settled the fare, Rachel stepped out and breathed in the chilly air. Number 55 had once been a substantial three-storey town house which, in its later life, had been converted into three separate apartments.

Joining her on the pavement, Darius checked, "Are you ready?" She nodded and together they walked up the short flight of steps to the impressively large communal front door, which was painted in glossy black with a prominent brass 55.

The intercom to their left had three buttons. Rachel followed Darius's index finger as it selected the button for flat B and pressed it.

The name of the occupant immediately caught her attention: Leon Bay.

Chapter 7

"Breathe," coaxed Darius. "Focus on one breath at a time and you will be fine." Rachel desperately hung on to the lamp post, fighting the overwhelming urge to regurgitate the morning's cooked breakfast.

Her head swam as she tried to grapple with the reality of what she had witnessed, of the events she had been party to. "Don't think about it too much. I will flag a taxi to take us back to the Vestibule." Rachel shook her head. After pulling herself upright and fighting down her nausea she replied. "No, I need to have some time to myself, please." Darius hesitated, before conceding, "Very well, Ms Minos. I will see you back at the hotel."

Rachel nodded and watched him proceed out of view. Maintaining a grim hold on the sturdy lamp post, she began to replay the bewildering experience, hoping to make more sense of it all.

The front door had been buzzed open without them being asked to identify themselves. They entered a communal hallway. Its spotless walls smelled freshly painted, the polished wooden floorboards shone brilliantly and fresh floral displays had been carefully positioned on each landing. "Nice place," Rachel commented; Darius did not respond.

On the second floor they stopped at the only door, painted ivory white, bearing a Gold B.

"Now, follow my lead - this could get a bit spicy." Rachel began to have second thoughts as Darius knocked on the door three times.

Leon Bay was six feet tall with long white bleached hair, dressed in very tight jeans and a tee shirt. A tattoo emblazoned on his neck simply read 'Leon'.

Rachel was reminded of the tattoo 'he' had convinced her to get on the small of her back. The reminder of it sent a shiver through her that emanated from that inaccessible spot. Despite the pain it would take, she resolved to get that tiny piece of 'him' obliterated from her body as soon as possible.

"Who the hell are you?" demanded Leon in an aggressive voice. "I was expecting... well, not you!"

Darius maintained a calm and even voice. "Good day, Mr Bay. We have been sent to discuss the issue of a contract involving you..." Interrupting, Leon firmly poked Darius in the chest and demanded: "Listen, I don't have time for you. Talk to my manager, Amanda, she deals with all my legal stuff."

Rachel watched Darius's admirable self-control as, without changing the delivery of his voice, he explained: "I don't think your manager is authorised to deal with this contract as it..."

Leon cut him off with several sharper pokes to the chest. "I said talk to Amanda! I am really not interested. Now, will you kindly get off my property before I get you kicked off it."

"This is in regard to your three-point contract."

Leon froze.

Rachel was reminded of a white rabbit caught helplessly in the blinding glare of an approaching vehicle. He stammered, "That contract... oh, right." And the colour rapidly drained from his face until it matched his hair. The swaggeringly confident man had been instantly swept away, leaving only a shadow of himself. "You better come in then." He left the door open and skulked into the apartment. Rachel closed the door as they followed him inside and into the living room.

Whoever had decorated this room had either thrown away their colour palate or had a fetish for white. Walls, carpet, sofa, chairs, paintings, porcelain naked female statues: all of them white.

Leon had already slumped into a large chair. Hugging a bottle of beer as if it were his baby bottle, he stared out of the window, consciously trying to avoid eye contact with either Darius or Rachel.

Taking a seat opposite, Darius opened his briefcase and removed a black file before setting the case back down upon the floor. Unsure what she should do, Rachel elected to stand behind Darius. It had the benefit of allowing her to look over his shoulder surreptitiously at the now open file.

"Can you please confirm that your full name is Leonard William Bay? You were born on the 13th July 1991 and currently reside here at 55, Montague Street." He paused, waiting for some reaction from the sullen-looking man. Leon continued to stare out of the window, deliberately avoiding eye contact as he grunted, "Yes... yes I am." Darius nodded, adding, "Excellent, we wouldn't want any mix-ups, would we?"

The cover sheet on the file was a neatly typed page of client information; the kind you would see accompanying a million similar files. Darius ticked and signed the entry at the foot of the form, confirming the client's identity and turned to the next page revealing a quite different sheet.

It did not look like paper; the yellow page possessed a fibrous texture. The text on the page had been handwritten in a dark red ink with a colour reminiscent of an aged claret. The alphabet used and the words they formed were utterly alien and unintelligible to Rachel and yet there was something about this strange script that was oddly familiar.

"Now, Mr Bay, you will recall that subsection 12A of the contract states that on fulfilment of the client's three requests the contract closure stipulation comes into effect. This stipulation being that payment in full be made to the provider upon the client's eventual demise." Darius paused, waiting for any reaction from Leon. The man continued to hug his bottle and stare out of the window.

"As per subsection 21D, if the client or provider breaks the terms of this contract either party may request external arbitration. This may result in punitive actions being enacted on either party up to and including immediate settlement or cancellation of the debt."

Colour had begun to flow back to Leon's face, his reply less timid and containing more bravado as he regained his composure. "Can we dispense with the preamble? I'm a busy man. I am expecting a sports correspondent to arrive soon and would prefer it if you were not here when she arrives."

"As you wish, Mr Bay." Darius turned over the next page, revealing a further sheet of this peculiar text. "The provider has found you to be in flagrant breach of the terms of the contract and has asked that my colleague and I intercede on their behalf as independent arbiters."

Leon leaned forward and smirked at them both. "Would you like a drink? I am going to have a whisky." He stood up, walked to the white bar and nonchalantly poured himself a double measure of Aberlour A'Bunadh. After adding a generous amount of cola, he returned to his seat, took a sip and requested to Darius, "Oh, please continue."

Darius now read directly from the mysterious text: "Mr Bay wilfully engaged the services of a Millwall warlock to change the client details on the said contract from Mr to Mrs with the intent to avoid the consequences of the contract by having his spouse unwittingly fulfil the contract's final settlement. This is in direct violation of subsection 17J: all transfers of the contract can only be made between parties who are a) aware of the contract's full terms and b) willing to participate."

Leon was the child caught with his hand in the cookie jar and he looked momentarily abashed by Darius's accusation. Then he threw his head back and heartily laughed out loud. "Boohoo, you caught me. Well, it was a calculated risk, but given what was at stake it seemed silly not to try. Serves me right, I guess, for trusting a Millwall supporter."

Despite his casual bravado, Rachel could sense the unease festering within the man even as he joked, "Well, slap my wrists. I promise I won't do it again." He put his glass down on the white marble table,

"Listen, I know you have a job to do so let's make this a bit simpler for you." He pointed to a white painting with a diagonal line bisecting it. "There is a safe behind that painting with ten grand in it. It's yours if you go back to whoever it is you work for and tell them that this has all been a misunderstanding and it's all cleared up."

Darius continued where he had left off, much to the visible frustration of Leon, "We are here to evaluate how best to fulfil the stipulations of the contract that you willingly entered into and subsequently gained full benefit from." Darius turned back to face Rachel. "I think it will help in your decision if you read about the three requests he made," and handed her the yellowed sheet.

The document had a rough, cloth-like texture with a fine weave that reminded her of starched sheets. She stared at the unintelligible script, her face betraying bewilderment at this complex alien language.

"Focus. You are of the Minos line. It is in your blood. Focus." Darius's commanding voice began to fade away as she stared down at the script.

The symbols began to move, causing Rachel to almost drop the page in surprise. As if rising from a long slumber, they began to stretch and move in unison. Slowly changing, the symbols altered their structure and pattern until, at last, recognisable English words began to form upon the page. Wide eyed, she watched transfixed as the transformed words jostled with each other for space upon the crowded page before finally coming to rest. "Good. Well done." Darius then encouraged her to read the page.

The title of the page read: 'Record of client's requests and resolutions synopsis'. There were three distinct sections, which Rachel duly read out loud:

13th April 2005: client requested that we remove footballing skills from his fellow club trainee Mathew Opoku and transfer them to himself.

Resolution: footballing skills successfully transferred to client. Mathew

Opoku suffered severe left knee injury from which he will never fully recover. Currently works in the provision of fast food in Balham area. Request fulfilled.

18th December 2014: client killed one Ron Silver on a pedestrian crossing outside Kings Cross railway station, London. Having not stopped at the scene, client requested that we 'make the mess go away'.

Resolution: all CCTV footage nullified. Witnesses of the event dealt with. Police records deleted. Vehicle involved in the incident purged. No action deemed necessary against victim's wife, Katherine Silver. Request fulfilled.

4th May 2016: client requested that we get rid of fellow club player, Paul Greave, and that his wife, Anika, become his.

Resolution: Paul Greaves was exposed by a tabloid paper for having a gay affair. Further damning revelations subsequently destroyed both his career and marriage. Opportunity taken to introduce the client and Anika in carefully choreographed encounters. Operation successfully completed. Paul Greaves counted as late casualty due to his committing suicide soon afterward. Request fulfilled.

Rachel looked up from the sheet and directly into the eyes of Leon. Deep inside her she could feel a growing coldness, an icy breeze howling within her inner darkness.

"What are you looking at? I deserved those skills far more than that stammering fool did." Leon picked up his glass and took another drink. "Unlike me, he had zero charisma and far too much love for the game. I look good on tv, the women love me," he flashed an unnerving smile at Rachel, "and the men want to be me. With those ball skills I became the perfect package. If wanting to improve yourself is a crime, well I am happily guilty as charged."

The bitterly cold wind grew stronger within her, feeding upon Rachel's pent-up anger. "Steady," counselled Darius as he placed a calming hand on her arm. "Keep it in check for now."

Leon was in full flow, "As for Anika: I think I deserve a refund on that one. When her darling Paul topped himself, she went completely to pieces. I wanted sexy eye candy on my arm, something to make other men jealous. What I got was a moody cow who spends most of her time crying. Not exactly what I had in mind."

Rachel struggled to keep the howling ice wind in check as she demanded, "And what of Ron Silver? What of his wife, Katherine Silver?"

He waved his hand in the air dismissively. "Listen, it was an accident. I didn't see the fool on the crossing. But the police wouldn't see it that way. So what if I had been drinking? It was Christmas, a man like me has the right to celebrate. Anyhow, let's be straight - who's more important: the young superstar who has made it to the national squad or a boring nobody?" He suddenly laughed. "Come to think of it, I should have sent his wife a bill for the damage he did when he bounced off my Bentley."

The ice storm raging within her struggled to break free from its confinement as, between gritted teeth, she asked Darius, "Now what?"

Darius withdrew his calming hand and explained the options. "Well, we can walk away and the contract will come due at the end of his natural life. We can elect to bring the due date forward by any number of years, or... we can enact immediate collection."

Leon jumped to his feet and pointed his finger at Rachel. "Listen lady, don't mess with me. I can make your life unpleasant. I have good friends that could mess up your home life if you don't..." He fell silent as Rachel glared at him. Something in her eyes once again swept the colour from his stunned face.

He stumbled forward, falling beside the marble table and landed on his knees. Looking up, he put his hands together as if in prayer and began to beg. "Please, I'm not a bad person. I wanted to be famous; I wanted to be the best. I made a mistake. Look, I've seen the error of my ways. I'll be good. I'll be like that Scrooge dude in the muppet movie. I'll go and look after that Katherine woman. I'll look after orphans and shit, anything, please don't…"

Rachel imperiously stared down at the sobbing wretch that now pathetically whimpered for its continued existence. She felt no compassion for it. There was no interest in the misdeeds it had perpetrated. No consideration for the suffering it had caused to innocent people. At that moment Rachel possessed no emotions at all. All that mattered to her was that this pitiful entity had broken the terms of its contract.

The monstrous power broke free from her body as, in an icy cold voice, she declared, "Immediate collection!"

Time, relative to Rachel, slowed to a snail's pace crawl. Leon's flood of tears now unhurriedly rolled down onto the white shag pile carpet, his abandoned whisky glass left to lethargically spin on the white marble coffee table.

Behind Leon, a crack suddenly appeared. It started as nothing more than a tiny cut in the air, only catching Rachel's attention as it grew larger. She watched, transfixed, as the fracture expanded before finally, with a pulsing surge, it grew into a man-sized hole. Inside, there was nothing, a non-reflecting matte blackness.

Thrusting out of this darkness came a long, thin, writhing appendage. Her first thought was of a large snake. But the smooth surface possessed no eyes or mouth. Perhaps it was the tentacle of some monstrous creature. But no. On an instinctive level, Rachel recognised this sinewy length as a tail.

Onwards it came, gathering into coils as it threatened to completely fill the white room with its apparently endless length. At last, the tip touched Leon. It drew back as if hesitating; tantalisingly, almost erotically, it began to delicately encircle the almost motionless man. Only when his waist and upper torso had been encircled with numerous loops of the tail, did it tighten its grip. The audible, sickening crunch of cracking ribs filled the room, as it firmly secured its victim.

Slowly the tail slid back into the dark portal, the excess coils unwinding in a dance of hypnotic synchronisation. At last, the remaining length unhurriedly dragged its helpless victim towards the closing portal. Leon's wide panicking eyes silently pleaded with Rachel, as he was finally dragged beneath the opaque surface.

Abruptly, time resumed its normal forward march.

Momentarily paralysed, Rachel stared at the now vacant area of space. The emotions which had been temporarily banished returned in a deluge as her mind desperately attempted to process the events she had witnessed - events she had somehow instigated and the fate to which she had apparently condemned Leon.

None of it made any sense and a rising tide of hysteria now threatened to completely overwhelm her.

In an act of self-preservation, she rejected it all and fled from the room. A solid wall of denial slammed down within her head, blocking out all thoughts of the events that had transpired as Darius's pleas for her to wait echoed in her wake.

Stumbling out onto the pavement, she had grabbed onto the nearby lamp post. "Breathe," coaxed Darius, "Focus on one breath at a time and you will be fine." Rachel desperately fought back the overwhelming urge to regurgitate the morning's cooked breakfast. "Don't think about it too much. I will flag a taxi to take us back to the Vestibule."

Rachel shook her head. After pulling herself upright and fighting down her nausea she replied. "No, I need to have some time to myself, please." Darius hesitated, before conceding, "Very well, Ms Minos. I will see you back at the hotel." Rachel nodded, and watched him proceed out of view whilst maintaining her grim hold on the sturdy lamp post. She decided to wait for a little while longer before attempting the feat of unaided walking.

"Got muw dow bwich" was all she heard as the heavy blow slammed into the back of her head, sending her tumbling downwards into the peaceful arms of unconsciousness.

Chapter 8

In the years Rachel spent in Barry's thrall she had learned to endure his tempestuous bouts of rage and to persevere under the verbal bombardment as he sought to continually degrade her.

Relief, when it came, were those periods when he lavished apparent tender care and love upon her. Even then, she would nervously await the inevitable transformation and ready herself to cower from his temper.

Barry ensnared her within a continuous cycle of deconstruction and reinforcement. Kept constantly off balance, she found herself lost between the fear of disappointing him and holding on to the hope that she could earn his love.

Yet, despite his physical superiority, Barry rarely resorted to physical abuse. That wasn't to say he couldn't be rough with Rachel, especially during sex.

When they had begun seriously dating, the occasional bit of aggressive sexual role play had been a thrilling and contrasting experience for her. It had all been part of the new adventure as they discovered their individual and mutual desires.

As the nature of their relationship changed, sex morphed into ensuring Barry's needs and desires were sated. She would endure his demands, comply with his orders, always hoping that her obedience would please him a little bit more.

For his part, Barry would always follow up a rough sex session by hugging and gently stroking Rachel. He would whisper into her ear, praising her beauty and purring how grateful he was that she really understood him.

Relentlessly, this cycle of deconstruction and reinforcement continued.

Perhaps Barry had known on an instinctive level that Rachel would not tolerate being physically assaulted. When, at last, he had violently struck her on that fateful evening, the cycle had been interrupted. In that moment of shock, Rachel had allowed herself to peer through the illusion and admit to herself that she had been suffering intolerable abuse.

The assailant who struck Rachel a surprise blow across the back of her head as she had hung on to a lamp post on Montague Street had shown no such inhibitions in their use of violence.

Rachel sluggishly emerged from the depths of numbing oblivion and dragged herself onto the shores of consciousness. The back of her head ached with a throbbing pain, the unfortunate result of being struck by something heavy.

An attempt to explore the extent of the wound was thwarted by metallic cuffs secured around her wrists. Cracking open an eye, she looked down at the ornate, decorated silver handcuffs attached by a sturdy chain to a hoop affixed in a concrete floor.

Rachel cautiously lifted her head to examine the surroundings. She had been sat upon a simple wooden seat placed in the centre of a large, empty room. Featureless concrete walls rose to a corrugated metal roof, in which a lone skylight framed the distant waxing moon.

As Rachel stared up at the celestial body, the silhouette of a low-flying plane passed noisily across it. Only when silence returned did she overhear distant, muffled voices engaged in animated conversation nearby.

'Barry's safe little apartment doesn't look so bad now, does it?' Her anxiety voice spat out the words with clear contempt.

Having frustratedly pulled at the handcuffs in a vain attempt to free herself, Rachel's mind momentarily wandered to the earlier events at Leon Bay's apartment. She immediately elected to leave the wall of denial firmly in position. This was not the time or place to attempt to deconstruct those disturbing events. Instead, she focused on how she had arrived here.

After the crippling blow, she could recall only tantalisingly fleeting snippets of time: being bundled into the boot of a car; handcuffs being roughly secured on her wrists; the car driving at speed and finally being pulled from the vehicle as the sound of a jet engine whined and roared nearby.

Her thoughts were interrupted as the large metal sliding door screeched open. Metal ground on metal, crying out for a little lubrication.

Backlit in the doorway, a man entered the chamber and walked to face Rachel. He stood around five ten in height, wearing a navy-blue two-piece suit and peach-coloured shirt. His head had been concealed under a loose black sack through which she could feel her captor's eyes watching and assessing her.

Silently, he walked one circuit around her, giving the impression of a man carefully evaluating a statue prior to the commencement of an auction.

"It was stupid of you to break concealment." She immediately recognised the voice as the occupant from the back of the Mercedes. "Once outside, you should have realised I would quickly track you down." He sighed as if disappointed in Rachel and began another slow, pacing circle around her.

"Let me tell you a story involving a dirty little blackmailer. A little over three years ago, I got an anonymous message - a demand, no less - pay up or else. They dropped hints as to the nature of my secret and threatened to expose me to Viath himself."

He stopped pacing as he mused, "Such a fate no sound man would countenance lightly." It occurred to Rachel that this man was clearly enjoying delivering this theatrical performance.

After the brief pause, he resumed his slow circle. "So, I paid this blackmailer and, month after month, they have bled me dry. Of course, I tried to work out who this weasel might be. I employed specialists, people skilled in rooting out the truth and we narrowed it down to a few key individuals."

He stopped directly before Rachel. "You, Rachel Minos, were top of that list. You had worked on the deal; you could have uncovered what I had done and, as I dug deeper, other subtle clues hinted at your complicity and treachery." Rachel was reminded of an amateur dramatics performance as her captor delivered his Shakespearean-style monologue.

His voice full of incredulity, he continued, "The preposterous cock and bull story about leaving to start a family. I mean, please, talk about acting suspiciously out of character." He threw his hands in the air to accentuate his disbelief. "The fact that the blackmail letter arrived almost six months to the day after you left had to be more than simple coincidence."

Another passing plane paused his flow; he resumed his pacing, waiting for the noise to subside. "The final conclusive piece of the jigsaw came when I tried to track you down, Ms Minos. Imagine my surprise to find that you had severed all contacts with friends and family. Can you understand my frustration at realising you had vanished from the face of the planet?"

He leaned towards Rachel, engulfing her in a cloud of lavender and jasmine cologne. "I was furious that, despite my best efforts, you remained an elusive ghost. But one that happily kept taking my money."

He resumed his prowl around his immobilised prey. "Imagine my surprise when a contact picked you up on CCTV, brazenly wandering through Camden without an apparent care in the world."

His voice became momentarily tinged with anger as he stopped once again. "Did you want to use my hard-earned money to buy a pretty dress? Well, that was your first and last mistake, Ms Minos."

"Though I am in something of a quandary. Not everything neatly adds up if you are the sole villain in my tale. And I don't like unbalanced accounts. The evidence leads me to wonder if you have a partner. Or, perhaps worse, you are an unwitting pawn in another's subtle game."

The hooded man stood silent for a moment before resuming his restless pacing. "Now, I want to be civil about this and I do have the greatest respect for your family heritage." Allowing his largess to sink in, he paused whilst examining his manicured nails.

"Give me the data you have on the Decem Fossas contract. Return my money and tell me who your partner is." He dropped his hand and focused on Rachel. "Do this and I may let you live."

Rachel wondered if the blow to her head had been harder than she realised. Perhaps critical memories had been jumbled and lost. The hooded man stood expectantly awaiting an answer to a question she was incapable of addressing.

As he impatiently glanced at his watch, Rachel decided she had no choice but to tell him the truth. He once again stalked around in a circle as she explained how she had made a mistake with her life. How she had been emotionally entrapped and isolated for nearly four years by a man who had beguiled her into loving him. That during this time he had severed all her contact with the outside world. She had been manipulated, controlled and, for four years, lost.

The admission of the total failure of her personal life to a stranger, the declaration that she had lost control, the embarrassment of the humiliation she had endured, it felt too much for one soul to handle. Like the Titan, Atlas, the crushing weight of her world pressed down upon drooping shoulders.

"Ms Minos, what a tragic story," he eventually replied, with no small amount of sarcasm. "How infantile do you think I must be? I watched you with keen interest at Sheol's and was impressed by how you handled yourself. It is a bitter irony that I had hoped to one day become your mentor. Of all people, who else would have spotted the irregularity in the contract and linked it to me. You had a rare talent and…"

He hesitated, changing his tack, having perhaps revealed too much about himself. "You have the audacity to cry a tragic story of how you were led astray by a bad man." He walked towards the sliding door and paused, turning back to face her. "I am going to give you ten minutes to reconsider your position. Use that time wisely, Ms Minos; reflect on the desperation of your situation." He looked around the empty warehouse to emphasize his next point: "No one is coming to rescue you. You are quite alone."

Slowly, he dragged the sliding door closed. "If you persist in denying me what is mine, I will turn you over to Mr Shank. I know he is extremely keen to have some alone time with you - especially after you broke his nose."

The door slammed shut and, apart from pale shafts of moonlight falling from the skylight, she sat alone in darkness.

Rachel futilely pulled at the handcuffs and chain; the reinforced steel remained stubbornly intact as she let out a loud, frustrated scream.

The attempt to focus her mind and ignite the flame within her darkness failed as, once again, that terrifying yet mercurial power eluded her.

After several more struggles to pull herself free, Rachel slumped down in the chair with the demeanour of a defeated woman. It made no sense to her. He was convinced that Rachel was his blackmailer and had information on him relating to Decem Fossas.

Who could have made her the patsy? Immediately her thoughts went to Barry. She toyed with the idea before discarding it. He had neither the knowledge nor opportunity to have orchestrated such a plan.

Perhaps there had been another person, from within Sheol, who had recruited Barry; the brains behind the partnership that...

Attempting to shy away from that train of thought, Rachel could already see the logical conclusion. Perhaps her meeting with Barry not been a coincidence? Maybe their falling in love and his subsequent control of her life had really all been part of an elaborate plan to blackmail someone?

Struggling to come to terms with the idea that her suffering may have been orchestrated for someone else's gain, Rachel leaned forward and dry-wretched bile from her stomach. It took several painful heaves of her guts before she flopped back into the chair.

How much time now remained of her ten minutes?

Rather than worrying about Barry and his improbable link to this mess, Rachel focused on who could have been involved within Sheol Publicity itself. That person would need to have access to the Decem Fossas contract and know enough about Rachel to embroil her in their planned deceit.

Hannah?

She had been bid leader and would have known the contract intimately and Rachel had ousted her as the company's rising star. Had Hannah engineered this as payback, a Machiavellian manoeuvre to clear her route back to a senior exec position?

Could this final scene be Hannah's endgame? Had their fun times together been a ploy to gain Rachel's trust? Did she hate Rachel so much for stealing her glory that a gruesome fate at Shank's hands was deemed to be acceptable recompense? She sadly shook her head in self-pity.

One other thought puzzled Rachel. He seemed convinced that Rachel had been blackmailing him but why, then, did he feel the need to conceal himself under a hood?

The moonlight surrounding her vanished: Rachel assumed that yet another low-flying plane was obscuring the lunar body when, unexpectedly, a pool of torch light momentarily illuminated her position from above before being extinguished.

Looking up aggravated the pain in the back of her head, but the reward justified the cost. Through the skylight, Rachel could make out the shape of a person silhouetted by the light of the moon.

The torch flicked back on, illuminating a large piece of cardboard on which had been hastily written in large capitals:

TELL THEM TO

After a pause, a fresh cardboard message replaced it, bearing the text:

TAKE YOU TO

Another sheet appeared with the words:

RED-STAR STORAGE

and another with:

HEATHROW

The final cardboard message read:

GOT IT? NOD!

The silhouette turned the torch beam back through the skylight to illuminate Rachel. She gently nodded, acknowledging she understood the message and the light was extinguished.

The silhouetted figure disappeared from Rachel's view and she readied herself for the sound of the metal door sliding noisily open once again.

Chapter 9

"For you, another half of cider," chirped the Australian barman, as he placed a fresh glass of cider on the bar in front of Rachel. Russell, as his name badge identified him, seemed in remarkably high spirits considering it was long past 7 o'clock in the morning and he had started his shift at 10 o'clock the previous evening.

As he swept away Rachel's empty glass, he asked, "So, you told them that everything had been stashed at Red Star Storage near Heathrow. Come on, you can't leave me hanging on this cliff hanger."

Rachel had begun to regret telling the tale of the night's adventures. But the sole member of the enthusiastic audience wanted to hear more and, most importantly, kept pouring her fresh glasses of cider.

Bag Head Man, as she had decided to christen him, had been understandably wary of taking her to the storage facility. Instead, he demanded that she provide the number of the locker so that they could arrange for the retrieval of the material.

"Nope," Rachel had bluntly replied. "You take me there, or when the clock runs down it all gets transmitted into the public domain." Rachel had decided that since Bag Head Man believed her to be a criminal mastermind it was time to act like one. "What are you talking about?" he asked with a hint of fear creeping into his voice.

Putting on a poker face that Mrs Thomas would have scored as an A-, maybe a B+, Rachel sprung her own surprise. "Did you think I would be stupid enough to emerge from hiding without some form of suitable insurance? I don't know how long you have been holding me but..." Rachel paused long enough to sow seeds of panic in his mind. "If I don't reset the computer's countdown, your dirty laundry will be uploaded to preselected web sites and emailed to a wide selection of involved people. Your dirty little secret will be public knowledge."

Rachel felt alive.

For the first time since escaping the Camden apartment she was thinking ahead, anticipating issues, strategizing. Damn, it felt good. Of course, this all hinged on the skylight silhouette having a viable plan or this would not end well.

Bag Head Man stared at her, clearly trying to decide if this revitalised Rachel was bluffing or not. "Bullshit," he sneered but with little conviction in his voice. "Give me the lockup number, Ms Minos, or you will get a bullet in the head."

'Got you,' thought Rachel. Now he was off his well-rehearsed script, her captor's demeanour and delivery had lost most of its previous polish. Time to double down on the bluff she decided.

She laughed at him, re-enforcing the façade of her contempt for his threat. "Go ahead. I suspect you intend to kill me regardless." Adopting her own theatrically whimsical tone she continued, "But I go to a far, far better place knowing that you will have to face the music... pardon me, face the wrath of Mr Viath."

At this point in the negotiation Mrs Thomas would explain, 'you must give them the impression that they have your best and final offer. They must believe that you're ready to walk away from the table, that you are happy to accept the consequences. That puts the onus on them to accept the outcome or face the repercussions.

He stared through his bag as another plane roared overhead. She could only guess at the thoughts going through his head as he desperately attempted to work out how the tables had been turned and why he was now in the defensive posture.

The silence between them had dragged on. Rachel began to fear she had over-extended. Perhaps she should throw him something to... 'No' came the clear voice of Mrs Thomas in her head. 'Once you play this gambit, you hold your nerve or fail'. So, Rachel smiled and said, "Tick

Tock."

At last, he cracked. "Fine, fine. My men will take you to the lock-up." His calm voice of control had been replaced with irritated tones as he petulantly added, "But if this is a ruse, I will lock you in a room with Mr Shank and let him do whatever he wants with you."

Rachel remained impassive despite his threat. She had been tempted to shrug her shoulders but thought better of it. Bag Head Man had capitulated and by ignoring his threat she continued to erode his belief that he remained in control.

"That was a pretty ballsy play," remarked Russell as he emptied the clean glasses from the bar's dishwasher. "What if he'd called your bluff?" Rachel took a long drink of her cider before answering. "I guess I had resigned myself to my fate. At least I would have gone down fighting." Russell laughed out, "Good on yah!" as he poured out a glass of wooded Chardonnay.

"So, what's with this Bag on Head name?" Rachel smiled at his question. "It's a bit silly, but a school friend of mine and I used to make up horror stories. One of those spooky tales we concocted was about a man who had been disfigured in a terrible accident. It drove him mad and, of course, this meant he would hunt down children at night. He wore a sack over his head to hide his horrific features and so we christened him Bag on Head." After emptying her glass of cider, she concluded, "It seemed as good a name as any."

Russell laughed in agreement "Kids' imagination, eh? So, back to tonight's adventures, what happened next?"

A darkly muttering Shank had eventually come to lead her outside. His nose was covered with a large plaster whilst dark bruising had spread across his face. From the back of his waistband, he drew an automatic pistol and began to wave it around. "Dew dink dis is bunny bwitch? Eh? Eh?"

Desperately suppressing the urge to say 'A little bit, yes' to the wildly unstable man with the deadly weapon, Rachel instead chose to look down and say nothing.

"Yer, dat's wight bwitch." He leaned forward and thrust the pistol into her face. "Yewl ged dis soom enuf," he growled. Apparently satisfied with his dominant act, he replaced the gun in the back of his jeans' waistband.

Still grumbling, Shank unhooked the chain from the floor and, with a sharp tug, brought Rachel to her feet. With a well-practiced demeanour of compliance, Rachel followed dutifully behind as he led her outside. With unwarranted, sharp jerks of the chain, he guided her to the waiting Mercedes and roughly bundled her into the rear seat. At least she had moved up from the boot, Rachel laughed to herself.

'It's not going to work: your plan sucks. They will kill you or worse. We should have stayed in the flat, we should have stayed safe with Barry. If we escape, let's go back and beg his forgiveness.' Rachel had grown ever more wearisome of her anxiety voice. She didn't bother to rise to its taunt and instead focussed on her surroundings.

There had been a short delay when the driver suggested that Shank get in the back with Rachel. Shank had flatly refused to give up his shotgun position for a Cobain seat and instead defiantly sat up front.

During the entire journey the driver, a sharply dressed Asian man, didn't look at her, or in any way acknowledge Rachel's presence. Shank, on the other hand, was paying too much attention to their captive: spewing out a constant spiel of hate-filled expletives, explaining in graphic detail what he would to do to her, how she would suffer and on and on. She added his monologue to her inner anxiety voice and tuned them both out.

Bag Head Man had watched them leave, having decided not to join them on this short journey. As they exited the complex of warehouses, Rachel noticed a card tag hanging out of the back of the seat pocket.

With the driver and Shank arguing about the best route to get to Red Star Storage, Rachel leaned forward and read 'Pull Me'.

Checking again that her captors were busily engaged, she carefully pulled at the card to reveal a short piece of string and finally a small shiny key, which she quickly palmed out of sight.

She sat motionless as the car sat stationary at a junction, the occupants of the front seats heatedly discussing how to programme the vehicle's sat nav.

Once they were in motion again, she opened her palm and looked at the mysterious key. Too small for a door and not a car key, but maybe...

She slipped the key into the handcuff lock. It fitted perfectly. With bated breath she turned it and 'click'. To Rachel, that tiny noise sounded like a bomb going off. Surely her captors would have heard it. Shank had returned to threatening numerous vile acts that he would perpetrate on her if this turned out to be a wild goose chase and, to her relief, hadn't noticed the faint sound.

"Those two jokers sound like a right comedic duo," interrupted Russell as he placed a glass of Chardonnay beside her. Rachel finished her cider and placed it on the bar and shook her head. "No, I may make light of them, but no mistake they were dangerous. A clown with a gun can still kill you with little effort."

Russell opened one of the many fridges under the bar and pulled out a chilled bottle of Weston's Cider. He waved it at Rachel, who nodded at him to begin pouring as she continued the tale.

As she had unlocked the cuffs, the Mercedes had pulled into the open-air carpark of the storage facility. Rachel left the cuffs hanging loosely, around her wrists. She hoped that the appearance of still being shackled would give her an edge when it counted the most.

The two men exited the vehicle and gave the area a quick scan to ensure they were alone before Shank dragged her out of the back seat with a "Wmich mone?"

Rachel had been about to say the first number that came into her head before she spotted a familiar piece of carboard propped up by the entrance to the closed portacabin office. "It's number twenty-one," she replied, hoping neither of them had the wit to spot what appeared to be a brazenly obvious notice.

They worked their way through the maze of containers, disturbing the night-time prowl of a feral cat, until they came to the red painted container with a large twenty-one emblazoned on it. Grabbing the combination padlock, Shank growled, "Whad's de mumber, bwitch?"

"It's eight zero zero. Now, put your hands up," came a new voice from the nearby shadows.

Standing around twenty feet away, they all saw the outline of a woman dressed in black combat trousers and jacket with a woollen balaclava slipped over her head. Pulled tight against her shoulder, she aimed an assault rifle in their direction.

The two men reluctantly raised their arms. They were clever enough to know that going for their pistols would result in a hail of bullets and probable instant death.

"You," the gunwoman motioned to Rachel. "Open the door."

Rachel dutifully complied. She turned the metal dials to eight zero zero, removed the padlock and pulled open the metal door to reveal a completely empty room. "Mew fuwkin lyin bwitch," Shank growled at her.

Rachel surreptitiously slid behind the men as the gunwoman walked forward out of the shadows, waving the assault rifle in the direction of the waiting lockup. "You two, get in."

That proved to be a mistake: now able to see the woman more clearly, the Asian man loudly exclaimed, "It's a toy gun!" He dropped his hands and moved to draw his pistol from its shoulder holster.

Since they had exited the car, Rachel had been planning her own surprise manoeuvre. Now she put it into action. Dropping the handcuffs from her wrists, she lunged forward, grabbing the pistol from the waistband of Shank's jeans and levelled the weapon at the back of his head, shouting, "Stop or I shoot him."

The driver hesitated, his gun trained on the now trembling black-clad woman. Shank bellowed, "Showt er, the safety's fuwkin mon." Rachel immediately spat back, "No it's not. I had a good look at the gun when you rubbed it in my face. Thanks to you being such a perv, I knew exactly where the safety was."

The driver's aim didn't waver as he stated, "You're not a killer. I'm going to take the shot unless you drop your pistol."

Mrs Thomas' voice echoed in Rachel's head. 'This is it. The critical point in closing of the deal. You have to prove to them that they have far more to lose than you do'.

"True, I'm not a killer by nature, but if I give you the gun, I know you will definitely kill me. That seems a good incentive to change my nature. But if you drop your gun I'll revert to type and just lock you both in the storage unit and walk away. So, it's your call how this scene plays out." Inside her head, Rachel began to panic as the situation escalated. Her anxiety voice didn't help: 'Oh! you shot a gun at a range once and now you're a killer? You're going to get yourself shot, but if you run away now, maybe you can save yourself.'

The driver readied himself to pull the trigger, murmuring, "Let's see how this plays out, then!" Rachel jammed the barrel of the pistol into the back of Shank's head, desperately hoping she didn't have to go through with the threat.

"Stowp. Dis fawking bwtich is cwazy man. Shewl dow it," pleaded Shank.

Time, on this occasion unaided by the warping of the fabric of space, ticked slowly by. Rachel quietly sighed with relief when the driver finally relented with a resigned, "Fine!" Dropping his arms, he placed the gun on the floor and calmly walked into the storage unit.

Rachel took great pleasure in jabbing the pistol into Shank's back. He dutifully responded by running forward to join his partner. Having demanded they throw over the Mercedes' keys, she felt a sense of power when the driver shrugged and tossed the key fob onto the floor before her.

As the black-clad lady pushed the door closed, the driver clapped his hands together and simply said, "Well played, well played indeed."

Shank, in stark contrast, raged at them with his usual tirade about how they were going to get theirs, etc, etc.

With the lock secured, Rachel relaxed her own aim and took in one long, huge breath before the two of them ran for the Mercedes.

"A toy gun! Did you really think that would work?" asked Russell as he placed a bowl of bar snacks on the table. Hannah pushed the bar snacks as far away as she could reach, picked up her glass of Chardonnay and indignantly replied, "Hey, I was doing the best I could. I am not exactly trained in special ops, you know."

Rachel leaned over and kissed Hannah gently on the cheek, "You saved my life, so you're pretty special to me." Hannah blushed rose red and protested, "Stop it! You're such a soppy tart! You will make me come over all weepy."

The two women clinked their glasses and took a drink as Russell asked, "But weren't you both scared?" They looked at each other and nodded. "Well, Rachel did throw up in the Mercedes as we drove here afterwards," Hannah cheekily revealed with mock accusation in her voice.

Rachel had been surprised and relieved when the balaclava had been removed in the Mercedes. She had been surprised since she hadn't recognised Hannah's much slimmer shape. She wasn't skinny, she still had those exaggerated curves lurking beneath the shapeless combat trousers and jacket. But the excess weight had been shed and now she looked altogether healthier and happier.

The relief came from knowing that someone she had thought of as a friend wasn't an evil mastermind who had orchestrated a horrible fate for her.

Brilliant light began to pour through the bar's ninth storey windows. They spun round on their stools to enjoy the magnificent view of the rising sun, its rays of light reaching across the city as it crested over the London skyline.

"Excuse me, ladies," apologised Russell as six more hotel guests entered the bar and seated themselves in a secluded booth. Russell approached the group, consisting of three women and three men, with drinks menus and greeted them with a "Good morning, folks. Trust you had an exciting night on the town and welcome back to the Djinn Bottle bar. My name is Russell; what can I get you?"

The older man in the group, pale skinned and formally dressed in a tuxedo, waved away the menus. "It was a pleasant night, thank you. We will have six of your special Bloody Mary cocktails. That is all."

Rachel turned to face Hannah and, after being momentarily distracted by the rays of sunlight accentuating her red hair, asked, "How on earth did you know where I was?"

"Funny story, that." Hannah put down her chardonnay, unbuttoned the top pocket of her combat jacket and pulled out a brown envelope. "Somebody left this in my office. It told me you were in trouble, gave me the address and where the skylight was." She pushed the envelope along the bar. There were two words written upon it: 'Read Me'.

"OK... So, what about the lockup?" Rachel asked. Hannah picked her glass back up and took a drink before explaining. "As I said, I was making it up on the fly. I had used the lockup for a couple of months when I moved flat. I had only cleared it out last week and its rent was paid up till the end of the month." She shrugged her shoulders. "It was the best secluded place I could think of."

Waving her glass at Russell for a top-up of wine, she added "The replica toy gun had been in my car boot for ages – it was supposed to be an upcoming birthday present for my nephew, Gareth."

Hannah turned ashen-faced and declared, "Ah shit, my car. I left it near the lockup on double yellow lines. I bet it's been towed away by now." Rachel laughed out loud and promised to pay for its safe return.

The events of the previous twenty-four hours were fast catching up on Rachel as she began to yawn. "Look, I'm done. It's late," modifying her statement to: "or is that early? Anyhow, I need sleep. I am heading down to my room."

Without asking, Russell placed a silver tray on the bar with their bill upon it. Rachel filled in the room number, added a generous tip, signed it and pushed it back towards the barman, adding, "Right then, thanks for listening." He smiled and wished them a pleasant sleep, as he beavered away creating the six special Bloody Marys.

Walking into the ninth-floor landing, Rachel pressed the lift call button and turned to face Hannah. "Look, I cannot believe what you did for me today. I don't know how I will ever be able to repay you for the risks you took." Hannah began to blush again, her cheeks quickly matching her long, curly locks.

Rachel continued, "But, as a friend, can I ask one more favour? I know this sounds a bit weird, so please say no if it makes you uncomfortable." She hesitated before asking, "Can you hug me to sleep? It's been a long time since I felt comfortable in someone's arms and I really want... I really need to feel safe tonight with someone that I trust."

With that, she meekly smiled at Hannah, awkwardly fearing a negative response to her request. As the lift doors slid open Hannah returned the smile and quietly said, "Sure, Rachel, I would love to."

Chapter 10

The soft pillow had become infused with a distantly familiar perfumed aroma. The designer fragrance evoking pleasant thoughts of fervent passion and luxurious indulgences.

Waking leisurely, Rachel kept her eyes closed, revelling in the guilty pleasure of a lazy emergence from a rare night's uninterrupted sleep. Or should that be a day's sleep, as they had come to bed as the sun started its ascent into the clear morning sky?

Tentatively, she stretched out her right arm. Hesitantly exploring the remainder of the expansive bed. Disappointingly, her tactile exploration revealed only a large expanse of Egyptian cotton.

She sighed as she accepted that Hannah must have slipped out; she did have a job and probably a life of her own. Rachel smiled to herself as she wondered if Hannah had left her telephone number behind on the nightstand.

For a while, Rachel fondly recalled snuggling into Hannah's arms. The tender feeling of another human wrapped gently around her, of being momentarily free of apprehensions; it had been an idyllically tranquil moment. Enveloped and watched over, Rachel had dropped to sleep within a minute.

With a loud yawn, she rolled over and plunged her face into the pillow. Deeply inhaling the evocative scent conjured up memories from long ago. Ghostly recollections surfaced of the Sheol Posse out in the city and living large; of dark and humid night clubs and perspiring girls dancing close together; of expensive bars and riotous drinking games; of roadside food stalls with deep fried food and then of unsteady journeys home, wrapped in tight embraces to prevent each other from stumbling.

Having wallowed in the past, Rachel grudgingly sat up and looked over at the room's clock. The dimmed green figures revealed that it was coming close to three in the afternoon.

Looking down, Rachel realised she still wore the only top she currently possessed. When they had undressed, she had felt clumsily shy, only removing her jeans and socks before climbing into bed. Hannah had followed her lead and slid in behind her. After she had asked if Rachel was ok and received a silent nod, she had wrapped her arms around her and breathed, "You go to sleep. Hannah's got you."

The last thing Rachel remembered before slipping into the realm of slumber had been her thinking, 'I'm glad I'm wearing new underwear.'

An abrupt unease gripped her: had she overstepped the mark with Hannah? Perhaps she should have told her more about the trauma of the last four years. Rachel had already hinted that things had not gone well but had avoided burdening her companion with unpleasant details. Maybe when she was ready to confront those memories herself she might be able to confide in others.

Now fully awake, her mind moved to planning what to do next. She started by creating a mental list of issues that needed to be addressed.

One: how the hell had she repelled the bikers? Rachel knew the power that had slowed time and flung them away had originated from within her. But how she had instigated it was a complete mystery.

Two: what had happened at Leon Bay's apartment? She would have to reluctantly lift the wall of denial to fathom what had been unleashed in that apartment. A shiver passed down her spine with the recollection of the bitter coldness that had momentarily possessed her.

Three: what of her parents' mysterious past? Were there more revelations to be uncovered? Where had they vanished to after leaving Partridge Way?

Four: What riddle lurked within the Decem Fossas contract? She had been implicated as a blackmailer; who had done this to her? Who was being blackmailed? What could be so dangerous if made public?

Five: what about the three bikers from two nights ago? How did they fit in? She could only guess at their interest in her.

Six: who was her secret benefactor and why had they limited their aid to crowbars and keys? Rachel was also intrigued as to how the benefactor had known these items would be needed and how they had been able to put them in place.

Having decided the list would do for now, Rachel focused on the single shaft of sunlight that had slipped through a gap in the heavy curtains and brooded on all these questions that currently had no answers.

Rachel nearly jumped out of the bed as the bathroom door unexpectedly swung open. It flooded the bedroom with brilliant light and released a thick bank of steamy fog which rolled into the bedroom. Like an apparition of the ancient mariner, a wet head emerged from within the billowing cloud and declared, "That shower is bloody awesome, Rach!"

Hannah strode into the bedroom, leaving a trail of soggy footprints behind her. One of the luxurious bath towels was wrapped around her body and secured under her arms. Hannah used another to towel down those long, curly red locks.

"Well, you slept like the dead! I half expected you to still be asleep when I finally dragged myself away from the Niagara Falls." Dropping onto the corner of the bed, she pondered, "How is it that I've never heard of this hotel?"

Hannah's ebullient presence had quickly dispersed Rachel's gathering clouds.

"I've been giving our problem some thought. Actually, given how long I was showering," she laughed, "a lot of thought. We need to get a copy of the Decem Fossas contract, then we can try and find out what has been hidden in there that's worth all this trouble." Hannah vigorously dried her hair as she continued. "Unfortunately, since I got shuffled sideways into client relationship management, I don't have access to those files anymore."

"How about the rest of the Posse?" ventured Rachel.

Hannah rearranged the towel wrapped around her which, with her vigorous drying, had come dangerously close to falling open. "Well, Lucy moved to the New York office. Apparently, she has a fantastic corner office overlooking the Hudson river and has a charming older American man who showers her with gifts and love." They exchanged knowing looks and simultaneously made light-hearted disparaging noises.

"Bethany, well, she grabbed the rising star position when Lucy moved on and she certainly embraced being the Queen Bee. She works closely with the Chairman now, so I assume she has access to the file." A hint of bitterness had crept into her voice as she continued: "We haven't spoken in a while. I think I'm too low on the corporate ladder for her to fraternise with. Still, I can test the waters and see if she would be receptive to helping, for old times' sake." They both agreed that it was the best strategy to adopt for now.

Hannah picked up her clothes and returned to the bathroom to dress. Rachel took the opportunity to slip back into her jeans, while making a mental note to expand her wardrobe beyond what she currently stood up in.

Having checked in the full-length mirror that her tee-shirt wasn't too grubby, Rachel ran her hands through her hair to make herself a little more presentable.

Emerging from the bathroom in her black combat trousers and jacket, Hannah exclaimed, "I think I may need to change into something a little more suitable for a luxury hotel."

Grabbing a pen and paper from the desk, Hannah wrote down her mobile phone number. "Just in case anything happens, call me." When Rachel sheepishly admitted she didn't have a phone herself, Hannah volunteered to buy her one.

"Rach, from what you have said, you should be safe here. So, I am going to head out, get myself a change of clothes, get you a phone and test out the waters with Bethany." She looked at her watch. "It's 3 pm now. I should be back around eight. We can regroup then."

Hannah stepped forward and gave her a hug goodbye.

Rachel felt inexplicably awkward as they embraced. An unpleasant mixture of conflicted happiness and irrational guilt boiled up within her. Hannah must have felt it as well, quickly stepping back before muttering, "Ok... right... I'll be off then."

Rachel felt furious with herself. She wanted to shout out 'wait' and give her a huge, warm hug back, but she remained frustratingly immobile as Hannah tried the door.

It wouldn't budge.

Hannah gave the door several more frustrated heaves before muttering, "I think the bloody thing is jammed."

"Let me try," suggested Rachel. The door swung open easily at Rachel's touch, to Hannah's bemusement. "Huh, I guess there's a knack to it, Minos," she grumbled.

"I'd better escort you out," grinned Rachel, "in case there is anything else that needs my special knack." Hannah responded with a playfully haughty 'Ha-Ha'.

Emerging from the lift onto the ground floor, Rachel asked if she wanted to grab something to eat first. Disappointingly, Hannah declined, saying she would grab a snack on her travels before adding, "Tell you what, let's get dinner tonight." Rachel readily agreed to the suggestion.

Crossing the foyer to the hotel's rotating door, Rachel spotted Mr Typhon with two men and a woman dressed in military garb. She presumed they were in costume for a fancy-dress party.

On spotting her, the manager excused himself from the squad and wafted across to greet her. "Ms Minos, I hope you slept well. In case you were thinking of lurking today, I have ordered a more luxuriant floral display." He directed Rachel's attention to the new plant pots being wheeled into place by the hotel porters.

Mr Typhon turned to face Hannah, asking Rachel, "Is this a guest of yours, Ms Minos?" Rachel felt herself blushing as she introduced Hannah to the hotel manager before clumsily adding that she was a good friend.

Shaking Hannah's hand Mr Typhon declared, "Ms Bates, may I offer you a warm welcome to the Vestibule Hotel. Any friend of Ms Minos I consider to be an honoured guest in this establishment." Hannah nudged Rachel in the side, whispering, "Well, get you!"

Returning his attention to Rachel the manager suggested, "Would you like Ms Bates to be given access to your room and to the hotel's facilities?" Rachel immediately nodded and with a click of his fingers Mr Typhon concluded, "Consider it done; please, if either of you need anything else, let me know."

The manager's attention was then drawn to a workman wheeling in a box which was around six feet long and two feet wide and deep. "Pardon me, ladies, I must attend to this. If you will excuse me."

Hannah now turned to leave as well but Rachel halted her in her tracks, throwing her arms around her, drawing her in for a tight embrace. Hannah reciprocated before observing, "Hey, I think the wanna-be squaddies are ogling us."

Rachel mumbled an apologetic 'Sorry'.

"What for?" asked Hannah.

"Oh...just things... and shit...you know." She replied, feeling a weight of embarrassment pulling her eyes down to the tiled floor.

With a final 'Minos, you are a mess. See you tonight', Hannah passed through the rotating door and left the Vestibule Hotel.

Chapter 11

It had taken a little under fifteen minutes to walk from the Vestibule Hotel to Nico's Coffee Shop on the corner of Tottenham Street and Charlotte Street. The Friday homeward rush had already got underway; the city's pavements were filling with pedestrians escaping from their places of work, each one looking forward to the upcoming weekend.

With increasing confidence, Rachel had successfully navigated through this surging mass of humanity. The walk would have proceeded more quickly if she hadn't paused regularly at clothing shops. Back in the Camden flat, securely locked away from the world below her, she would stare down on people going about their daily lives and often fantasise about window shopping. Now the opportunity had presented itself, she took the time to longingly gaze at the displays, her attention focussed on potential tops, skirts and winter footwear.

The final shop had an extensive display of winter shoes and boots. Women's styles had certainly moved on in the last four years. Rachel keenly anticipated wasting an hour or two trying on various designs and styles, before settling on one that would need to be practical, warm and stylish. But, as she had no money, for now she would have to just window shop.

Thankfully, the cold weather meant that no one would question her disguise: a dark brown fedora and a thick, woollen football supporter's scarf wrapped tightly around her face. As the best options from the hotel's lost and found box, neither of these items would normally find space in her wardrobe. Though, looking at her reflection in the coffee shop window, the chic look of the fedora had grown on her. Rachel hoped her disguise had proved sufficient to deceive the city's ever watchful camera network.

The warmth of the coffee shop proved a welcome contrast to the chill outside. A man's waving arm, protruding from a booth at the back of the shop, caught her attention. She waved back and Darius beckoned her forward to join him.

Earlier, having watched Hannah leave the Vestibule, Rachel had set her mind to testing out the suite's oversized bath. She had formulated a cunning plan to add excessively liberal amounts of complimentary Dead Sea bath salts and Japanese herbal oils. She would slide into this heavenly concoction and...

"A moment please, Ms Minos!" Bursting the fragrant bubble of Rachel's bathing fantasy, the hotel concierge, Dean, waved a slip of paper at her.

It was a handwritten message: 'Ms Minos, I will be conducting business at Nico's Coffee Shop, on the corner of Tottenham and Charlotte Streets. Please come as soon as you are able. Darius Long.' Only when Dean confirmed that Darius had personally handed him the message this morning did she put to rest the suspicion that this could be a trap to lure her out of the hotel.

Sadly, the bathing extravaganza would have to wait.

Back in the coffee house, a man in his early thirties vacated the bench seat opposite Darius. He was tall - six foot two at least - with short, dark hair, wearing a green bomber jacket, jeans and a pair of well-worn walking boots. With an affable smile and a south London accent he greeted Rachel. "Hello there. Please take the seat. I was just keeping it warm for you."

With a slight bow and flourish he ushered Rachel into the vacated bench seat before bidding both her and Darius farewell. Rachel smiled back and thanked him as she slid onto the seat, her eyes lingering on him as he called out a cheerful goodbye to the barista.

As she unwrapped the team scarf from around her head, Darius gave her a sideways look and with mirth in his voice teased, "Ms Minos, I hadn't taken you for a Chelsea supporter." Darius himself was impeccably dressed in a tweed three-piece suit with a brown cashmere coat neatly laid out beside him on the bench seat.

Folding the football scarf neatly and placing it onto the table, she explained, "I am keeping a low profile and this was the best I could do. Given that I have no money." She pointedly highlighted the last sentence.

"Ahhh. Yes. Here you are." He pushed a small thin, white envelope across the table towards her. Rachel had been expecting a more substantial package, stuffed with numerous bank notes. Instead, it contained what appeared to be two credit cards, prompting her to admit that she had been hoping for cash.

"How long has it been since you were last in London, Ms Minos?" he wondered. "Lots of places don't even accept cash anymore. Even buskers on the Underground have tap and go machines." Pointing at the cards, he continued, "Each one of these has been preloaded with one thousand pounds."

Rachel looked unconvinced, warily staring at the two plastic oblongs. "But couldn't someone still track me using them?" He smiled and shook his head. "I generously pay a pair of elderly spinsters to register these cards for me. Those two old birds are superb at dealing with nosey calls and misdirecting them on drawn-out wild goose chases. But, if you're worried, use them in a hole-in-the-wall machine. Type 9191 and withdraw all the cash."

Grudgingly, as the waitress approached, Rachel took the two cards and slipped them into her leather coat's inner pocket. The waitress was young - probably no more than twenty - with a quiet voice and timid mannerisms. Rachel hadn't eaten since yesterday's breakfast and some of that had been unfortunately deposited into the footwell of the Mercedes. So she ordered two slices of carrot cake in addition to a black coffee.

The waitress retreated, leaving the two of them to sit in silence. Rachel debated with herself whether to take the money and leave or lift the mental wall and face up to the events at 55, Montague Street.

'Get out,' advised her anxiety voice. 'Let's run back to the hotel, pretend nothing ever happened. That's the safe thing to do.' But she knew that wasn't an option and, instead, demanded to know, "So, who the hell are you really?"

Darius initially appeared distracted. He quickly refocussed his attention and handed her a business card. The plain white card had his name: 'Darius Long', a title: 'Freelance Redemptore' and his contact telephone number. Returning it, with growing irritation in her voice, she asked "Ok, so what is a Redemptor?" Darius immediately corrected her. "Ms Minos, the correct pronunciation is Redemptore." In an Italian accent, he had highlighted the e at the end of the word, so that it sounded like Redemtoray.

Rachel felt irked by the pedantic correction. This man had encouraged her to unleash something terrible, so she didn't feel inclined to suffer his grammar lessons. It proved to be a monumental struggle to hold back her temper as she snapped back, "That doesn't tell me what you bloody well are."

He maintained that same increasingly irritating calm tone as he explained, "Redemptore are employed as mediators for contracts between recipients and suppliers. When either party breaks the conditions of a contract, we decide, based on the agreed penalties and forfeits defined within the contract, what the outcome of an infringement should be."

Darius sounded like a cheap television advert offering the no win, no fee services of a law firm ready to help with your recent accident.

"Sorry, suppliers of what, exactly?" she demanded. Darius paused emptying his cup of cold coffee before answering, "The supply of unique services that break the rules of what most people believe is possible." Rachel stared at him for a moment before asking, "You mean wishes, don't you? Is that what Leon Bay got? Three wishes?"

Darius calmly looked around to ensure no-one could be eavesdropping. "That is a simplistic word for what I understand is an extremely complex process, but it will suffice." Leaning forward and with a low hiss in her voice, Rachel demanded, "So these suppliers, are they devils? Are these people selling their souls? Did I bloody well send Leon Bay into Hell?"

Darius drummed his fingers on the table five times. He considered abruptly ending the increasingly antagonistic conversation. Perhaps in deference to his old friendship with her parents, he elected to remain seated and continued:

"There is no Devil or Hell. Or at least not in the classical way that you have been taught. Those archetypes were constructs of the Church, created in an attempt to restrict people's access to suppliers of these unique services."

He paused as the waitress approached with two large slices of cake. Only when she had moved out of earshot did he continue. "The Church, in medieval times, desperately wanted to limit supplier access to themselves. After all, one person's miracle is another's deal with the Dark Lord."

She fought to keep her guilt at Leon Bay's fate in check, trying to absorb this information. "Does everyone suffer the same fate as Bay did?" Her mind replayed the image of that desperate face as the tail had relentlessly dragged him into the darkness.

"It depends on the terms of the contract. But my experience has shown that the more self-interested the requests, the harsher the completion terms stipulated by the supplier." Darius paused before presenting examples.

"Take Leon Bay. He used his contract to improve his life at the expense of others. He stole their futures; he took their lives and all for his own benefit. Does he deserve our sympathy if the completion terms are unpleasant?" Rachel sat impassively, choosing not to comment.

"Arthur Pickering is a man who selflessly used the services he acquired to provide help for London's lost and homeless. I happen to know that the completion terms for his contract are extremely generous."

"Is there a God?" Rachel blurted out. Why had she asked that question? She had never been religious and neither had her parents.

"I have no idea, Ms Minos. That's certainly above my pay grade," Darius answered.

Deep down, Rachel knew why she had asked about God. She was stalling. Trying to avoid the question she hadn't wanted to ask: "Darius, were my parents Redemptore?"

The answer was delayed by the delivery of two cups of black coffee. Once the waitress had again retreated, Darius confirmed, "Yes, they were. But those two were also so much more."

He picked up his fresh coffee and began to sip the hot beverage. Rachel stared at him, terrified to ask, but desperate to know more.

Eventually, the desire to shed light on this newly discovered realm overwhelmed her hesitance. Questions began to tumble from her like water cascading over a waterfall. "What did my parents do? What do you mean they were so much more? Where are people taken when contracts end? What the hell was that tail? Why do I have this power within me?" She paused for breath as more questions surged into her mind.

Darius raised his hand to halt the verbal deluge.

"I have said far more than I should and can say no more on these subjects." He dropped his hand and, after a short pause, added, "But... if you were to join the Redemptore, that would be a different matter."

From the briefcase sitting beside him, he produced a thick document and placed it between them on the table.

"Ms Minos, were you to join the ranks of the Redemptore, you would have the opportunity to seek answers to your questions. They would train you, harnessing and moulding your unique capabilities." He opened the contract, placing a pen next to a long, dotted line, then concluded, "You would also gain protection from outsiders that may wish you harm. Sign here and your life will be changed."

The offer was appealing. She would gain information, training and protection. The easy solution to her problems. All it would take was her signature on the contract.

The memory of Mrs Thomas's course echoed through her mind: 'Beware the salesman who offers you plenty of inducements - there may be a barbed fishhook buried amongst those juicy morsels.'

Rachel replayed Darius's pitch inside her head.

'The opportunity to seek answers': not the actual provision of answers to her questions. 'Harnessing and moulding': for whose benefit and to what end? 'Gain protection from outsiders': but not protection from those within the Redemptore? 'Your life will be changed': for better or worse?

Rachel leaned back, closed her eyes, and attempted to calm herself. One by one, she gathered up the desperate panics, the paralysing fears and irrational emotions, corralling them together into a corner of her mind. Only when a semblance of mental order had been restored did she open them again.

The thick contract remained between them.

The more she thought about it, the less it seemed to be an opportunity. To Rachel it looked like the trigger mechanism of another trap, its bait consisting of nothing more than vague promises.

"Thanks, but no thanks," she finally responded.

Pushing the contract back towards Darius, she picked up her coffee and, with relief in her heart, took a long drink. Perhaps the Redemptore would have assisted her. Or perhaps they had more sinister intentions. But at that moment there were two indisputable facts. One: she wasn't ready to surrender her hard-won freedom so quickly. Two: she was extremely hungry, so Rachel picked up the first cake slice and began to munch on it.

Curiously, rather than disappointment, a relieved expression spread across Darius's face. He also resumed drinking his coffee and, with some amusement, watched the rapid consumption of the cake.

'You should have taken the offer,' whinged her anxiety voice 'You're too pathetic to survive on your own much longer. You need other people to protect you. It's the easy solution to our problems, take it.'

Darius put down his cup and asked, "Ms Minos, doesn't that annoy you?" With a mouth full of cake, Rachel could only look confused in response. He continued, "That voice, constantly undermining you. Don't you find it intrusive?"

Rachel gulped down the remainder of the cake. "You can hear it?" she asked in astonishment.

'Oh shit!' whimpered her anxiety voice.

He nodded. "I am not sure what it is. I'm no expert in these things, but you really should think about getting it looked at." He may as well have been discussing a red spot that had broken out on her face. "I know a reliable person who can probably help you with such a problem."

He scribbled a name and address on the reverse of his business card and handed it over. "She is particularly good at these kinds of things and is very discreet."

Rachel thanked him for the suggestion before adding, "Look, I'm sorry for turning you down. Perhaps in a..." Darius interrupted in a barely audible, hushed voice. "Ms Minos, do not regret the choices you have made. It is a rare thing to regain your independence. Do not squander it."

Returning to his more usual, measured demeanour, he continued, "It was good to see you Ms Minos, but I do have other business to attend to." He glanced towards the coffee shop's front door and at an elderly lady who had just entered. "Until we meet again, Ms Minos."

With this sudden dismissal, Rachel slid off the bench seat, wrapped the scarf around her face and pulled the fedora low over her brow. With a simple 'Bye then', she worked through the crowded shop and out into the street beyond.

Darius motioned to his next appointment to wait as he pulled his mobile phone from his jacket pocket. "Hello… No, I am afraid she wasn't interested in the offer… I am not sure that would be a prudent approach… Well, that is your choice, but I think it would be ill-advised… Very well… goodbye."

Chapter 12

"Plain or the sequins?" Rachel pondered. Checking in the mirror, she held each top up against her chest. "Definitely plain."

The glittering top was placed back on the hanger, the other into the shopping basket already holding an assortment of tops, trousers, skirts and lingerie. A reasonable start to her new wardrobe.

Earlier, after leaving the café, she had made her way straight back to the shoe shop. For nearly an hour and a half, Rachel had lost herself in shopping nirvana. It had been a pleasure she had taken for granted just four years previously. Now she revelled in the rediscovered joys of retail therapy.

She had been dismayed to discover that attempting to walk any distance in high heels proved to be far more difficult than she recalled. Wobbling and teetering with the unfamiliar elevation, she realised it might take some time to get used to them again.

A gold-trimmed pair of flat, strappy sandals had then caught her eye. But, despite looking fabulous, they were hardly practical winter wear. Instead, a pair of black court shoes, along with a pair of sneakers were added to her growing purchase pile.

'He' had long ago convinced her that boots, stilettos and their like didn't suit her. When she wasn't in his cast-off outsized trainers, 'he' wanted her to wear teeteringly high platform heels. She was never comfortable with them but persevered to prove her love for 'him'. Luckily, she was never expected to walk anywhere in those things.

Given 'his' dislike of them, it was no surprise her large collection of slender-heeled shoes and boots had vanished during the move to Camden. Rachel hoped they had found an adoring home and not been lost in a dump.

Liberated from 'his' constraints, she had tried many styles of boot: high heeled, over knee, calf length, ankle high, thin heeled, chunky heeled and so on. She loved the look of them. She adored how they made her feel. She wanted all of them.

But, given her situation, they hardly ticked the practicality box.

Instead, a pair of black mid-calf, low-heeled, biker-style leather boots were selected. They looked good, were easy to walk (and run) in and boy did they keep her feet snug and warm.

"Excellent choice," the young shop assistant agreed. "My girlfriend is saving up for that very style but in brown." The young man was now surrounded by a wall of boxes built from the shoes and boots Rachel had rejected.

"Is there anything else I can do for you?" He had remained genuinely enthusiastic to help, despite the long, drawn-out selection process. "One more thing," Rachel added, an idea having occurred to her. "Add another pair of these boots, in brown." He nodded as she continued, "But in your girlfriend's size, since you'll be giving them to her tonight."

It took a moment for the proffered gift to register with the young man. Once the penny dropped, as he bagged and rang up her purchases, he thanked her repeatedly, his excitement nudging Rachel into a good mood.

Back in the clothes shop, Rachel worked her way through tightly packed displays. This wasn't a sparsely decorated haute couture boutique like those of her past life. Here, the garments were stacked high and sold for a reasonable price.

The assistant coughed loudly, pointedly gesturing at the clock above the counter. It was seven thirty-two. Wrapped up in her first shopping spree, Rachel had lost all track of time. She realised she had better get a move on; Hannah could be back at the hotel already.

Under a cloudless winter sky, the temperature in the city had already dropped below freezing. She exited the store with her fresh clutch of bags and a new white woollen scarf wrapped tight around her face.

The pavement teemed with late workers finally starting their journeys home. Revellers were out in force, enjoying the pleasures that night-time London had to offer. Cars and taxis sluggishly made progress along the road, scooters and cyclists daringly weaving through treacherous gaps. It was the usual vibrant Friday night in London.

Rachel stood for a moment and soaked up the atmosphere.

There was a refreshingly carefree bounce to her step as she finally strolled along Foley Street and it wasn't just down to her new boots.

She had dodged a proverbial bullet in the coffee shop, rekindled her passion for shopping, made a young man's day and was now looking forward to her first evening meal in a restaurant.

"Hey, love! Does a good-looking lady like you fancy a drink with us?"

The three men were smoking outside the Pig and Whistle pub. Heavy brown coats draped over work suits protected them from the bitter cold. Each looked to be in their late thirties, their muscular six-foot frames hinting at long hours spent with personal trainers.

The tallest had stepped directly into Rachel's path, blocking her jaunty stride. As he asked if she wanted a drink, his co-conspirators chuckled in admiration at his bravado.

He leaned uncomfortably close and she could smell the hoppy odour of ale on his breath.

She froze.

Her good mood was smashed; its slivers cut through her like icy shards.

Horrible memories of long evenings with a drunken Barry forced their way into her mind. She felt a sickening churn in the pit of her stomach. A feeling that had become all too familiar when she had tried to anticipate his needs, tried to placate his desires, tried to show that she was a good Babs.

But no matter how hard she had tried, there was always something wrong. Some tiny detail she had forgotten; a part of his prescribed rituals she had missed; perhaps responding too slowly to a request or perhaps too quickly.

Each time, she would feel his disappointment. She would lower her gaze in shame. Lament her continual failure to please him and vow to do much better next time.

The drunken man clumsily asked again, "Hey beautiful, do you want that drink or not?"

Someone was screaming at the top of their voice.

Someone was howling profanities that would make a docker blush.

The crowded street of people paused, staring towards the source of the commotion.

They were looking at Rachel.

She was yelling at the drunken man, who now backed away to seek shelter with his stunned work colleagues.

Hysterical tears streamed down her face. With an increasingly self-righteous tone, the drunken man yelled at her "Crazy woman, I only asked you if you wanted a drink."

Rachel didn't respond. She ran.

She ran to get away from the drunken man.

She ran to escape the memories of Barry.

She ran to leave four wasted years behind her.

She ran headlong into the familiar red coat of Billy.

Tears continued to stream down her cheeks. Relentless sobbing choked back her words.

Billy looked up and down the street whilst worriedly enquiring "Ms Minos, are you ok? Are the local vermin bothering you again?" His huge frame tensed; his substantial hands balled into fists, ready to deal with any threats.

Dropping her bags of shopping to the pavement, she grabbed onto his huge arm. It felt like the solid trunk of an oak tree. She gripped it tightly. Drawing strength from its steadfastness.

The tears subsided. The sobbing faded.

The perilously thin veneer that was Rachel was restored.

"Are you ok now, Ms Minos?" His deep voice gently enquired. Releasing her grip, she nodded. "Thank you, Billy. Sorry about that. Bit of a moment."

With a concerned look, he helped to gather up the discarded shopping bags and assured Rachel that it was not a problem. Wishing her a good evening, he ushered her through the rotating door and into the safety of the Vestibule Hotel.

Mr Typhon had been talking to a gentleman who wore a tweed cape and deerstalker hat as Rachel stumbled into the reception foyer. Sensing something was amiss, he immediately crossed over to her and summoned a porter to take her shopping bags up to the suite.

The bags safely removed, he handed her a fresh handkerchief and suggested, "Ms Bates has already gone up to your suite. You may wish to freshen up in the washroom before meeting her." Taking her silence (apart from the loud blowing of her nose) as acceptance, he guided her into the washroom.

Her reflection in the mirror looked rough. Red eyes peered at her through puffy eyelids. Tear streaks on her cheeks were counterbalanced by a running nose. "Looking sexy there, girl!" she sarcastically croaked at herself.

The extensive application of running water and the facial wipes, soaps and creams saw a marked improvement. Finally, a faint smile valiantly battled its way back across the reflection's face.

It was a hollow smile.

The speed with which she had emotionally crashed had been frightening. The blunt-edged reminder that she had a long road to recovery ahead of her. 'He' had inflicted deep scars on her psyche. 'He' had tried to break her. But she had endured, and things couldn't get any worse, could they?

With a resigned 'Good enough' she left the washroom and headed to the lifts.

Outside her suite, Rachel paused. 'How much should you reveal to Hannah?' she asked herself. The episode with Leon Bay and the discussion with Darius, that she would keep to herself for now. Primarily since she had no idea how to even explain it to herself, let alone her friend.

What of the four lost years with 'him'? For a while she weighed the pros and cons, finally resolving that, if the opportunity arose, it could prove cathartic for her and illuminating for Hannah to explain what had occurred during that dark time. The decision made, with trepidation she opened the door and entered the suite.

Hannah was looking through the shopping bags with keen interest as Rachel removed her red leather coat and slung it onto the bed.

"Well, someone has been busy shopping!" She held up a matching set of bra and knickers and gave them a disapproving look. "Rach, you are not going to ignite a passionate fire with those!" she laughed. The joyous sound immediately lifted Rachel's spirits.

Hannah had changed into a svelte two-piece work suit, ivory silk blouse and four-inch black heels, her hair now pulled back and secured with a single large clip.

"My god, this is all bit mundane," Hannah protested. "I mean, where is the Rachel Minos we knew. Where is the 'bow chicka bow wow'?"

Feeling chastened by the critique of her purchases, Rachel noted: "Well I bought these boots." She watched with envy, as Hannah moved with poise and grace on her high heels. "Well, Rachel," began her critic, "Next time you are kidnapped or kicking down a door, those will be the perfect footwear."

Folding her arms defensively across her chest, Rachel responded with a long, drawn-out raspberry. "Fair enough," laughed Hannah in response.

Her voice became serious as she added, "I bring news of how we are going to get into Sheol Publications. Grab a seat and I'll explain."

Sitting in one of the room's armchairs, Hannah had laid out the details of the plan as she cracked open a bottle of Pinot Grigio. Having removed her boots, Rachel sat cross legged in the other chair. After digesting the plan and taking a sip of the wine, she dryly observed, "It seems to be... a bit complicated?"

Hannah had kicked off her heels and draped one slender leg over the chair arm. She looked at her watch and nodded in agreement, "Yeah. Look, I barely managed to bully my way in to see Bethany. I owe her admin Linda a big old favour." Rachel quietly pondered what that favour would entail. "Anyhow, after I explained what had happened and what we wanted, I thought Beth was going to call security."

As Hannah checked her watch, Rachel mentally struggled to marry the description of this haughty employee with her recollection of the mousey member of the Posse.

"Eventually Bethany agreed. But only if we followed her plan and only if she takes all the credit for anything that is exposed." Hannah took a long drink of white wine as Rachel added, "Presumably, we take the blame if everything goes wrong?"

"Naturally," Hannah confirmed. She shrugged her shoulders adding, "It's not like we have a lot of options here." Removing her hair clip, she shook her head allowing the red locks to tumble free across her shoulders. "Unless you have developed amazing cat burglary abilities?" They both laughed as Rachel suggested that a catty demeanour probably wasn't a suitable substitute.

Hannah checked her watch and noted, "For the plan to work, you are going to have to look the part." With a wave of her hand, she dismissed the bags on the bed. "Those, my dear Rachel, are just not going to cut it."

The ringing of the suite's telephone cut short Rachel's objection to Hannah's critique. "Ms Minos, Front Desk here. We have a visitor for you."

In the background, she could hear a familiar voice objecting to the introduction. "A visitor? Pfft. Serge is an artiste! I have been summoned to work my magic and to bring forth beauty and elegance."

"Right on time," smiled Hannah.

Chapter 13

"Champagne, white or red wine or orange juice, madam?" The alcohol had been tempting. Sheol Publications would have spent a small fortune on catering for this event. Rachel knew the wines would have been handpicked by respected sommeliers to perfectly compliment the evening's hors d'oeuvres. But a clear head may prove vital, she sighed to herself and selected a glass of orange juice from the large silver tray.

An area normally filled with easy chairs and desks had been cleared. Dark drapes now lined the frosted glass walls of the adjoining offices. Tall tables were strategically placed for guests to gather around and chat. In the far corner, a DJ played quiet tunes as employees and guests drank and talked. Later in the evening the DJ would change the music. The volume would be ramped up and people of all ages would be giving it their all on the makeshift dance floor.

Positioned at the edge of the large gathering, Rachel could comfortably observe the other attendees without drawing attention to herself. She watched people's interactions and observed the pecking order of seniors and subordinates. It didn't take her long to construct a mental register separating the Sheol employees from their clients and guests.

Less than fifty percent of the employees were known to Rachel. Given the company's merciless replacement of underperforming staff, the figure was not entirely unexpected.

She had spotted the twelve senior execs, none of whom had been replaced during her four-year absence, though some were now looking considerably older and greyer as they charmed the blue-chip clients. Rachel assumed that the lack of wastage amongst the twelve would almost certainly have been a great source of frustration for Beth. Until one of those twelve positions became vacant there would be no opportunity of further promotion for her.

Account managers focussed on keeping the remainder of the client base entertained, while junior staff fussed around their allocated charges, ensuring their needs and desires were quickly sated.

All the time, sales leaders glided between the tables of guests. They were corporate sharks in expensive suits. They smelled money in the water and kept on moving as they sought new opportunities to strike a deal.

Two of these sharks had already circled around Rachel. They had been drawn to her unfamiliar presence. Intrigued to gauge her wealth. Inquisitive to see if the embryo of an opportunity could be conceived with this potential new buyer.

Mentioning that she had come as the special guest of Bethany Hopkins dampened their enthusiasm and they quickly moved off in search of less complicated prey.

"Canapé, madam?" Another waiter presented a large tray heaped with a wide variety of shrimp-based finger food. The artistic creations looked delicious, but Rachel's eye was drawn to the waiter. He had to be at least six foot two with short dark hair. She immediately recognised him from the coffee shop: he was the man who had vacated his seat to allow her to converse with Darius. He had swapped his bomber jacket and jeans for a white tuxedo jacket and black trousers, but there was no mistaking him.

He, however, had failed to recognise her.

The previous evening, on entering the hotel suite, Serge had cried out in mock pain, "Rachel, my love, has a barbarian been allowed to assault your head with a lawn mower?" After spending twenty minutes tidying up Rachel's earlier hack job, he declared, "Darling, Serge can only do so much. But do not worry." After he had taken Rachel's measurements, Hannah had briefed him that Rachel needed to look like she belonged at the exclusive event but had stressed that she wasn't to attract too much attention.

When Serge returned the next day, he had presented them with four different dress options. They selected a simple yet elegant grey cocktail dress. There followed a titanic battle of wills over the footwear, Serge insistent on matching high heels, Rachel preferring the stability of low-heeled court shoes. On this occasion, Rachel emerged triumphant.

Only then did Serge lay out a selection of four wigs upon the bed. After a brief modelling session, Hannah agreed with Rachel and they selected a long, voluminous black wig.

Serge concurred with their choice and set to work styling the opulent black hair. When combined with the selective application of makeup, Rachel's reflection had become that of a stranger. The waiter's failure to acknowledge her vindicated Serge's claim that 'Today I have created a new woman!'

Reassured that her disguise was working, Rachel removed several deep-fried shrimps and a napkin from the waiter's silver tray before he moved on to tempt others with his seafood selection.

Hannah, dressed in a familiar silver sequined dress, had spotted that Rachel was now finally alone and approached her table. She then engaged her in general business conversation, as she had already done with at least ten other clients that evening.

Surreptitiously checking they were alone, she whispered, "Beth is waiting in an office. Take the corridor behind you, first left, office 805." Rachel nodded. Hannah concluded their conversation and excused herself to engage with a newly arrived guest.

Rachel regretted not taking the alcohol. It could have proved useful in bolstering her flagging self-confidence. She didn't enjoy all this cloak and dagger activity, but, if it allowed her to get a copy of the elusive contract, she would continue to play along.

The opportunity to slip away presented itself as the Chairman, John Viath, made his customary dramatic entrance. With all eyes focussed on him, she was able to pass unnoticed through the drapes.

Memories of her time spent in the corridors of Sheol Publicity flooded back. The coffee machine where vital business decisions had been made. The break room - the perfect place to eavesdrop on the admins' gossip. The photocopying room where... well, best not to dwell on the variety of functions that the windowless room had been used for.

She paused at the frosted glass door to office 805, checked she had not been followed or observed and gently knocked. "Come in," came Bethany's familiar voice.

Perched on the corner of an office desk, her diminutive frame struggled to fill the brown leather skirt and jacket. Her thin legs barely touched the floor despite the tremendous height of her heels. She looked curiously at Rachel before asking, "Sorry, are you lost?"

Rachel pulled aside the long hair falling across her face, revealing herself before saying, "Bethany, thank you so much for agreeing to help us. Hannah said you would give me access to where the Decem Fossas contract is currently stored?"

Bethany smiled as she replied, a cold smile devoid of real emotion. "That is what I told Hannah. But that's not the reason I wanted to meet you." She slipped down from the corner of the desk and slowly paced around behind it. "Rachel, I think you are being misled. I think you are being used."

Rachel quickly looked around the glass-walled office. Apart from the desk and two chairs, it was bare. The only exit was behind her and there were no obvious cameras. That, of course, didn't preclude hidden ones. "What are you talking about, Beth?" she asked.

Bethany gave a visible facial twitch in response to her truncated name. "I only go by Bethany now," she firmly stated. "Tell me how you came to believe you had been framed for extortion." It wasn't an unreasonable question, so Rachel gave a summary of the events in the warehouse,

Hannah's intervention and their eventual escape.

Bethany listened intently. At the conclusion of the tale she asked, "So you never saw Bag Head Man's face? You have no clue who he was?" Rachel agreed that was the case. "Did you ever see Hannah and this Bag Head Man at the same time?"

Quickly running through the evening's events in her head, Rachel answered "Well no, but…" Bethany cut her off as she forged on, "I assume you don't actually have any proof that it was Hannah at the skylight?" Agreeing that she didn't, Rachel became increasingly uncomfortable at the line of questioning.

Bethany pulled open a drawer in the desk, extracted a thick brown file and held it up in her left hand. "You see, Hannah doesn't know that I've been investigating her for some time." She dropped the thick file onto the table and flicked over the cover. "Activity unbecoming of an employee was brought to a senior exec's attention and I was tasked to launch a covert investigation into Hannah."

Checking her manicured fingernails, she innocently asked, "Has Hannah told you that she is planning to leave Sheol Publicity?" Rachel remained silent. "No, I didn't think so. The Decem Fossas contract comes up for renewal next year. Of all people, I don't need to explain to you how valuable the information in that document would be to rival bidders."

"I don't believe you!" blurted out Rachel. "She has helped me, she has…" Her voice trailed away as the possibility that Bethany might be correct began to take root.

The contents of the file were spread out across the table. Photographs of Hannah in meetings. Telephone transcripts. Copies of emails. "I wanted you to come here today and see this, the evidence of her duplicity."

Bethany resumed her damning narrative. "Did Hannah mention her access to view contracts such as Decem Fossas had been revoked? No?"

Rachel again remained silent.

"I have a theory. I think Bag Head Man and Hannah are one and the same. I think she orchestrated an elaborate ruse that made you believe that you were in danger. She intended to play on our old friendship. She would use you to convince me to give you access to the contract data."

Bethany paced back around the table to stand in front of Rachel and handed her a photograph. Rachel swallowed hard as she stared down at the picture of Hannah in apparent conversation with Shank and the Driver.

The damning photo dropped from her hand tumbling to the floor. Rachel could feel the familiar knot forming in her guts as she tried to decide if this story of betrayal was true. Hadn't Hannah helped her? Hadn't she supported her emotionally? Could it all be yet another lie? Another person twisting Rachel to do their bidding?

'You see?' her long-silent anxiety voice observed. 'I told you not to trust her. You wouldn't be in this mess if you had listened. How can you trust your own judgement? You fell for Barry's lies, now you have fallen for Hannah's duplicity and both have always just wanted to use you.'

Leaning back against the table, Bethany concluded: "If you don't believe me, ask her yourself. See if she is leaving for a rival. Find out if she is taking clients and information from Sheol with her."

Finally, Bethany's stern exterior softened as she added, "Look, we were never as close as you and Hannah, but you are still a dear friend to me." She handed over a business card with her private number. "I think it best that you don't hang around the party. Take the service elevator - I am sure you recall where that is. It will allow you to slip out unnoticed. When you are ready to talk and if you want to add your statement to this file, call me."

Awkwardly hugging Bethany, Rachel thanked her for being a good friend and left the office in a daze. Half of her mind had begun to weave the threads of the conspiracy together, forming a disturbing tapestry of Hannah's guilt. The other half pulled at the tapestry's many loose ends, pointing to half-baked theories, the possible digital alteration of the photo and questioning how her voice had been disguised.

As she progressed down the corridor towards the service lift, Rachel noticed a small plastic card lying on the tiled floor beside a solid-looking metal door. Curious, she bent down and picked it up.

The card bore the name of Sheol's IT supplier: Universal Service Enterprises. Below that, the card owner's name: Martha Edwards. She stared at the card, then at the card slot in the metal door.

The sign on the door read 'Server Room − Strictly no admittance without authorisation.' Rachel thought to herself, 'Why not?' and, with a firm shove, pushed the card into the slot. Disappointingly, nothing happened. She pulled it back out. There followed the satisfying sound of muffled clunks: substantial locks within the metal door were disengaging.

The volume of noise in the server room surprised her. The cacophony formed by hundreds of spinning hard discs, numerous cooling fans and the constant drone of the powerful air-conditioning system.

The overhead lights were off; the only other light sources, the multitude of green and red LED flashes from rack-mounted equipment. Her assumption that she was alone was dispelled when torchlight flickered at the far end of the room.

Inexplicably, Rachel felt emboldened to investigate the source of this light. Removing her court shoes, she carefully tiptoed in stockinged feet towards the source of the flashlight. Upon reaching the end of the racks, she could hear, above the ambient sound, typing on a computer keyboard. Carefully leaning around the corner, Rachel spied a waiter working at a standalone computer rack. Not just any waiter. The man from Darius's booth.

Perhaps sensing Rachel's observation, the waiter spun around and met her gaze. "What the hell are you doing here?" she demanded to know, attempting to sound as if she had every right to be there.

"It's not what it looks like!" he feebly exclaimed.

"You mean you're not downloading sensitive data from Sheol's stand-alone ultra-secure server?"

Looking abashed, he admitted, "Ok, maybe it is what it looks like. I just don't want any trouble." A tremble of fear in his voice, he opened his arms wide showing he had no weapons. For a moment Rachel considered how cute he looked, before getting back to the task at hand.

"You'll get no trouble from me if you retrieve the data I require." From deep within her cleavage, Rachel retrieved a USB stick and tossed it over.

A look of recognition came over his face as he caught the stick. "Hang about, you had a meeting with Darius, didn't you?" He smiled, "It is a genuine pleasure to meet you again. Sorry for not recognising you earlier." He turned back to the keyboard. "Very good disguise, by the way. Ok, what are you looking for?"

Rachel joined him at the screen and the soon the Decem Fossas file had been transferred to the USB stick, which, in turn, had been returned to its secure hiding place. 'Well,' she thought to herself, 'Even if Hannah turns out to be an evil, manipulative genius, at least I have the file."

Securing the keyboard and switching off the computer screen, they both turned for the exit. As if they were strolling down a public street, he casually remarked, "The name is Alex, by the way; and you are...?" For a moment, she considered using her Alice pseudonym. But Alex knew Darius, so, presumably, he would eventually learn her identity. "It's Rachel. Oh, you dropped this by the door."

She showed him the plastic key card. He looked puzzled and drew an identical card from his white jacket's breast pocket. "Err, nope. I have got mine here."

"You two! Stop right there! What were you doing in there?"

Two burly security guards had unfortunately witnessed them emerging from the server room. Rachel took control and immediately stepped forward. "Gosh, I'm so sorry. This is all very embarrassing," she giggled in her best I've-been-caught-being-a-naughty-girl voice.

"I am afraid I took a shine to this nice waiter." She pinched Alex's bottom, causing him to utter an involuntary yelp. "Well, the photocopying room seemed to be occupied, if you get my drift."

She paused to allow the security guards to slowly connect the dots.

"Martha was a darling and lent me her card so I could…get to know this charming young man, a little more intimately." Rachel was enjoying her little performance and the glazed look overtaking the security guards meant it was having the right effect.

"Your name, madam?" the burlier one demanded.

"Of course, gentlemen. I'm Alice Liddell. I was invited by Bethany Hopkins." The mere mention of Beth had the desired impact, hastening the guards to ask via their portable radios for confirmation that she did, indeed, appear on the invite list.

"I do hope I can count on your discretion, gentlemen. It would be unfortunate for innocent, hard-working people to be caught up in a scandal… if you know what I mean." The radio crackled back with confirmation.

Keeping hold of the initiative, Rachel thanked the guards, firmly took Alex's arm, and hurried back towards the increasingly loud music of the party.

"I can't believe you got away with that," an impressed Alex remarked.

Rachel didn't reply; she knew it wouldn't take long for the guards to recall that they had been in the secure server room. More confusion would be required to cover their escape.

Passing a red fire alarm box, she casually cracked the glass. The building immediately began to reverberate to the sound of alarms and an automated voice calmly advised the building's occupants to evacuate in an orderly fashion.

Slipping through the drapes and back into the party, no-one had moved. The guests and staff continued to talk and drink, oblivious to the loud alarms. Rachel feared her improvised plan was about to go horribly wrong, until John Viath's unmistakable voice boomed out: "Ladies and gentlemen, please can you leave in an orderly fashion by the fire door. I promise food and drink will be available at the evacuation points."

Merging with the compliant crowd of evacuating people, Rachel lost touch with Alex. Around her, guests and staff still chatted and drank their champagne as they filtered into the bare concrete evacuation stairway.

It was at that moment that Rachel fleetingly smelled lavender and jasmine cologne. She immediately tried to stop, to attempt to locate the source of the distinctive scent. But the momentum of the evacuating crowd prevented her doing so, the mass of people pushing her forwards, driving her down the stairs.

As she descended the eight storeys towards the ground floor exit, Rachel desperately looked around hoping to once again detect the smell or grab a glimpse of someone familiar or perhaps overhear a voice that could give a clue as to the source of the cologne.

Only the crackling sound of a security guard's radio at the exit below refocussed her attention from the search. She assumed the security guards were looking for her. By now they would have been warned to be on the lookout for a guest with long, black hair. As they passed the second floor, Rachel removed and dumped her wig before finally exiting into the cold night air. She smiled cordially at the security guards, who ignored the woman with short, blonde hair.

"Hey, you!" came Hannah's familiar voice. She draped a warm blanket over Rachel's shivering shoulders. It must have been already close to freezing outside and Sheol staff were handing out warm blankets to all their guests.

Leading Rachel to one side, Hannah asked, "How did it go? Did you get the contract?" and began to wrap her arms around Rachel in a warming embrace.

Rachel stepped away from her, putting a few feet of distance between them. Hannah looked confused and hurt by the sudden movement. With concern in her voice she asked, "Is everything ok?" Steam rose as her breath condensed in the chilled air.

"Are you leaving Sheol and joining a rival firm?" Rachel asked, her voice beginning to crack with pent-up emotion. Hannah hesitated, her eyes clearly betraying concern as she asked, "What do you mean?"

Trying to keep her voice level, Rachel tried again, "It's a simple enough question, Hannah. Are you planning on leaving Sheol? Are you joining a rival firm and are you taking clients and their data with you?"

Again, Hannah hesitated before, in a meek voice, she admitted, "Yes I am." She stepped forward, attempting to grasp Rachel's hand. "I meant to tell you, but I..."

She never managed to complete her explanation, as Rachel stormed off into the cold darkness of the city.

Minos Rising

Chapter 14

"Well, that was a traumatic evening," Rachel muttered to herself. Having walked from St James's Square, she'd taken a moment to sit down on the porch step of a Victorian house and rest her weary feet. The unfamiliarity of walking, even in her modest court shoes, had taken its toll and she was certain that a blister was forming on her right foot.

As an unseen bell chimed out the hour of 11 pm, she watched her breath form billowing white clouds in the increasingly frigid night air. The thick blanket Hannah had given her only partially offset the scant thermal protection provided by her dress. Unfortunately, to preserve her anonymity from the ever-present CCTV, she'd draped it over her head rather than snugly around her shoulders. Now stationary, Rachel began to shiver as Jack Frost's arms drew her into its bitter embrace.

She hadn't seen a single free black cab since storming away from Sheol Publicity and from Hannah. A helpful passer-by had earlier suggested she call an Uber - whatever one of those might be.

Unfortunately, Rachel now had to admit to herself that she was lost. She felt sure the Vestibule must be close by but couldn't be sure in which direction.

Leaning forward to massage her right foot, she thought back on how the evening's unusual events had started even as she had prepared to leave for Sheol Publicity. Having dressed her, styled her wig and applied her makeup, Serge had announced that he must go urgently. He'd received a text from his wife saying that the children were in bed and that she was now preparing a candle-lit dinner for their Saturday date night.

Hannah and Rachel had exchanged surprised looks, their presumption of Serge's preferred partner having been completely subverted by this revelation.

As the wailing siren of a speeding ambulance pulled her back to the icy present, her anxiety voice smugly observed, 'Well, it's really no surprise. No-one is what they seem. Apart from you. You're just Ms Gullible. Everyone knows it. Everybody is able exploit you'.

"Oh, why don't you just fuck off and leave me alone," Rachel growled out loud.

"If that's what you want, but it's only a cup of hot soup."

Surprised, Rachel looked up.

Before her stood a man wrapped in a green anorak with a red scarf and matching bobble hat. His face was almost square in proportion and covered with a grey and white peppered beard. With a friendly smile plastered across his face, the oddly familiar stranger held out a large Styrofoam cup, a column of steam rising lazily from the piping hot contents.

Behind him, a large urn and a metal container were strapped to a makeshift trolley. The entire structure was held together with rope and large amounts of duct tape. On its side, a hand-printed sign declared: 'Arthur's mobile soup kitchen for the lost and homeless of London'.

"I'm sorry for being rude. It wasn't directed at you." She looked longingly at the Styrofoam container. "But I'm not really homeless. I'm just looking for my hotel." The man laughed as he countered "So I think you qualify as a lost of London, don't you?" He proffered the soup again and Rachel this time gratefully accepted it, wrapping her trembling hands around it to soak up the welcome warmth.

"So luv, what hotel you looking for?" Opening the metal container, he pulled out a large bread roll and offered it to her. She declined the kind offer, "No thanks, I'm not hungry, just very cold." He returned the offering to its container as she answered, "The Vestibule Hotel. Do you know it?"

"Oh yes I do, I am heading that way myself. Mr Typhon always has some supplies waiting for me." Rachel took a sip of the unexpectedly delicious soup as he continued, "I can give you directions, but you're welcome to walk with me if you want a bit of company on your trip?" Rachel nodded to his latter suggestion and stood up, ensuring the blanket continued to conceal her face.

The spreading warmth of the remarkable soup rapidly revitalised her. Arthur gave her evening attire a quick once-over and warned, "I got a couple of stops along the way. But it won't take too long. You look cold, luv; you should borrow my coat." As he began to unzip his parka, Rachel insisted that he keep it on. Grudgingly he pulled the zip back up, adding, "If you feel the chill help yourself to more soup." He tapped the top of the urn and pushed the cart forward.

They had walked around one hundred feet when Arthur halted the trolley by a recessed shop doorway. The urn was full to the brim as he scooped the contents into two large Styrofoam cups. "Grab a couple of bread rolls, would you?" he asked.

Emerging from under a mound of sleeping bags and plastic sheeting came two old ladies. They fondly greeted Arthur as the soups and bread rolls were eagerly accepted. "Any sign of Betty?" he asked them. The women forlornly shook their heads. "OK, I'll keep an eye out, but let me know if she turns up." They agreed and thanked Arthur again for the supplies.

On the move, Rachel enquired who Betty was. "One of the older regulars; she went missing nearly a month ago. Not unusual for them to disappear and return sometime later. But over the last few years, a lot of me regulars seem to have vanished. No trace of them to be found. I checked in with the shelters, the hospitals, other charities: nothing. Right, next stop."

Coming to a halt, he opened the urn. The soup was marginally below the top of the brim as he filled the cup and took out another bread roll.

Curled up by a stairway lay a man in a sleeping bag. After explaining to

Rachel that this man suffered a hearing problem, he shouted, "Evening, Peter!" The man, no older than his early forties, snatched the soup and roll before ranting, "I'm late. Very late. It's Important. You'll see. I'm late." Arthur nodded and shouted back, "Course you are, Peter."

Wheeling the trolley forward, Arthur explained, "I heard he used to work in the City. Came from nowhere and a bit of a billy whizz. He got himself the corner office, the posh car, the house in Hampstead and the beautiful wife. Livin' his dream, he was."

He paused his tale as a police car pulled alongside them. The officers checked after Arthur, asking how he was doing, to which he replied, "You knows me, I can't complain." They then asked if he had noticed any more of the rough sleepers missing. "Not so far, fingers crossed, eh. Anyhow seems to be only around the end of the month, which is a bit odd." The policemen agreed and said they would pass the observation on. He wished them a good night and they were gone into the darkness.

Leaning on the heavily strapped handlebars, he pushed the heavy cart forward. "Where was I? Oh yes. Peter," he continued. "So, he's livin' his dream and it all blows up. Insider tradin' or summat. Huge stink. Big money lost. All a bit murky. The city people, they take him for everything. His job, his car, his house, all gone. His wife, she moves on to a new Rolex wearer. Peter loses his marbles and, like so many, ends up out here."

Once again, they halted and two more cups were filled from the brimming urn, before Arthur checked on two young men huddled near a large air-conditioning vent.

Her curiosity piqued, Rachel reopened the urn. Again, it was full to the brim. She berated herself for not paying proper attention, recalling her previous conversation with Darius. "Arthur Pickering is a man who selflessly used the services he acquired to provide help for London's lost and homeless."

Arthur returned, joking, "I assume they're both ok; they don't speak a word of English. Not seen 'em here before. They look like nice blokes though." He paused, conscious that Rachel was standing staring at him. "I got something on me face, luv?"

"This may sound a bit strange," she said, "but did you sign a contract for what you might call special services to help look after the homeless?"

The concern of asking an absurd question quickly evaporated as Arthur replied with a tinge of sadness in his voice. "Oh, is it that time already? Have you come to collect on it?"

"Oh God, no!" she exclaimed. "If...if you could, can you tell me how you did it? I have kind of got involved with this stuff and it's all a bit confusing." She realised she probably wasn't making a lot of sense, but, before she could clarify, Arthur began to push the cart and joked, "So, you're tumbling down the rabbit hole as well, eh? Look, it's a bit like one of those posh exclusive men's clubs." Rachel gave him a blank look. "First rule of the club is: don't talk about the club."

He smiled mischievously, "But I think of it less as a rule and more as a flexible guideline, really." Rachel laughed. "So anyhow, way back I met this guy in the One Tun pub and he told me about this other guy, who knew about a geezer who could grant wishes. Course I thought he's selling me a pound of pork pies. But, a long story cut short, I eventually found the geezer, on a bench next to the Griffin Tazza in Regent's Park." Arthur paused and checked an empty office doorway for an occupant, before moving on.

"So yeah, we have a chat and the geezer, he offers me this big contract and bloody well offers me three wishes. Lots of legal talk about payments due and the like. I think it's all bollocks at first, but then I gets a spooky feelin' about him and his offer. So, I ask for a never-empty urn of hot vegetable soup for me cart."

Arthur patted the urn on its lid. "The man in Regent's Park, he's a bit surprised and asks if I was sure I didn't want the other two. I turned him down flat. Told him the urn was all I wanted. So, he amends the contract and in the completion terms he writes 'To be agreed with client'. I signs it and thought that was it."

He laughed out loud. "You could have knocked me down with a feather when, next morning, I find this 'ere urn on the cart. Never runs out of hot vegetable soup and it tastes bloody good as well."

Rachel agreed it did and asked, "Why not use the other two wishes to, say, end poverty, or homelessness, or enforce world peace, or something like that?"

He shook his head as he explained, "You know, way back I used to watch those black and white American science fiction TV shows with me dad. You know, the ones with a spooky twist at the end of the story?" Rachel nodded despite not really having a clue what Arthur was talking about. "I know what happens when you do summat like that. Ask to end poverty, all the money disappears from the world and chaos and death ensues. Ask for world peace, a nuclear war gets accidently kicked off and kills everybody. Bingo, we now have world peace. Those shows taught me that these things always get twisted in the way you never expect. I figured the worst they could have done with me one wish was give me an always-full urn of awful-tasting soup."

As they turned a corner, a familiar top-hatted man in a red coat came into view. "Hello Billy, still keeping your lonely vigil, mate?" called out Arthur. The doorman returned his greeting and held up a large clear plastic sack bulging with bread rolls.

Arthur turned to Rachel. "Delivered to your hotel, safe and sound. As you are no longer a lost of London, this is where our journey together comes to an end, luv."

Rachel thanked Arthur, asking if she could give him money to help with his work. He smiled. "Nah, I'm good. I just ask that when you next see someone in real trouble, wade in and help 'em. Ok?"

She nodded and gave him a big hug as a thank you. Arthur gently patted her on the back and warned, "Careful, miss, you'll get Billy all emotional, and his hugs can crack people's ribs." Finally, she let go and, as Billy handed over the bread rolls to Arthur, she passed through the revolving door and into the hotel.

Stepping into the welcome warmth, Rachel was confronted by Mr Typhon, who stood waiting in the empty foyer. With a wry smile on his face, he presented a large, round silver tray to Rachel. At its centre, a small square of chocolate.

"Would you care to try a Lemon and Cabbage Mint, Ms Minos?" Rachel stood stunned, trying to imagine the eclectic taste combination. "Our chef is indulging in a creative phase; he seeks to expand our clientele's culinary experiences."

Rachel politely declined the opportunity.

With an almost choreographed move, he handed the tray off to a passing bellboy whilst conceding, "Quite understandable, Ms Minos. I suspect this creative phase may have more to do with the chef being off his medications." With an expansive gesture towards the lifts, he concluded, "Welcome back to the hotel. Please enjoy your rest."

Walking towards the lift, she cautiously enquired, "Mr Typhon, has Hannah - Ms Bates - gone to my room?" The manager walked beside her as he confirmed that she hadn't yet returned to the hotel.

Perhaps it was Rachel's concerned look that prompted him to ask, "May I enquire if everything is ok, Ms Minos." Arriving at the lifts she paused and confusingly answered, "Yes...no...maybe... I don't really know." The manager slowly shook his head saying, "I see."

After a pause, perhaps expecting Rachel to expand on her response, he asked "Perhaps you wish Ms Bates' hotel access privileges to be revoked?"

Rachel's answer was as confused as her first: "No... yes... well, maybe..."

The manager held his hand to his face and observed "I see. I must confess, Ms Minos, that I detect the merest hint of uncertainty from you in this matter. Perhaps we should suspend Ms Bates' privileges pending your firm resolution on the matter?"

Rachel nodded. "It is done!" exclaimed Mr Typhon and clicked his fingers. Behind him, the lift door slid open to take Rachel up to her suite.

Chapter 15

Hannah stared with undisguised hatred across the dining table. Her flame-red hair, harshly pulled back into a ponytail, highlighted the scarlet flush growing in her cheeks. Worryingly, she now held one of the silver dinner knives in her right hand. She repeatedly turned the blade end over end, reminding Rachel of the circus knife thrower carefully judging the weapon's balance before hurling it at a target.

The focus of Hannah's anger sat directly opposite, across the white, linen-topped table. Bethany was calm, almost completely devoid of expression. The dining room lights reflected off her shoulder-length platinum hair giving her an almost machine-like appearance, the curl of her lip into an unpleasant sneer the only visible trace of human emotion.

Alex sat directly opposite Rachel. When organising the meeting, she had hoped an impartial person might help in keeping things civil - in addition to the ulterior motive of being interested in seeing him again. She couldn't put her finger on it, but there was a certain something about Alex. That said, his pink tuxedo and frilly dress shirt - apparently the only smart outfit he owned - didn't score him any style points.

The sommelier stood behind Rachel and presented the selected bottle of wine: a 1995 Petrus Pomerol. At three thousand pounds a bottle, it was by no means the most expensive wine in the hotel's extensive cellar. But, given there was a reasonable chance some of it may be hurled across the table by one of her guests, it would suffice for tonight.

In response to the nod of her head, the sommelier withdrew to uncork the wine.

"I know tensions are high, but I'd like to..." Rachel's attempt to start proceedings in calm manner were about as successful as putting up a tent during a category five hurricane in a swamp as hippopotamuses stampeded through.

"You're a manipulative, lying, cold-hearted bitch!" Hannah yelled at Bethany. The unexpectedly loud outburst solicited an 'oh my' from the adjacent table and a general murmuring from the other diners. "You set me up," continued Hannah, "You manufactured lies to frame me with your Machiavellian bullshit."

Bethany remained almost statue-like in her pose as she observed, "Oh please. You're like the little child caught with their hand in the cookie jar. Bwahh bwahh, it's not me, big girls did it and ran away. It's like all your recent sales deals: no-one's buying it."

Rachel wondered how long it would take before Mr Typhon arrived. She momentarily entertained the mental image of the hotel manager stepping up holding a red fire extinguisher then calmly hosing down the two battling women.

"Ladies, I think it best if we let Rach..." Alex's attempt to calm the situation was brushed aside as Hannah, now firmly gripping the knife, raged, "I know the real Beth." Bethany's icy calm demeanour twitched at the truncated name. "She is filled with envy. She wanted to be the rising star. She wanted to be Viath's golden girl. How unfortunate that there were so many better people in her way."

Rachel winced as the fiery redhead slammed the knife, point first, into the table. "You screwed up my career, sabotaged Rachel's life and drove Lucy to flee to America. You're a social cancer, eating away at people's lives because you don't have one of your own."

The sommelier placed a tasting glass of the Pomerol beside Rachel. She looked down; it had tiny bits of cork floating in it. After she pointed this faux pas out, he removed the glass.

"Bwaaa, Bwaaa, poor Hannah can't hack it, cos other people are better than her. Get a grip, girl." Bethany's eyes betrayed the seething anger barely contained behind the doll-like stillness. "You can't deny you're running off to a competitor. It's obvious that the Decem Fossas contract gives your otherwise pathetic street value a real boost." She leaned forward, resting a painfully thin hand on the table. The pale skin almost blended in with the white tablecloth. "You tried to use poor, sweet Rachel to get it for you. You used one of your typically over-complicated plans. After all, photos don't lie."

Engrossed in the increasingly heated exchanges, without looking, Rachel picked up the refreshed glass of wine. Taking a sip, she immediately spat out a mouthful of cork. Examining it, the glass was now a swirling morass of wine and cork fragments.

"Of course, photos lie! Ever heard of photoshop, you stupid cow?" Hannah pulled the knife out of the table and now gripped it firmly in her right fist. "It's true, they do," agreed Alex. "I have a fantastic photo of me on stage dancing with Ginger Rogers. I look just fabulous in that silk dress."

Trying to block that disturbing mental image from her mind, Rachel directed her anger towards the lurking sommelier. "Excuse me, this is utter rubbish, I'd like to see your manager." The voice that replied was chillingly familiar: "I think madam will find that she got exactly what she deserves."

A sudden movement across the table distracted Rachel. Hannah and Bethany were now kneeling on each side of Alex. Slowly, provocatively, they ran their tongues along his neck. Their probing hands pulled at his frilly dress shirt, slipping dangerously low beneath the table. Alex wore the facial expression of an eight-year-old who had just been told he would be going to Disney World for a whole month.

As Rachel tried to stand, with the intent of breaking the three of them up, a firm, muscular hand thrust her back into the seat. "Dream time's over now, Babs," Barry whispered into her ear. "It's time to wake up. It's time to come back home." Rachel could only squirm under his oppressive grip as he promised. "Babs, do I have special plans for you …"

Rachel sat bolt upright in her bed.

The alarm clock on the bedside table was buzzing loudly. The green display indicated it was just gone midday. Her brow was glistening with sweat. The damp bed sheets had been dragged into twisted disarray.

She pulled her knees tight under her chin and tried to block out 'his' ominous words from her mind. 'It's fate,' sneered her anxiety voice. 'You're going to end up back there. You will get on your knees and beg for him to take you back. You'll see.'

The weight of four lost years combined with her fears of the future pressed down unbearably on Rachel's shoulders. 'Why delay the inevitable?' it whispered. 'It's time to go home; you know I'm right'.

"That is fucking it!" Rachel shouted defiantly into the gloom of the empty bedroom. Rolling out of bed, she turned on the lights and began to search the writing desk. For a moment she feared that room service may have thrown it away, but they had placed it neatly within the desk tidy.

Flicking Darius's business card over, she read out loud the handwritten name and address: "Madam Lachesis. 20B, Greens Court, Soho."

Located between Peter Street and Brewer Street, it had taken her twenty minutes to walk there through the quiet Sunday afternoon streets. Having donned the Fedora, scarf, leather coat, black jeans and boots, Rachel felt protected. Not just against the biting cold or the Orwellian cameras. She felt a comforting inner security that was difficult for her to put into words.

Turning into Greens Court was a trip back into 1960s London. Narrow, with three storeys of flats above the shops, the short alley proved to be an eclectic mix of a café, a barbers, a dry cleaners and several adult shops.

The door to 20B nestled between the café and the barbers. It desperately needed attention - the cherry paint was badly faded and patches of exposed wood had begun to rot. There was no buzzer, just an incredibly old doorbell.

Despite there being no audible sign that the bell had worked after she had pressed it, Rachel waited patiently. A bearded man stepped out of an adult shop brandishing an innocuous brown bag. Seeing Rachel, with a somewhat flustered look, he turned and left the alley in the opposite direction.

Assuming the doorbell may not have worked, she was about to bang on the door with her gloved fist when an electronic buzz sounded and the lock was released, allowing the door to swing slightly ajar.

Tentatively pushing the door wide open revealed a long, narrow corridor. Probably fifty foot in length; a single low power light bulb provided scant illumination.

After closing the front door behind her, Rachel's boots clunked noisily on the bare floorboards as she proceeded along the corridor. Ahead stood an old four panel interior door. The brass covering of the handle had been worn black from numerous years of use and the peeling paintwork revealed it had also been repainted far too many times.

'This is a very bad idea,' warned the anxiety voice. 'Looks like a drug den to me. You don't want to get gang-raped by crackheads, do you? Let's run away, now!'

The room she entered was probably forty foot on each side. Four large tables groaned under the weight of assorted folded garments, statues of strange creatures, books, small bottles containing curiously bright liquids and many other curios. On a fifth table was an old mechanical cash register and a modern credit card machine.

Three of the walls were lined from floor to ceiling with shelving, all tightly packed with a bewildering array of glass jars, earthenware containers, metal tins and many other receptacles.

The fourth wall was festooned with Persian rugs and oriental tapestries.

Pushing between this wall of cloth emerged a woman. Rachel guessed she would be in her mid-fifties, maybe older. She wore an elaborate black gown festooned with silver mystic symbols. Black permed hair hung loosely over her shoulders. Despite the dim light, she wore a pair of small round sunglasses.

"Welcome to Madam Lachesis's Soho emporium! This is a palace of the darkest arts. Here we learn the truth that lurks beyond the veil. Wait... I can sense that strong forces are at play. Perhaps the fate of the world itself depends on you and... oh."

The woman abruptly stopped when she laid eyes on Rachel.

"I was expecting a Chinese tour group. Are you the guide?" Rachel shook her head. "Oh well," she lamented, removing her sunglasses and replacing them with a pair of normal glasses. "What can the learned Madam Lachesis do for you?"

"Well, Madam Lachesis, Darius said you may be able to help me." Upon hearing Darius's name, the older woman's expression changed and her voice dropped all theatrical embellishment. "Oh. You're trade. You should have said so earlier. Let's have a look at you and, please, my name is Janice."

She approached Rachel, first looked at her left profile and then her right. "Can you open your mouth, please," she requested. Somewhat bemusedly, Rachel complied. Janice stared inside her mouth, muttering a few 'hmms'.

"Ok, your hands please." As requested, Rachel held out her hands; she began to feel like a piece of livestock being evaluated at a marketplace. "Well, that's not good," muttered Janice with a hint of concern in her voice. "What isn't good?" asked an apprehensive Rachel. "You should really be using hand moisturiser, especially with your dry skin." It was Rachel's turn to mutter a confused 'Oh'.

"Nothing you can't sort with a trip to the chemist," Janice smiled. "Now, given your icy heritage, I think you're of the Minos lineage - I'd say on your father's side. But you're much more than that..." She paused, turning over Rachel's hands to examine the palms. "Oh yes. Mother is of Norse celestial descent; the fire leaves me in no doubt about that."

Rachel asked, "What do you mean, Norse celestial descent?" Janice released her hands with a questioning look on her face. "Don't you know your lineage? Did your parents never share it?" Rachel shook her head. The older woman took a step back. "As a rule, I don't meddle in your kind's business. It can lead to a significantly shortened life span. If you came here to find details on your past, I am afraid I can't help you. I am sure your parents had good reason to keep you in the dark. It's really not for me to get involved with such lofty affairs."

It occurred to Rachel to push this woman for answers before recalling the actual purpose of her visit. "It's not the reason I'm here. I keep hearing this voice. I thought it was my imagination until Darius claimed he could hear it."

Janice led Rachel to a floor-length mirror. "Now, that I can probably help you with." She manoeuvred her to stand directly before her own reflection. "Right, now let's get a good look at your problem. Please stay perfectly still."

After rummaging along the shelves, she returned with a glass jar packed full of tiny grey leaves. Removing a handful, she stood next to Rachel. "Now, let's see what we see," she announced and released the leaves to tumble over Rachel's head.

The falling leaves began to shimmer and emit a dull, silvery light. An eerie glow formed around Rachel's reflection and an additional ghostly image began to coalesce into view.

Rachel could barely believe her eyes. Draped around her shoulders, the shadowy outline of a scrawny cat could be clearly seen. From its spectral paws, long silvery claws penetrated deep into Rachel's shoulders. The translucent scrawny cat's face bore a distinct look of displeasure as it hissed, "Fuck off, you old hag. This one's mine."

Frozen in fear, Rachel asked in a trembling voice, "What the hell is that?" Janice smiled reassuringly, patting her hand. "It's just a passion lich. These little buggers like to feed off the negative emotions of powerful people like you." She then cooed at it as if it were a small pet. "This one has had a good old long feed, haven't you? You have been a very naughty boy."

As the leaves reached the wooden floorboards, the glow faded and the outline of the scrawny cat began to vanish, its face being the last part of it to disappear as it spat out a 'Screw you, crone'. Janice laughed as it vanished. "Now, he is a feisty one."

Her voice still trembling, Rachel implored, "You can get rid of it, can't you?" Janice nodded as she returned the glass jar to its place on the shelves. "It's not trivial, but it's not a complex ritual."

"How much will it cost?" Rachel didn't have a lot left of the two thousand pounds she had received from Darius. But to get rid of that thing she would beg, borrow or steal the rest. "Don't take this the wrong way, but, in your case, I don't want money," Janice cryptically answered. Looking cautiously at her shoulders, Rachel asked what would be required in payment?

"Well, given your potential, I'll take an IOU for reciprocal services at an undefined future date."

Rachel hesitated, concerned at what she might be committing herself to. She considered walking away, but the image of that hate-filled feline kept her rooted to the spot and she agreed to Janice's terms.

"Right then, let's make it all official then," stated Janice, pulling a piece of paper from within her robe. Resting on the table next to the register, she began to write down the details of the agreement. It occurred to Rachel that of course there would have to be a contract.

Having read it and not found anything obviously untoward, Rachel signed it and handed it back. Janice rang a sale up on the mechanical register and placed the folded contract into the cash drawer.

"Right then. This is going to take a bit of time. Let's get the kettle on and have a cup of tea before we get started," suggested Janice.

It was 7pm when Rachel finally returned to her hotel suite. After throwing her coat onto the freshly made bed, she placed a glass jar with a new wax-sealed stopper on the bedroom's writing table.

"Do you want to keep it, or shall I dispose of the little bugger for you?" Janice had asked at the end of the ritual. For no obvious reason she could think of, she had decided to keep hold of it.

The ghostly, scrawny cat face of the passion lich appeared in the jar. It stared out at Rachel and silently hissed. "How d'you like your new digs?" Rachel asked. "I think I'll call you Cheshire," she decided. The cat face glowered at her before abruptly disappearing once again.

Rachel slumped into one of the leather armchairs and pulled off her boots. The removal of the lich had lightened her mood and she felt boosted with a bit more energy.

But the crushing emotional weight remained. It still pushed down on her weary shoulders. She had held out a faint hope that her emotional problems and so many other woes were all Cheshire's fault. Perhaps, by removing the lich, those complex issues would be banished forever.

The truth was that Cheshire had fed on the fallout of those four lost years. It had greedily lapped up her fears and snacked on her deep anxieties. It may have pressed her buttons to illicit a tasty meal, but they were still all her own creations, still her own mental issues.

Rachel sighed out loud. "Guess there is no shortcut to solving those." She leaned back and wriggled her tense shoulders whilst pondering Janice's inadvertent revelations as to her family background.

Across the room, a mobile phone buzzed.

Hannah had gifted Rachel the phone after Serge's first visit. "Let's drag you back into the twenty-first century," the redhead had joked. But Rachel had viewed the device with suspicion. She feared this gift could perhaps be used to track her movements. So, it had been left charging but otherwise ignored.

Placing her boots and coat in the wardrobe, Rachel picked up the phone and examined the little screen. There were fifteen texts and eight missed call from Hannah.

Looking towards the glass jar, Rachel mused out loud, "Well, Cheshire. It looks like I may have to deal with this next." She returned to the writing table, slid open the side drawer and placed the jar inside.

"But first, I need a bath and you, my little friend, don't get to have free peeks at me anymore." And with that, she pushed the drawer firmly shut.

Chapter 16

Translucent pearls of water were flung from her arm as Rachel reached out to touch the side of the pool. Her pulse raced as another length was completed. Despite the fatigue building in her arms, she didn't pause to celebrate or to catch her breath. Instead, she flipped over and pushed strongly off from the tiled wall, commencing yet another length.

Thrusting her right arm forward, Rachel quickly resumed her rhythm. Having lain dormant for many years, she could at last feel her swimming muscle memory beginning to return.

As a child, on most Saturday mornings her father had taken her to the Chadderton leisure centre. He had been a diligent teacher, ensuring she mastered the crawl, breaststroke and even the butterfly by the age of ten. By the age of thirteen, Rachel had proved herself capable of swimming almost two lengths underwater.

Today, Rachel had only managed to complete twelve lengths of the hotel's compact swimming pool and muscles that had grown unaccustomed to any form of prolonged activity were already beginning to groan in protest. Steadfastly, she refused to concede to their distress as she drove herself forwards.

After two more lengths were completed, Rachel sensed she was probably coming to the limit of her rather feeble endurance. Determined to finish with a flourish, on this turn she dived deep and pushed off from the lower edge of the wall.

Skimming along the tiled pool bottom, she kicked out one final time towards the other side. Down here Rachel was isolated from the noises of water splashing, the whir of the air conditioning and the repetitive tones of the monotonously relaxing South American panpipe music from the sound system. Down here there was only one sound: that of her own strenuous physical exertion.

Far too quickly, the desire to take a breath grew within her. She ignored it, pressing herself onwards. Picking a spot on the bottom of the pool, she would commit herself to reach it. Then she would repeat the whole process. Dragging herself onwards as her lungs began to cry out for air.

Deep inside, a spark unexpectedly ignited.

Her pulse began to pound noisily against her ears as the fledgling spark grew into a smouldering flame. Yet this felt quite different. The flame didn't immediately run amok, allowing Rachel to focus her mind upon it, to attempt to arrest the flame's development.

Passing the halfway line of the pool, her body pleaded for her to take a single breath. Rachel resolutely ignored the need, her focus now firmly upon controlling the flame.

Gently relaxing her mental grip, she allowed the fire to swell, growing a little bit larger. Its captured heat mirrored the burning sensation spreading throughout her oxygen-starved body.

The limit of her endurance had at last been reached and, despite the desire to stay submerged, her tortured body began to arc upwards towards life-sustaining air.

Bursting out of the watery depths, she gently released the modest flame, allowing it to pass through her exhausted body.

The surge of water displaced as she spectacularly breached the surface hung impossibly frozen in place. The pool's lights glistened off the myriad tiny spheres of water, now moving imperceptibly slowly through the air.

Despite it continuing to writhe and struggle in its attempt to break free from her grasp, Rachel's bid to prevent the blaze from fully escaping her body proved to be successful.

Around her, the waves of pool water lethargically moved away. Within them, she could see intricate, beautiful patterns slowly form, merge, and vanish. These spectacular displays of natural beauty were moments normally hidden away within a blur of motion.

To her left, a large sphere of water hung improbably in the air. She reached out and touched the gelatinous surface which deflected inwards as she gently pressed upon it. With a girlish laugh, she drew a smiley face on the glistening surface.

The flame continued to seek escape, but this time Rachel willed it back down within herself. Eventually the flame relented, although Rachel felt she sensed its disappointment.

As the blaze finally vanished into the darkness, she felt elation at having held back the wave of destruction whilst enabling the passage of time to be slowed to a crawl around her.

All too soon, the wonderous moment of slowed time abruptly ended. The displaced water grudgingly agreed to obey the law of gravity and commenced its inevitable collapse back into the pool.

Exhausted by her exertions, Rachel swam a lazy breaststroke to reach the edge of the pool. Having taken a moment to catch her laboured breath, she flipped onto her back, closed her eyes and floated freely.

Her extremities continued to tingle from the afterglow of the enormous surge of energy that had passed through her body. She had controlled the flame. It was a quite different sensation to the icy cold that had gripped her after summoning the mysterious tail that dragged Leon Bay away.

Adrift in the pool, Rachel bathed in her moment of personal glory. It felt like the first real step in achieving some form of control over this power, whatever the hell it was. Mind you, she thought, being able to summon it at will would also be a useful skill to develop.

Opening her eyes, Rachel stared up at her floating reflection in the mirrored ceiling. She took a moment to admire herself in the new red and black swimsuit, though the high cut thigh now seemed to be a little excessive.

Drifting aimlessly across the pool, Rachel's mind floated back to this morning. Sitting alone in the hotel room, she'd pondered what her next steps should be. After spending a few pleasurable minutes watching Cheshire angrily bump around in his new jar, she had come to a decision.

She would comb through her copy of the Decem Fossas contract. If she discovered evidence of something worthy of blackmail, it would point to Hannah possibly being innocent of Bethany's accusations. If she found nothing, regretfully she might have to concede that Hannah had indeed actually used her.

There remained one tiny little problem. The contract had been stored on a USB stick and she didn't have a computer to read it. The hotel did have four approach-and-use terminals located in a room beside reception. Unfortunately, loading a sensitive document onto equipment which would likely be monitored wasn't her preferred option. Her cash reserves certainly wouldn't stretch to the expense of a laptop.

Mr Typhon had been sympathetic to her suggestion that a portion of the family's substantial credit be turned into cash. But his hands were tied. Her father had made specific provision that the money deposited with the Vestibule was only usable within the hotel and for its services.

Rachel needed money fast and, so far, there seemed to be only one other option. But had Rachel irreparably burned that bridge with the refusal to join the Redemptors or Redemptore or whatever they were called?

Deciding that she had no other choice but to test the waters and see, Rachel recalled Mrs Thomas' advice on opening negotiations: 'It is always vital not to appear overeager or, God forbid, desperate during those opening exchanges'.

A casual conversation with Dean, the hotel concierge, had revealed that Darius would regularly spend an hour in the hotel's poolside jacuzzi, resting amongst the bubbles from midday until one o'clock.

The plan had begun to form in her head. She had headed out to the nearest sports shop and blew her remaining money on the extravagant swimming costume and then an excruciating bikini wax at a beauty parlour. Barely making it back to the hotel in time, she had squeezed herself into the new acquisition and made sure she was swimming lengths long before midday came around.

Now the time had come to put the next step of her plan into action. She rolled off her back and, at a leisurely pace, swam to the other end of the pool and climbed out. After picking up her towel, she deliberately stretched her tired arms high over her head and yawned loudly.

Using a lazy towelling action to dry her hair, Rachel slowly sashayed back along the poolside towards the changing rooms.

This route coincidentally took her past the now occupied jacuzzi.

Rachel had prepared a couple of opening lines to use in case he didn't take the bait. They were a little clichéd, so she was relieved not to have to use them, as Darius called out, "Good afternoon, Ms Minos. Did you have a good workout in the pool?"

Feigning surprise, she turned to greet him, remembering to adopt a casual stance, whilst continuing to slowly dry her hair. "Oh Darius. I didn't see you there. How are you doing?"

"I am doing well, thank you. As, it appears, are you." Rachel shifted her weight onto her left leg, revealing the high-cut thigh of the costume as she replied, "I am feeling a lot better than I have in a long time. Thank you so much for recommending Madam Lachesis to me." Darius nodded in response.

She considered dropping the towel and retrieving it with an exaggerated bend from the waist. Then discarded that idea as probably overplaying her hand.

"I'm certainly enjoying my downtime," she continued. "I have a few days' pause in between things. You know how it is when you have nothing to do." He nodded in agreement.

Now she played her final card and hoped it would complete her winning hand. "Well, I better get going. I thought I'd wander down to Leicester Square and see if there's anything of interest on at the cinemas. Or perhaps I'll just wander around the West End." If he didn't respond, Rachel had already planned out her next line. It would be a casual enquiry, 'do you have any work to fill my spare time with?'

Thankfully, after a moment's reflection, Darius asked, "Ms Minos, I don't suppose... but if you're free, I could use a lady of your talents on a job. Strictly off the book. Not Redemptore business."

Doing her best not to appear overeager, after a suitable pause, she said, "It would probably be a lot less boring than wandering around the West End. So, what exactly are we talking about?"

Darius smiled, thinking he had cunningly snared Rachel's interest. "This is an unusual but, I think, interesting engagement. The client's...let us say...exotic pet has escaped, and he needs it rounded up before...well, before it causes too much trouble."

Slowly rubbing the towel along the length of her arms, she disinterestedly asked, "Exactly how exotic are we talking?" Darius smiled. "Let's say it is certainly not native to this neighbourhood." Rachel forced a look of concern. "Is it dangerous?" He laughed as he pointed out, "I wouldn't think of it as being terribly hazardous, but if there wasn't some risk the client would hardly need to hire us, would he?"

Rachel nodded. "Ok. It does sound intriguing, but I'll want six thousand for the job." Darius shook his head. "Too much, my dear. I'll split the reward fifty-fifty with you. That would be a tidy sum of five thousand pounds each."

After forcing herself to pause, as though she was giving serious consideration to his offer, Rachel finally relented and agreed to join him.

Darius stood up from the jacuzzi to shake her hand on the arrangement. Rachel attempted to suppress a sudden blush and quickly averted her eyes. He was now standing proudly before her, sans any form of swimming costume.

"Ms Minos, I look forward to the hunt and I'll see you at 10pm in the foyer."

Rachel hastily agreed, keeping her eyeline rigidly fixed at shoulder height as she shook his hand and then briskly retreated to the women's changing room.

Chapter 17

"Why does everything happen at the dead of night?" Rachel grumbled into her scarf.

Moonlight reflected with an ethereal glow off the frozen surface of the boating lake. On the far bank, a dimly illuminated fox pawed forlornly at the ice. It let out a mournful bark before padding off to find an alternate source of drinking water. It all seemed a bleak picture to Rachel.

During one of the hottest summers on record she had remained locked up in that tiny Camden apartment. Desperately, she had tried to keep cool as the oppressive humidity dragged on for weeks without end. It felt cruelly ironic that now, as London descended into one of its coldest spells on record, she had been outside most nights. Every day, the forecasters advised it would get even colder and, with serious voices, warned there was no end in sight.

The footpath around the lake to the Regent's Park Boathouse Café proved to be treacherously slick with ice. After several close calls, she had taken to walking along the frost-covered grass verges. Falling over and twisting something would not have made their mission any easier.

Soon after entering the park, Rachel had only just managed to avoid park security on their patrol. Huddled out of sight in a clump of bushes, she'd tried not to yelp as a pair of fat rats scurried by. One of them had paused to sniff at her before following the other into the darkness.

The thought of those rats made her shiver almost as much as the icy, still air that tried to penetrate her trusty leather armour. Rachel was convinced it was much colder in the park than on the street. Also, the gritted street pavements had provided some purchase for her boots, so walking wasn't such a test of her natural balance.

Arriving at the Boathouse Café she glanced around but could see no sign of Darius. "Bet he's buggered off back to the hotel," she mumbled.

"Probably sitting in the Djinn Bottle having a warming brandy."

She pulled the peculiar-looking fruit out of its bag and wafted it in the air. Six inches long, it resembled a pear with the skin of an orange, yet mauve in colour. Darius had assured her that their quarry loved this fruit and would be attracted to its unpleasant scent.

Still, after two hours of creeping around the park waving the damn thing in air, there had been no sign of the beast. They had agreed to split up and meet back at the café with Rachel searching around the lake and Darius taking the open grassland near the Hub.

"I wonder if we're even in the right bloody park," she complained into the still night. It wouldn't have surprised her if they should have been in Hyde and not Regent's Park.

Peering through a frosted window of the boathouse, she could make out piled-up tables and parasols in the gloom, securely stored until the return of better weather, but there was no sign of the elusive quarry.

Hoping that Darius wouldn't be much longer, Rachel rubbed her gloved hands together. If she hadn't desperately needed the money, she would have headed back to the hotel and sod the payoff.

A loud crunching noise from amongst the trees behind the boathouse put her on alert. Stepping around the corner of the building, she peered through the bare tree branches. Someone was running towards her, crashing through the brittle undergrowth. Darius appeared and he seemed to be running at speed from something. Whatever it was, it must have been far behind him as she could see no sign of it.

"Stop it!" he gasped, clearly exhausted by the chase. It was at that point in the evening that Rachel realised the client's briefing on their prey had missed out some critical information. Something unseen, the size of a large dog and extraordinarily strong, had barrelled into her at speed.

Flung off her feet, Rachel completed a twisting half-somersault in the air, her fedora disappearing into the shadowy undergrowth. Letting out an involuntary yelp of pain, she crashed down onto the ice-covered pathway.

Staring up into the clear black sky, she lay on her back, thinking how much her life had changed in a few short days. Darius stumbled past, helpfully gasping, "I declare, the damnable thing's invisible."

Confirming that nothing had been broken in the collision, she rolled onto her hands and knees and looked around. Darius now circled a clump of bushes, the beast presumably having gone to ground within them.

Carefully regaining her feet, Rachel trotted over to join Darius. Her back would be bruised in the morning, but she felt that little else, apart from her pride, had been damaged. Pointing towards the bushes she whispered, "Is the bugger in there?"

Darius nodded and motioned for her to circle to the left. Cautiously she paced in that direction, Darius in turn circled to the right. With slow, deliberate movements Rachel retrieved the fruit from her pocket. Waving it towards the bush, she muttered, "Dinner's up, you little bastard."

She had only covered perhaps five paces when the beast burst unseen from out of the bushes. She focussed on the puffs of frost being disturbed on the grass, and the streaming cloud of its steaming breath. As it charged towards Rachel, those scant visual clues allowed her to gauge its course and speed. Almost too late, she realised it was heading directly towards her.

Issuing a noise that could be best described as a cross between a dog bark and a cat howl, it leapt from the ground towards, she presumed, her throat. Rachel held her arms out and tried to grapple the unseen beast. By pure luck, her gloved right hand slipped around its studded collar, allowing her to grab a firm hold.

The combined mass and velocity of the charging beast proved too much and, for the second time, she found herself crashing backwards onto the ground. The small mercy of the impact being onto grass was unfortunately offset by the earth being rock hard from frost.

Hanging onto the collar with her right hand, she managed to punch her left fist into the side of its face as it lunged forward. The smell of its breath churned her stomach, but the sound of its jaws snapping closed mere inches from her face was of greater immediate concern.

She fumbled with her left hand, trying to find some purchase as the beast squirmed to free itself of her grip. "Oh no you don't, you bastard," she shouted as it tried, in vain, to pull away. It frustratedly roared in response, splattering Rachel's face with its foul-smelling and corrosive saliva. Only by chance did her new white scarf bear the brunt of the unpleasant soaking.

The beast again lunged forward, pitting its bulk and strength against Rachel's tenuous grip on its collar. She could hear its jaws repeatedly snapping shut perilously close to her face.

She tried to trigger a spark within herself. Tried to create a flame so she could give herself time to deal with this creature. But, despite her best attempts, nothing at all happened.

With a painful squeak, the beast's writhing began to weaken. Beside her, kneeling on the grass, Darius had driven the fast-acting tranquiliser into its back. Looking up, Rachel could see the empty syringe apparently hanging in mid-air above her. In its weakened state, at last Rachel could grip the collar with both hands and roll the increasingly limp mass off her chest.

The appalling stench of its saliva was filtering through her scarf. Trying not to gag, she pulled it off her face and tossed it as far away as she could manage. It would take her a long time to forget that smell.

Panting, Darius dryly observed, "Well, that could have gone a tad more smoothly." With pains now shooting up her abused back, Rachel could only grunt in agreement.

Eventually, the growing cold permeating though the ground overcame her desire to lie still. With help from Darius, she staggered to her feet and stretched out her twisted back.

He had rolled their quarry into a large bag, which he now struggled to hoist over his shoulder. "Right, I'll take this thing back to the client and get our payment. Ms Minos, will you be alright heading back to the Vestibule on your own?"

Rachel nodded. She kept her concerns private. Having lost her hat and scarf, she would have to carefully avoid the numerous CCTV cameras during the thirty-minute walk back to New Cavendish Street.

For a moment she toyed with the idea of staying with Darius. Seeking his protection against the unknowns of the night. She quickly dismissed the notion. She had already survived several trips through the city on her own and Rachel was determined to prove to 'him', Cheshire and herself that she was an independent woman.

Leaving the ice-decorated park, Rachel watched several empty black cabs whisk along Marylebone Road. Annoyingly, she didn't have a penny left to pay for one. "Should have got a loan off Darius," she wistfully announced to no-one.

Avoiding a cluster of cameras, she turned onto Portland Place and halted in her tracks. A black Mercedes was double parked further down the road, its hazards flashing, its engine running. Perhaps Shank and the Driver had acquired another vehicle? Rachel knew it was probably nothing to do with her. It was more than likely a taxi waiting to pick up a fare, but, regardless, she doubled back to find an alternate path.

Her route to the hotel became ever more torturous with the constant changes of direction to avoid those ever-watchful cameras. The tourist map of London that the hotel concierge had supplied proved to be an

179

invaluable tool in navigating her way around the city.

Turning onto Hallman Street, at least she knew that the comfort and warmth of the hotel was just around the next corner. As she passed a row of parked cars, she made up her mind to drop into the Djinn Bottle, grab a cider and maybe flirt, just a little bit, with Russel the barma...

Too late, Rachel saw the car door as it swung violently into her, sending her sprawling onto the floor. Her abused back sent further spasms of pain through her body.

Using a lamp post to drag herself back onto her feet, Rachel's fears crystallised as a man in a black balaclava leapt from the vehicle.

She thought she had been so careful in avoiding those cameras; had she missed some? Or perhaps the assailant had been parked, waiting, hoping for her to pass by on the way to the Vestibule Hotel. As he charged at Rachel, it made little real difference now.

His gloved hand smashed into her right eye with bone-crunching force. Stunned, Rachel fell sideways, slamming into a parked car.

Hanging onto its wing mirror, she failed to see or avoid the second blow as it drove hard into her jaw. Tumbling to the pavement, she could feel the metallic taste of blood filling her mouth.

Now sprawled across the floor, a heavy boot slammed into her chest. The bone-cracking force of the impact drove the wind out of her. Scarlet blood sprayed out of her mouth and across the icy white surface. It bizarrely reminded Rachel of a modern art painting she had seen recently.

"How'd you like it, you fuckin' bitch?" Her assailant bent over her and grabbed a fistful of her hair, pulling her head off the ground. Rachel's attempt at a pithy comeback was limited to a gurgle of blood.

Maintaining a firm grip, her assailant dragged Rachel to her feet. "Not so fuckin' tough without your top-hatted boyfriend, are you?" Throwing her back into the side of the car he leaned forward, bringing his covered face to within inches of hers. There was animalistic fury in his voice as he sneered, "You must be so fuckin' stupid being out here without a disguise."

He punched her hard in the guts with his right hand. Her pitiful cries for help were smothered by his left. "I've been told to take you in alive. But they didn't say I couldn't have some fun first!" She weakly tried to push him away, but he brutally slammed her left wrist back against the car roof.

Leaning forward again, he menacingly whispered into her ear, "Time for you to pay the Shank his due." Still smothering her mouth with his left hand, his right began to unbutton her leather coat. Her attempt to summon up some form of resistance proved to be futile.

She tried one more time to light a spark.

She began to sob as nothing happened.

Shank grunted in satisfaction as he flung open the coat and began to paw at her belt buckle.

"Now, now, my love. You're just not doing it right." The familiar voice emanated out of Rachel's line of sight. "You have to realise it's not a thing you can just turn on or off. It is not like a light switch." Rachel recognised her mum's Lancashire accent, but she couldn't see her. "Little one, you have to call to it. You must summon it to you. You have to ask it for its help."

Fumbling open the belt buckle, her assailant smirked as he grabbed hold of her jeans zip. Her mother's fading voice implored her, "Now, my little girl, call it to you."

Rachel called into the darkness.

She pleaded to it to come to her aid.

In the darkness, a spark flashed brightly.

Rachel desperately breathed life into it, creating a fire. She fed it with the pain from all her injuries and it surged into an intense fireball. She fanned it with the terror that gripped her and it swelled into a firestorm.

The assailant hesitated, perhaps sensing something was not quite right. He released Rachel and moved to grab the pistol tucked into his waistband.

He never reached it.

Space and time were bent to her will.

Each second was stretched into a minute as she allowed the flame to surge freely from within her body.

Gracefully the attacker lifted into the air, his helpless body tumbling in slow motion. Ever so gradually, his mouth opened in surprise at his unexpected predicament.

Although she struggled to hold on to consciousness, Rachel had never felt so powerful. In that moment she knew that, with a mere thought, she could demand that the fabric of space be violently twisted, tearing Shank into a million bloody pieces.

Why not? After all he had done, he deserved it.

Instead, she allowed him to be slowly smashed through an upper storey window of an adjacent office block. As he vanished out of sight, the broken shards of glass gently twisted in the pale moonlight, reminding Rachel of twinkling stars in the night sky.

Rachel released the flame. She took a moment to thank it for its timely intervention. With the flow of time returning to normal, Rachel sensed that she would soon lose consciousness. It wasn't far to the hotel; perhaps she could make it there.

Dragging herself along the line of parked cars, glass began to noisily shower down onto the street behind her. Car and building alarms noisily rang out their warning. The cacophonous noise masked her violent coughing as Rachel sprayed the shiny metal vehicles with her blood.

Her broken body wanted to lie down and rest; instead, she kept going. Reaching the end of one car, she would set a goal to reach the end of the next vehicle and so forced herself onwards.

Darkness began to swim through Rachel's head. Where was her mother? She must have been close by. Why didn't she come to Rachel's aid? She wanted to fall into her mother's arms. To once again be a little child. To have her cuts and bruises tended to with plasters and to listen to her mother's soothing words.

Heaving herself to the end of Hallman Street, Rachel struggled to recall if she turned left or right. Her heart sank with the realisation that she had dropped the map when Shank had landed his first punch.

Dropping to her knees, she burst into tears and wiped the constant trickle of blood from the corner of her mouth. "Please mum, help me!" she cried out between her sobs.

The only response, the faraway blaring of an angry car horn.

The calming embrace of numbing darkness now flooded over her. As consciousness fled, she slumped forward and tumbled face first onto the frost-covered pavement, blissfully unaware of the sound of approaching footsteps.

Mr Typhon stood in the Vestibule's foyer, studiously examining Antoine Careme's sketchpad. After several considered 'hmms', he politely observed, "Well Antoine, no-one can accuse you of lacking in imagination."

He handed the pad of paper back to the head chef. "But I think an ice sculpture centrepiece of Dante's 9th level of inferno may be a little much for some of our more traditionally minded clientele."

The manager never heard Antoine's response, as Arthur Pickering and Billy passed through the hotel's revolving entrance and staggered into the foyer. Slumped between them was Rachel's bloodied, battered and worryingly limp body.

Keeping his concerned gaze locked on Rachel, Mr Typhon clicked his fingers at the reception desk and requested that Tina 'Please get the Physician here now'.

Chapter 18

With frustratingly slow progress, the second hand continued its laboured journey around the clock face. With each sweep of the hand past twelve, a loud clunk heralded the passing of yet another sixty seconds and the lethargic progression of the minute hand.

No matter how desperately Rachel had willed it to move quicker, the clock had relentlessly continued at its precisely measured pace. It had been a long, boring afternoon spent counting down the remaining moments of their cruel incarceration.

The ringing of the bell finally echoed through the building and her heart jumped at hearing the joyous sound. That bell was a celebration of liberation. A sign that freedom beckoned.

"Ok everyone, home time. Don't forget chapter twenty-one for your homework. There will be a test on Monday afternoon. Have a good weekend." Mr Bhatti also reminded the classroom of excited children to walk and not run, as they rapidly surged towards the door and freedom.

Squeezing into the corridor beyond, the throng of kids shouted their goodbyes to sir. The late spring sunshine had been calling out to them all afternoon and it was the start of what promised to be an extremely hot weekend. For those nine-year-old students, the test on Monday was now an eternity away.

Once in the playground, Rachel met up with her best friend Alison. In appearance they couldn't have been more different. With long blonde hair brushed neatly down her back, her blouse tucked into her skirt, school tie neatly knotted and white socks pulled up to just below her knees, Rachel could have been posing for the school brochure. By contrast, with short, mousey brown hair, her blouse hanging out, the tie already stashed in a pocket and socks rolled down to her ankles, Alison could have been a comic book characterisation of the school's wild child.

Walking to the school gate they huddled conspiratorially and animatedly exchanged their afternoon news. They discussed the kids they liked, the kids they didn't like, the kids who they thought were weird and the boys who were a bit dreamy. They had so much to discuss, despite having last met only a few hours earlier at lunch time.

Reaching the school gate, the quickest way home for both of them was to turn left. They, of course, turned right. It was too glorious a Friday afternoon to be indoors, so it would be the long way back home today.

Strolling down Laurel Avenue, some children shouted goodbyes at them, some waved enthusiastically and some deliberately ignored them. It all really depended on your standing within the complex social structure of Mill Hill primary school.

"He's following you again!" Alison whispered into Rachel's ear.

She glanced back and sure enough, Scott Macey was trailing some ten feet behind them. He was only eight years old. A whole year younger than Rachel! He was also a good few inches shorter than her.

Rachel flashed her meanest glare at him. In response, the boy blushed with embarrassment at having been spotted and crossed over to the other side of the road. There he deliberately averted his gaze, but Rachel suspected he was sneaking a few peeks towards her.

At the bridge, the two girls took the steps down to the canal and turned right along the towpath. They laughed and chatted while meandering at an ever-slower pace. A canal barge overtook them, its engine chug, chug, chugging as it worked its way north.

"I am so jealous. I bet they're going up to Rochdale or Huddersfield or maybe even as far as Leeds," Alison thought out loud. "It's ages before I go away again."

Rachel was unsympathetic as she moaned, "Pffft, you get to go on holiday to Spain and France every year. The furthest my family ever go is Manchester. My parents are just soooo boring - they don't ever want to go anywhere."

They entered the cool shadow of a huge brick mill standing on the opposite bank. In a history lesson, Mr Bhatti had told them that the Malta mill had been built in 1905 for making cloth. Apparently, they were going to go and see a working mill later in the term. Maintaining her good student persona, Rachel had appeared keen on the idea. But in truth it sounded very boring to her.

The appearance of a couple of springer spaniels elicited whoops of excitement from the two girls. The dogs' owner, an elderly woman with a walking stick, explained that she had only wanted a single dog, but when she went to choose a puppy, she found the two of them were inseparable and, in (as she called it) a moment of madness, took both of them.

Alison kneeled on the towpath and hugged and stroked the excitable dogs. Rachel was more reserved, not wanting to get stray dog hairs on her still pristine uniform.

Once the dogs had moved on, they stood on the towpath throwing stones into a reed bank, much to the annoyance of the local water birds. As they threw, they listed their teachers in order of preference, before moving on to pop singers and finally actors.

Climbing up the slope from the canal, they paused next to the huge electricity pylon. As a small child, Rachel had often fantasised that the towering metal structure would one day come to life. It would sweep her up in its huge metal arms and carry her away on exciting adventures in the nearby and very mysterious Pennine Hills.

Today it remained stationary, providing shade from the glaring sun while the girls chatted about music, boys, makeup and their plans for the weekend.

Finally, they entered the housing estate and made their arrangements to meet up after tea. After further prolonged and drawn-out goodbyes, Alison continued up Saxon Drive and Rachel turned onto Partridge Way.

Mrs Thompson, who lived at number thirty-three, was standing in her driveway with Mrs Bhat from number forty. Both had their arms folded as they stared further up the road. As Rachel passed them by, Mrs Thompson whispered into the other's ear, who nodded back sagely.

Parked outside Rachel's home was a long grey limousine. She had seen similar vehicles on TV shows set in exotic faraway places like America, California, or London. She had never thought to see one herself and certainly not in Chadderton, parked outside her house.

Approaching the glamorous vehicle, Rachel spotted three motorbikes, one parked in front and two behind the limousine. There were boys in her class who could have reeled off the detailed Top Trumps stats for each of those machines. She just thought they were big and intimidating.

Two riders, dressed in full black leathers with black helmets and dark tinted visors, stood motionless by the car. She thought they must have been boiling standing out in the late afternoon sun.

They silently watched her as she approached. She thought they looked very creepy so, holding her school bag up to her chest, she quickly trotted by them and through the front door of her home.

Entering the modest nineteen seventies three-bedroom detached house, Rachel could hear people talking in the kitchen. She paused in the hallway, straining to listen in on the conversation.

"I don't care," said her father. "It is not going to happen." Rachel could detect both concern and determination in his voice. Similar to when, as a five-year-old, she had demanded to have pony lessons. On that occasion, her week-long sulk had failed to sway his final decision in her favour.

"I understand your concern, but I don't think you are being rational about this." The stranger's voice was female with a posh-sounding accent. "You must realise It has the potential to far exceed your joint accomplishments."

Her mother's broad Lancashire accent sounded uncharacteristically angry. "It has a name and Rachel is <u>my</u> daughter, and <u>we</u> decide what's best for her." Outside, the distant rumbles of an approaching thunderstorm could be heard echoing across the sky.

"My apologies, you are, of course, correct." There was the sound of a mug being placed on a table. "But consider this: your daughter is unique, the impossible progeny of two utterly different lineages. She may prove to be nothing more than a normal woman, or perhaps she will be something quite different, perhaps even something truly magnificent."

Rachel jumped at the sound of a fist slamming into the table as her father bellowed, "I don't care! My daughter deserves a normal life and that's what I vowed at her birth to give her. We had this same argument with the Redemptore and we accepted their compromise of exile to ensure that Rachel was safe from them. Why on the earth do you think we would now hand her over to the likes of you?"

Rachel had never heard her dad sound so furious. His anger when she had accidentally set fire to the garden shed didn't even come close. On tiptoes, she crept forward to the partially open kitchen door and tried to peer through.

The stranger's voice remained calm. "I understand, but you cannot shield her forever. Eventually she will flee this little nest. Will you have prepared Rachel to be part of our world? Will she be ready for what she could eventually become?" Her parents remained silent, the only sound the rumbling thunder of the approaching storm.

"Perhaps we should ask Rachel herself what she desires?" the stranger asked.

The kitchen door was flung open. Rachel let out a scream and jumped in the air. She dislodged her mother's favourite painting – a seaside hotel perched on a tall cliff – sending it clattering onto the floor.

Standing before Rachel was another biker. This one was shorter than the other two and dressed in a white, one-piece leather suit with black flashes down the side. Rachel stared up at her terrified image reflected in the white helmet's mirrored visor.

With a voice of crashing thunder, her mother surged forward shouting, "Get away from my daughter!" The white-clad biker wisely stood aside as Rachel was swept up into her mother's arms and carried out of the kitchen doorway and into the living room.

Slamming the door closed behind them, her mother sat down upon her large easy chair, perching Rachel on her lap. "Mommy, what were you talking about?" Rachel asked with a lump forming in her throat. "They are not going to take me away from you, are they?" Tears were welling up in her eyes at the thought of being snatched from her parents, of being taken from her home and away from her friends.

He mother hugged her tightly and, with a soothing voice, comforted her. "My darling Rachel. Whilst you're my baby, no- one is _ever_ going to take you away." Rachel snuggled into those encircling arms as her mother began to sing a nursery rhyme:

>Polly put the kettle on,
>
>Polly put the kettle on,
>
>Polly put the kettle on,
>
>We'll all have tea.

A wave of heat surged from her mother's body. Rachel's eyelids felt heavy and she struggled to keep herself from falling asleep. Much as dew on a hot summer morning evaporates, so too did her fears of being stolen away.

Sukey take it off again,

Sukey take it off again,

Sukey take it off again,

They've all gone away!

Rachel's left eye cracked slowly open. Her vision swam and swirled as she tried, unsuccessfully, to focus on the ceiling. She coughed, her mouth feeling as dry and rough as sandpaper; sharp stabbing pains in her chest punished the sudden movement.

"I think she's awake," came a distant voice to her right. It was vaguely familiar, but she couldn't recall who it was.

Something was preventing her right eye from opening. Rachel tried to lift her left arm to remove the obstacle but was only rewarded with further intense pain. An unseen hand firmly grasped and gently lowered the wayward arm back down to the bed.

"If you can hear me, Ms Minos, I need you to stay perfectly still." The female voice coming from her left was unfamiliar. "You have been badly hurt. But you are strong. With my aid you will recover."

Rachel's mind began to drift on pharmaceutically driven currents. Snippets of the attack flashed into her mind and as quickly dissolved away. She wondered what had become of Shank, how she had found her way back to her hotel room and where that unfamiliar childhood memory had been dragged up from.

How could she have forgotten such an event in her then young life? Until this moment, she had possessed no recollection of what had occurred on that sunny Friday afternoon. Perhaps the shock of the attack or the numerous chemicals now swimming through her body had somehow dislodged the event from a dark recess within her memory.

Blinking her one working eye revealed the blurred outline of a figure bending over her from the left. "I'm going to inject you with something to speed your healing process. I am afraid this will hurt a lot." A large syringe, filled with a luminous yellow substance, came into view. The blurry figure leaned forward and injected Rachel in the arm.

She moaned as wave after wave of intense pain surged through her broken body. "Is she ok?" came the now distant voice to the right. It was filled with concern and compassion for Rachel's plight. "She sounds much worse. Isn't there anything you can do to help her?"

"It's unfortunately part of the regenerative process. But I can put her back under and spare her any further immediate suffering." The voice on the left was casual and matter of fact. She could have as easily been discussing the respective merits of curry or an oriental meal for tonight's dinner.

The morass of Rachel's confused thoughts became submerged by the smothering power of a sedative.

She drifted away to a place of happier memories.

To a time of long and lazy summers.

Of games and fun with her best friend Alison.

Of her first real kiss, in the shadow of the giant pylon, with a young boy called Scott.

Chapter 19

"Now raise your arm. Good, and now you can lower it. Excellent. You do appear to have regained your full range of motion." The Physician finished scribbling in her red leather notebook, placed it on the bed and retrieved an ophthalmoscope from her medical bag. "Look straight ahead and do not blink," she curtly instructed.

Rachel sat cross legged on the edge of the bed, dressed in pink and white cotton pyjamas. Three days had passed since she had fully regained consciousness. Remarkably, apart from bruises, aches and twinges, she had mostly recovered from the grievous injuries.

"And blink. Look up. Look down. And look straight ahead." The well-practiced, calming smile on the Physician's face provided no hint of her thoughts as she moved to examine Rachel's left eye.

Average height with a slender build and wispy blonde hair, the Physician wore a pale grey blouse, a rose-coloured pleated skirt, and flat, black, laced shoes. The appearance struck Rachel as more country GP than mysterious, city-based medical practitioner.

"Now look straight ahead..." As her left eye was being thoroughly examined, the scrawny cat face appeared across the room in its jar. Cheshire grimaced at her, perhaps disappointed that its captor had made such quick progress in her recovery. The Physician recovered her notepad and added additional lines of illegible scrawl. "Now, Rachel, how do you feel?"

Rachel stretched her arms over her head as she replied, "Actually, surprisingly good all things considered. Still some aches and pains, but, yeah, I feel ok." As more notes were added to the page, Rachel suggested, "Whatever that stuff was you treated me with, you should think about marketing it. It seems to be amazing."

The Physician responded with her unflappable bedside manner:

"Regrettably, the majority of the populace could not endure the trauma of the procedure." The answer surprised Rachel, who wondered, "How did you know I would survive it?"

A different smile, obviously deployed when dealing with patients' tiresome questions, now graced the Physician's face. "Having been present at your difficult birth, I felt confident that you would... cope with the compound. Now, stand up please."

"You were at my birth? Did you know my parents?" Rachel uncrossed her legs and slipped off the end of the bed. "Yes, I was and yes, I did. I am sure that you will understand that I am oath-bound not to discuss the specific details of that event." The Physician pulled Rachel's top up and examined her back. "But I will say that you were a fascinating case study. Given your parents, I assumed your chances of survival were, at best, no better than thirty-three percent. Now, stand on your left leg, bend your knee, and touch your nose with your right hand."

Much to Rachel's frustration, the Physician refused to be drawn into revealing further details about their shared past. "That all looks satisfactory, Rachel. I would request that you avoid pushing yourself too hard and you should be fully recovered within the week. Please contact me immediately if you suffer any serious setbacks."

Given the catastrophic injuries sustained five short days ago, Rachel remained amazed that she now only experienced aches and strains. "What if I feel any new severe pain or similar?" The physician paused, before pulling a small black spray canister from her bag and handing it over to Rachel. "Spray this on any regions where you feel pain." The black canister proved to be devoid of any labels or writing. "So, I just spray this on the skin and it will help any problems?"

Picking up her bag and heavy winter coat, the Physician bluntly replied, "No. It's just a placebo. It has no medical benefit whatsoever. But double-blind controlled trials show that thirty percent of people often find relief in using such products. If you believe you are in pain, perhaps it will also help you." Rachel struggled to decide if the Physician's answer had been meant to be sarcastic or serious.

Having thanked the Physician for the treatments, Rachel escorted her to the door. "Goodbye Rachel. It was good to see you again. I shall check on you in a week's time."

Closing the door behind the Physician, Rachel crossed the room and pulled back the drapes to reveal the late afternoon view. To her surprise, a blizzard of golf ball-sized snowflakes swirled past the frost-stained window.

Leaning forward, she peered down through the murk to the street below. Figures wrapped in heavy layers pushed their way against the blast of arctic wind that mercilessly howled down New Cavendish Street. A jogger wrapped in thermal running gear could barely keep their footing on the treacherously slick surface.

Vehicles' horns were sounded in frustration as they crawled along at a snail's pace; windscreen wipers fought a losing battle against the relentless build-up of snow; motorbikes slithered their way forward, lacking their normal gung-ho, traffic-weaving bravado.

An unexpected sickly feeling gripped her stomach as she peered down at the scene below. Rachel could have been staring down at Camden Road. She could have been watching the passage of commuters, shoppers, children, buskers, dog walkers and joggers outside that tiny apartment.

The pervasive odour of mouldy carpet and mildewed walls unexpectedly assaulted her nostrils. Fearful memories began to emerge from that bleak period of her life. What's the time? Barry might be home soon. Had she completed everything on his to-do-list? Did she have time to make herself pretty for her loving boyfriend? Perhaps he would...

Pssssssssssssssssssssssssssssssssssssss

The spray was icy cold and wet. Rachel gave her face a good dousing before replacing the cap on the matte black can. Placebo or not, she certainly felt better.

After placing the can on the writing table next to the new laptop, she headed into the bathroom for a towel. Cheshire watched her with a smirk plastered across its scrawny face.

The reflection in the bathroom mirror still bore the aftermath of the vicious attack. The bruises on her cheeks and around her left eye were beginning to fade; her lower lip had almost returned to its normal size. But she certainly wouldn't be winning a beauty pageant any time soon. Returning to the writing desk, she darkly hoped that Shank looked a good deal worse.

Pushing Cheshire's jar to one side, she lifted the laptop lid and resumed her review of the Decem Fossas contract. It had proved quite a chore to get the computer to work without connecting to the internet. It had taken the intervention of the hotel's technical support staff to finally get it all working. To Rachel's relief, they had shown no interest in finding out why she didn't want the device to be connected to the rest of the world.

The seven hundred and twenty-nine page contract plus twenty-seven extensive appendices could not be described as a light read. During her first pass through, she had begun to recall the document's structure and content. It seemed like a lifetime ago that she'd sat in that tiny office, wrinkling out the those niggling issues and crafting her elegant solutions.

The appendices had been added to the document after her involvement had been completed and so required a great deal more of her attention. Her fresh A5 notepad was already full of copious notes as she commenced her second pass of the document.

Frustratingly, apart from some novel interpretations of local charity laws, Rachel had uncovered nothing outwardly untoward. Certainly no trace of a scandal that could be used for extortion.

She sat back in her chair and sighed in exasperation. Cheshire momentarily appeared in its jar; its face bore a wide, smug grin as it lapped up her obvious frustration. Rachel opened the table drawer, placed the jar in it and - with a parting 'Lights out for naughty Cheshire!' - slammed it shut.

Another hour ticked slowly by with no significant progress. With a loud yawn, Rachel rubbed tired eyes. Perhaps, she postulated, the information she sought had been secretly encrypted within the document. Could the answer to her riddle be tucked away amongst the digital ones and zeros?

Standing up, she reached her arms over her head. Stretching her back generated several worryingly ominous clunks. To her right, the snow-blinded view through the large plate window gave no hint of the time. According to the bedside clock it was fast approaching 5pm.

"Time to practice," she announced to the room.

Lowering herself to sit on the floor adjacent to the toasty radiator, she crossed her legs, closed her eyes, and attempted to empty her mind. It took nearly a full five minutes to achieve the final clear state, beating down her stray thoughts like tiny fires springing up on a tinder-dry moor.

She called into the darkness.

Nothing happened.

Again, she called out, asking it to come forward.

Nothing happened.

Now feeling apprehensive, she called a third time and was rewarded with a feeble spark that appeared within the void. Breathing life into the flame, she noticed how reluctantly it began to burn, the pale flames growing sluggishly.

This was the third consecutive day she had summoned the flame from the darkness. Today something was clearly amiss: it looked weaker and lacked its previous intensity. The dark red, roiling flames had faded to a bleached yellow.

It had never even occurred to Rachel until now, but did the flame require time to regenerate? Did it need to regather its power between uses? Or perhaps, more worryingly, was there only a finite amount of energy that she could extract from it?

The previous practice sessions had already seen a marked improvement in her ability to contain and control the power of her inner flame. Yesterday she been able to successfully slow time down within the confines of her hotel room for a whole four minutes, whilst outside forty had passed by as normal.

It wasn't as if she had a user manual to consult or a telephone help line to contact regarding her... performance issues. Until she had a better understanding of how it functioned, it would be foolish to potentially squander its remaining power on a practice session.

She released the flame, thanking it for appearing.

With growing concern, she watched as the flame lethargically vanished back into the darkness. "I'll leave you for a few days," she told herself, "and by then hopefully you will have recovered." She didn't want to consider the repercussions of it failing to regain its potency.

The knock on the door roused her from deep thought.

Standing up took a good deal longer than usual: her left knee still refused to articulate properly. Eventually, she hobbled over to the door and peered through the peephole. A familiar mop of red hair waited outside.

Mr Typhon had taken it upon himself to contact Hannah soon after

Rachel had been returned injured to the Vestibule. "It is the Vestibule's policy to reach out to a family member or designated contact in the event of such unfortunate circumstances," he had explained when Rachel fully regained consciousness. "I felt this was the correct course of action due to your circumstances and given that she was the only viable contact we possessed for you. But you may rest assured that there was always a member of hotel staff present during this period."

He recounted that, as Rachel had languished between the realms of the living and the great beyond, Hannah had sat in constant vigil at her bedside, barely leaving her for the three days and two nights.

"If you feel that I have acted in error, please accept my most humble apologies and I will arrange to have Ms Bates ejected from the hotel without further hesitation." Rachel wondered if she asked him to eject Hannah from the roof of the hotel, would he do so? Chillingly, part of her felt certain that the hotel manager would accommodate her request without a moment's hesitation and with his customary flourish.

The unexpected benefit of her brush with death had been the restoration of a modicum of trust between Hannah and herself. If she had orchestrated a complicated subterfuge to manipulate Rachel into acquiring the contract, why had she subsequently ignored the USB stick sitting on the desk?   If she had managed to copy the data during her three-day vigil, why would this allegedly cold, manipulative monster continue to look after her?

Obviously, Hannah's omitting to mention her pending departure and change of corporate allegiances cast a continuing shadow of doubt. Rachel concluded that she would, for now, closely scrutinise Hannah's actions, in case the redhead was attempting to use her in an even more convoluted scheme.

Her decision made, she had thanked Mr Typhon for taking the initiative and requested that he delay the ejection of Hannah from the Vestibule.

At least for now.

Rachel swung the door open. Hannah wore a heavy, padded winter coat, its shoulders damp with snowmelt. "It's firkin' freezing out there," was all she muttered as she bustled into the room.

Rachel ordered a pot of coffee and biscuits from room service before following Hannah into the bathroom. Leaning against the door jamb, she watched intently as the redhead's damp coat, ankle boots and dark work trousers were removed and hung up over the heated towel rail to dry. Now stripped down to her sky-blue blouse, panties and ash black hold-up stockings, Hannah began to vigorously dry her hair. Still dressed in the pink and white pyjamas, Rachel suddenly felt uncomfortably frumpy. A sure sign she was on the way to recovery.

Handing Hannah one of the cotton towelling robes from the wardrobe, Rachel recounted the Physician's medical assessment but carefully omitted the discussion regarding her birth.

Wrapping a towel around her head, Hannah leaned towards the mirror and touched up her makeup. "So, you're cleared for light duties, eh? So, it's your choice: the restaurant or the Djinn Bottle bar?

Rachel made some feeble excuse about having to get back to work on the contract. Hannah admonished her, "Ms Minos. You have been cooped up in this hotel room in your PJs for a week. It's time to put on some proper clothes and to boldly venture out at least as far the hotel foyer."

Swapping her pyjamas for real clothes, even for a few hours, did feel like a good idea. The change of scenery might also help her tackle the contract with fresher eyes.

Before she could answer, there came a knock at the door. One thing that she had learned, being stuck in her room, it was uncanny how quickly room service requests were delivered in this hotel.

Having poured the coffee, Rachel sat on the end of the bed. Hannah paced up to the window, leaned against the back of one of the leather armchairs, and looked out on the wintery scene below. "I poked around the office as much as I could get away with. No-one was obviously behaving strangely - at least, no more than usual. I dropped hints with a few people that you had been involved in a bad traffic accident. I made it clear that it was still touch and go if you would make it."

She sheepishly turned around to face Rachel and admitted, "I actually have a drawer full of Get-Well cards from people who remember you. Oh, and some chocolates to speed your recovery." Rachel suspected she would never get to taste those chocolates. "Anyhow, let's see if that little rumour changes anyone's behaviour."

Finishing off her coffee the redhead enquired, "How has your contract research gone? Have you found the secret message yet?" Placing her empty coffee cup on the compact lounge table, Hannah paced back across the room as Rachel recounted the fruitless labours of her investigation.

"Trousers or skirt?" asked Hannah. Confused, Rachel turned around to find the redhead standing by the wardrobe holding in one hand a pair of jeans and the other a pencil skirt. She considered objecting to going out - perhaps pointing out that there may be spies in the hotel reporting back on their movements. Or that she would like maybe a day or two or more to heal properly. The truth was, she felt oddly terrified at the prospect of leaving the security of her room.

Hannah stared expectantly and eventually Rachel blurted out, "Trousers." "Good choice," observed Hannah. "Since my own trousers are soaking wet, I shall squeeze myself into this particularly alluring skirt." It occurred to Rachel that it would make sense for Hannah to store some of her clothes in the wardrobe, given the amount of time she was spending in the Vestibule. Instead of making the offer, Rachel dumbly nodded.

Given the lingering bumps and scrapes along her legs, back and arms, it proved to be a boon that the jeans were not a skin-tight/spray-on pair.

Regardless, it had been a drawn-out and delicate exercise to pull them on. The loose-fitting, long-sleeved sweatshirt proved a less daunting prospect. With a joint effort and some welcome hilarity, they eventually squeezed Hannah into the pencil skirt. Finally, with a bit of makeup applied over the facial bruising, they were ready to head out.

"Good evening, ladies." The hotel manager had swept across the foyer on spotting their emergence from the lift. "Ms Minos, it is most gratifying to see you out and about. Housekeeping will be ecstatic to finally have unfettered access to your room."

Rachel was fascinated by Mr Typhon's paisley tie and pocket square. The intricate, almost fractal-like pattern created an optical illusion of constant movement. The remnants of the Physician's pharmaceutical concoctions may have also played a part in the beguiling animation.

Pointing towards the dining room, Mr Typhon suggested, "As the weather has turned somewhat inclement, will you ladies be dining with us this evening?" The women agreed and, after escorting them to the dining hall entrance, he summoned the maître d' before conspiratorially whispering, "Given that you are still in recovery, Ms Minos, I would recommend avoidance of the chef's signature dish this evening. It is… let us say… adventurously avant garde… even for him."

He excused himself to intercept a group of six guests dressed in smart tuxedos and formal evening gowns. Without winter coats, they were making a beeline for the revolving door. "Count, one moment of your time please. You may not have seen, but the weather has turned inclement whilst you slumbered."

Packed full of diners, the restaurant's ambient noises of cutlery on plates, glasses being clinked, general conversation and laughter filled the vast space with an energetic atmosphere.

"I can't see an empty table anywhere," Hannah worriedly observed. The maître d' exchanged words with two of the waiting staff who swiftly disappeared amongst the throngs of diners. "Pardon the delay, ladies.

You will be seated in just one moment."

As they waited, Hannah nudged Rachel's arm and surreptitiously pointed to a large, circular table in the centre of the hall. "Talk about a bling mountain," she commented. The woman in question, who had the appearance of a country dowager, proudly displayed a large gold and diamond necklace cushioned on her ample bosom. Holding a champagne coupe as a permanent fixture in her right hand, she loudly told her guests, "And I said, off with his head!". The six young men who made up her dining guests laughed rather too enthusiastically with her. Rachel thought out loud, "Wonder what her story is?" Hannah replied pointedly, "Dunno, but at least she's having fun."

"Ladies, if you would please follow me." The maître d' nimbly weaved through the maze of diners, guiding them to a table beside the water feature. "I could have sworn this wasn't here earlier," Hannah observed as they were seated. "Perhaps it's time to get those ageing peepers checked," Rachel cheekily responded. Hannah's retort of their customary, loud raspberry elicited laughter from them both.

A swarm of staff descended to provide menus, fill their tumblers with water, supply bread rolls and light the table's candles, before quickly retiring.

Hannah squirmed in her seat, as the pencil skirt's tight waistband dug into her. "If you dramatically burst free during the meal, I am out of here," laughed Rachel. With a mock sullen voice, Hannah accused Rachel of being such a mean friend, before opening the expansive menu and reviewing the long list of offerings.

They ordered a starter of a sharing seafood platter, followed by a sirloin steak for Hannah and a Caesar salad for Rachel. Their dining options sorted, the sommelier approached. Rachel had a good, long, hard stare at his face. Just to be sure.

A glass each of the house Sauvignon Blanc was ordered to accompany the salad. For the steak, they decided on a red wine, Hannah preferring a merlot. The sommelier's suggestion that they had a rather fine Pomerol was cut abruptly short by Rachel's 'Oh God, no!' Memories of Hannah and Bethany licking Alex's face raced through her mind as she ordered an Australian Moss Wood merlot.

The exquisite food, the drink and the conversation proved to be exactly what Rachel needed even if she involuntarily tensed with each approach of the increasingly apprehensive sommelier.

The crowd in the dining room had thinned out as the cheeseboard and two glasses of tawny port were placed on their table with a crisp 'Bon Appetit'.

Rachel cut herself a slice of Norwegian Jarlsberg as Hannah stealthily undid the pencil skirt's top button and relaxed with a heartfelt sigh. Rachel gave her an 'oh really' look, to which Hannah responded with a childish, "Don't judge me," and took a drink of the port.

"Girls, darlings! May I interrupt?"

The Dowager from the central table had tottered her way up to the two of them. Her tight gold lame dress and ostentatious necklace created a stir amongst some of the other diners, while the animated coupe proved barely capable of containing its champagne payload.

"I must say, you two look such a darling couple." Rachel's protestations that they were only friends was completely ignored as the Dowager forged on. "I was saying to my gentlemen companions, if you two dears fancy teaching an old war horse some new tricks..." She suddenly stumbled on her heels, catching herself on a conveniently passing waiter. After complimenting the young man on his athletic physique, she turned her attention back to Rachel and Hannah. "As I said, new tricks, if you get my drift, ladies." There followed an exaggerated wink. "I'd be game. So, you know... let me know," she concluded with a passable impression of Eartha Kitt.

Rachel and Hannah could barely suppress laughter at the Dowager's suggestion. They both glanced at each other with wide-eyed amusement plastered across their faces before Rachel told her that they would give the suggestion serious consideration. Hannah then cheekily added that they were still in the early stages of their relationship and not yet ready to indulge in the experimental.

Rachel kicked Hannah under the table.

"Well, if you sweeties change your mind…" She turned to stagger away. Rachel leaned forward, preparing to berate Hannah, before quickly sitting back as the Dowager spun back around.

"How dreadfully rude of me. I failed to introduce myself. I am Mary Scharlach. Duchess. The title. That is." She emptied her coupe as Rachel and Hannah introduced themselves, before weaving away with an "Au revoir, my pretties. Keep me in mind" and meandered through the dining room in search of fresh champagne.

Having returned to her room, Rachel flopped down onto the writing table chair with a contented "I am so stuffed and vewy dwunk". Hannah laughed in agreement from the bathroom. Peeling off the skirt, she grabbed her own clothes from the heated towel rail, preparing to face the harsh winter's night.

Dressed, she emerged, glancing over towards Rachel, who was staring open-mouthed at the laptop screen. "Are you ok, Rach?" Hannah asked. Rachel excitedly waved her over and pointed at the screen.

Leaning over her shoulder, Hannah examined the LCD display. The document had been zoomed out, so that all twenty-seven pages of appendix nine appeared on the screen as small rectangles.

"Errr, what exactly am I looking at?" Hannah asked, confused. "Don't you see it?" Rachel animatedly asked. "Errr, see what?" came her even more perplexed response. "The pattern. The entire appendix forms a pattern! Don't you see it?"

Hannah screwed up her eyes and stared at the screen. To her it looked to be little more than a lot of little rectangles. "So... what does it mean?" she finally asked. Rachel leaned back in the chair, accidently brushing cheek against cheek, "I don't know. I think I need to print them and lay them out. But it has to be something, doesn't it?"

As she asked the question, Rachel turned to find Hannah's face only inches from her own. Perhaps it was the drink or the evening's fun or the Physician's chemicals or pent-up emotions struggling for release or a combination of all of them that drove her to tenderly kiss Hannah on the lips.

Both immediately pulled back, surprised by the sudden, gentle exchange. The room descended into a strained silence as a multitude of emotions were quickly processed. "You could stay the night... if you wanted to." Rachel finally ventured.

Hannah stood up, a look of pain on her face. "Oh God, Rach, you don't know how long I have wanted to hear you say those clichéd words." She paused, gathering her thoughts. "Bloody hell, Rachel Minos, I have wanted to be with you since the day you arrived at Sheol Publications. Secretly, I held out hope that someday you would see me in the same way." Fumbling for a handkerchief, she wiped a tear that rolled down her cheek.

"But the crap you have been through, the shit you are sorting... I don't know. I don't want to be your experimental rebound lover, something to help you get past your crap and then move on." With a tremulous grip, she picked up Rachel's hand. "I would rather fancy you from afar than shatter our friendship, Rachel Minos."

For what felt an eternity they held hands, each struggling with this unexpected tangle of emotions. Finally, Rachel broke the silence with a croaky voice, "Wow... I guess... I don't know. I'm sorry... I've been so blind." She coughed to clear her throat. "If you want, let's take it slow." Hannah nodded in tearful agreement as Rachel added, "But why don't you at least store a spare outfit in the wardrobe? I don't think my clothes can take the strain."

With a bitter mixture of laughter and tears, Hannah bent back down and they embraced each other, desperately resisting the primal urges that begged them to go a little bit further.

"Right." Hannah abruptly stood back up, drying her face and buttoning up her coat. "I'll see you tomorrow evening at the same time." With that, she quickly left the room before her tenuous wall of willpower collapsed under the enormous strain of her desire.

Rachel sat still at the desk, staring forlornly at the closed door, secretly willing Hannah to re-appear, to run over to her, to embrace her, to make it all better.

The door remained obstinately closed.

Sensing that Cheshire again mocked her from the darkness of the drawer. Rachel kicked the table with a, "And you can shut the fuck up!"

Chapter 20

"We can have those printed within two hours, Ms Minos."

"Thank you so much, Dean." Rachel handed the concierge the silver USB stick. "That'll save me from having to brave the outside," she added with much relief.

The concierge moved on to the next guest and Rachel surveyed the crowded hotel foyer. Mr Typhon was overseeing two burly hotel maintenance staff as they rolled out long rubber mats across the marble paved foyer. The black mats may have marred the aesthetic look of the Vestibule's reception area, but concern for his clientele slipping and falling due to snow-covered shoes outweighed Mr Typhon's artistic sensibility.

Earlier that morning, Rachel had awoken after a disturbed night's sleep. She had lain motionless in the dark recalling vague snippets of her nightmares and dreams: Barry had forced her to clean the Camden apartment bathroom with a worn-out toothbrush; she'd drunk champagne with the Sheol Posse as they watched the sunset from atop the London Shard; she'd fled in terror while pursued through an endless maze of London streets, her pursuers unseen, her destination unreachable; finally she'd been tied to a chair and watched Bag Head Man remove the disguise, to reveal a grim-faced Hannah.

Oh, Hannah.

Rachel's thoughts drifted to the previous evening's close encounter. To the alcohol-fuelled kiss. To the revelation of a love long unrequited. She felt both elated and confused by the emotions she was experiencing. Rachel had always felt close to Hannah. But could she, did she feel more?

Sliding off the edge of the bed, Rachel padded through the gloom to the window and pulled back the heavy drapes. Clumps of snowflakes continued to drift lazily down from the leaden clouds. The street below had been transformed into an uninterrupted river of white, along which intrepid or foolhardy pedestrians, braced against the bitter wind, valiantly fought their way through the thickening snow.

On the morning news, a smartly dressed weather reporter described the snowstorm as 'gripping the country in an unprecedented freeze'. Pundits were comparing the deteriorating situation to the big freeze of 1962-63.

Her original plan of locating a copy shop and having them print out appendix nine was no longer an enticing prospect. With a replacement hat and scarf she could travel without fear of being recognised, but she had decided against daring to venture outside the hotel.

Rachel left the concierge's desk and made her way to the dining room for breakfast. A waiter quickly seated her at her usual table by the water feature.

Perusing the breakfast menu whilst the waiter poured her a cup of English tea, she enquired, "Excuse me, but what are Huevos Rancheros?" The waiter smiled and, with a strong hint of a Mexican accent, replied, "Ah madam, a personal favourite of mine. Fried eggs served on lightly fried flour tortillas, topped with a salsa fresca made from freshly chopped tomatoes, chilli peppers, onion and cilantro." Placing the teapot on the table, he added, "My mother would make them for the family on a Sunday morning."

His eyes became misty with the recollection of happy breakfast memories. "Our chef, he does a fine Huevos Rancheros, it never fails to take me home to Nogales. But, in truth, it's not a patch on my sweet mother's cooking."

Rachel felt doubtful about a spicy Mexican dish for her breakfast, but, having listened to the waiter's passionate description, she would have felt narrow minded ordering sausage and bacon.

Later, dabbing the final blob of sauce with a slice of toast, she complimented the passing waiter on the recommendation. Perhaps a little heavy on the chillies for first thing in the morning, but still a revelation. He beamed with satisfaction, happy to have introduced another gringo to his homeland's cooking.

Strolling out of the dining room, she considered what to do while the document was being printed. Rachel thought about a swim. Her face appeared almost completely healed and what bruising remained had been covered with makeup. But her arms, back and legs were a completely different story. It seemed unlikely that guests of this hotel would care about her appearance, yet Rachel remained self-conscious at the idea of revealing those battle scars to strangers.

"Ahh, Ms Minos, a word?"

The hotel manager balletically dodged between three guests dressed in ill-fitting green suits and approached her. In a lowered voice, he explained, "Ms Minos, there is a member of the local constabulary here to see you. I have asked him to await you in my office."

Rachel stood frozen, her eyes widening in panic. A policeman. Here in the hotel. Wanting to speak to her. Why? Her imagination ran wild.

Sent on behalf of Barry? Had he spun his lies and convinced them that she was a danger to herself? That she should be brought back home. Back to his squalid Camden apartment. Where he could... look after her?

Perhaps her breaking into the server room at Sheol Publicity had been reported. Had they deduced that Rachel had lurked beneath the black-haired disguise? Did they want to press charges for corporate espionage?

It could be to do with Leon. The disappearance of such a famous sportsman would have rung alarm bells. Had they connected the dots and found their way to her? Did they think she was involved in his kidnapping or maybe even worse?

The blackmailer or Bag Head Man - could they have decided to cut their losses? Were they throwing Rachel to the authorities, attempting to cover their own misdeeds?

"Ms Minos, are you feeling unwell?" earnestly enquired the manager, "Can I procure you a glass of water?" Rachel tried to clear her mind of futile speculations. "Thank you, Mr Typhon, I'm fine. Do you know why he wants to see me?" As the manager led her to his office, he confessed that despite his best efforts, the sergeant hadn't revealed the purpose of his visit.

Mr Typhon's office was larger than Rachel expected. Its dimensions measured at least fifty foot long by thirty foot wide. To her left was a large polished oak boardroom table with matching chairs precisely arranged around it. To her right stood substantial teak desk, covered with intricate carvings that wouldn't have looked out of place on a cathedral's gothic pulpit. In the centre, four chocolate-brown leather armchairs were artfully arranged around a green jade table.

Dominating the room, however, was the fish tank. The entire fifty-foot length of the far wall provided a floor-to-ceiling window into an aquatic world where living collages of multi-coloured fish slowly worked their way through thick forests of sea plants. Larger shadows hinted at more ominous beasts lurking amongst the gnarly rock formations.

With his back to the tank, next to a leather chair, stood the policeman. He was tall, perhaps around six foot three in height. A stab vest covered his snow-dampened uniform and a custodian helmet was held under his right arm. He looked to be in his late fifties, with extremely close-cropped hair and beard.

Introducing himself as Sergeant Barkham, he asked, "And you would be Rachel Minos, correct?" As Rachel confirmed her identity, Mr Typhon excused himself from the room.

The sergeant invited Rachel to take a seat and then seated himself directly opposite. "Not an easy place to find, this hotel. We have sent several colleagues over the last few days to contact you. Strangely, they couldn't find it." Rachel shrugged, feeling disappointed that he had proved more capable in locating the Vestibule.

The sergeant continued, "Thank you for seeing me. Normally we would have asked you to come to the station, but there is some pressure to have this matter cleared up quickly." Rachel nodded, her heart beginning to beat faster, and said she would be glad to help.

Several fish, seemingly curious, gathered at the tank wall directly behind the policeman, their fins gently waving as they maintained their station. Rachel fancied that they were watching the developing discourse.

"I'd like to take your victim statement from the recent assault on you by one Philip Aubrey Brown." Rachel looked blankly at the policeman and responded with a simple "Who?" The sergeant reassuringly smiled before explaining "You may know the late Mr Brown by his alias of Shank."

Rachel fought to keep her emotions in check at the sound of that name. With a flash of pain, she could feel his gloved hand as it smashed into her right eye with bone-crunching force. She felt helpless as she relived falling sideways, slamming into the parked car.

As several more fish joined the growing shoal, Rachel latched onto the sergeant's last sentence: 'the late Mr Brown?' A tight knot formed in her guts as conflicting emotions wrestled within her. Part of her was ecstatic that the nasty piece of work was now dead. Another fretted that she had killed him when she'd thrown him through the first storey window.

In the dark hours of the night, during her recent recovery, Rachel had fantasized about taking her revenge on him, but to have taken his life, that was something completely different.

Through her haze of confusing emotions, Rachel realised the policeman was still waiting for her answer. "Er, yes," She blurted out, "Yes, I was unfortunate enough to encounter him." Sergeant Barkham gave her a curious look in response to her answer, scribbled in his notebook and stated, "Before he was murdered, Mr Brown stated that he had perpetrated an assault upon you. I was hoping you could tell me what happened."

A long eel joined the gathering of fish, slowly coiling and uncoiling its long, sleek black body. Its mustard-yellow eyes focused on the unfolding proceedings. Rachel stammered in response, "Murdered?"

The sergeant leaned forward. "You may have seen it in the news? Mr Brown was shot in his hospital bed three nights ago." A sense of relief flooded through Rachel as she realised Shank's death wasn't her doing. The moment of respite was short lived as she realised that someone had still shot him in cold blood.

Rachel's mouth was dry as a sandpit as she began to describe her encounter with him. "It was a number of days ago; I was walking past Euston Station. He was the passenger in a car, a black Mercedes. He told me his name and repeatedly asked me to get into the car with him. He was eventually scared away by a police car." Rachel swallowed hard, hoping they could focus on this earlier meeting and ignore their later unpleasant encounters.

Two reef sharks emerged from the murky depths of the tank and joined the growing throng to watch the ongoing exchange. Rachel thought it curious that the smaller fish seemed unperturbed by the sudden presence of these predators.

After adding to his notes, Sergeant Barkham continued, "Thank you, Ms Minos. But I don't believe that that is the incident Mr Brown was referring to. The event in question happened around 11pm, six nights ago. Do you recall anything from that evening?"

Rachel gave her best performance of attempting to recall the events of that night. "Let me see. I think that's the night I had trouble sleeping. If it was, that night I walked up to Regent's Park and back."

Sergeant Barkham looked quizzically at Rachel. It was bad enough he had been pressured from on high to come and take this witness statement, something he hadn't done since he was a constable, now the supposed victim of the assault was clearly being evasive in her responses. "Ms Minos, are you saying that the late Mr Brown did not assault you?"

"Well. Yes. Ok." Rachel stammered before deciding on her story. "I am ashamed to admit this, but I narrowly escaped a mugging." The sergeant again asked her to describe as best she could the events of the incident. "It's a bit of a blur, I'm afraid. A man in a balaclava jumped out. He hit me and demanded money. I panicked. I threw him my purse and ran back to the hotel. That's about it, I am afraid."

"Thank you for telling me that, Ms Minos. I realise it can be difficult recalling such an encounter. Did you recognise him during the attack?" The sergeant flicked over a page in his notebook. "No, he wore a balaclava, so I never saw his face." Despite having mustered her best theatrical effort, Rachel felt that the policeman might prove to be a severe critic of her performance.

A large octopus, its skin ochre-red and gnarly in appearance, leisurely drifted up to the shoal of watching fish. Maybe it was intrigued by the aquatic gathering, maybe it wanted to join in watching the unfolding drama.

His voice calm and even, Sergeant Barkham enquired, "Ms Minos, do you have any idea as to how Mr Brown knew your name?"

Rachel could clearly picture Shank as he lifted into the air; his helpless body tumbling in slow motion; ever so gradually, his mouth opening in surprise at his predicament.

In a flash of inspiration, she blurted out, "Oh, my purse! It probably had old business cards of mine. That must be how he got my name."

The gathered watery crowd became animated, fish turning to face other fish, creating the illusion of animated chatter between them. More than likely, Rachel thought, in response to her blatant lie.

The sergeant nodded. "That would make sense." As he completed his notes Rachel asked, "Sergeant Barkham, how exactly did Mr Brown die?"

The policeman closed his pad before replying "Obviously I am not at liberty to divulge the details of an ongoing case. But, as the newspapers have already reported, Mr Brown was being held in hospital, under detention for several parole violations. The working assumption, given he was starting to provide us with valuable intelligence, is that someone arranged to have him silenced."

In response to the word 'silenced', among the twisted rock formations at the rear of the aquarium a large scarlet eye flicked open. The gathered marine crowd immediately dispersed, frantically swimming to seek cover within the kelp forest.

Sergeant Barkham stood up and concluded, "I am sure you would be able to find more information online, but I am obviously not in a position to expound further on the subject."

Watching her closely, the policeman instinctively sensed that there was something not quite right here. The pressure to quickly close the Brown case was unusual, though not unprecedented. But now his curiosity had been piqued as to how this apparently unassuming woman really fitted into Shank's strange saga.

"Thank you very much for your time Ms Minos. If anything comes to mind in relation to this case, these are my contact details."

Rachel barely noticed that the sergeant had stood up. Her gaze was drawn to the single eye that had, in return, focussed on her. Only when he placed his card on the table before her did she break her attention away.

She wished Sergeant Barkham safe travels given the atrocious weather. In return, he wished her a good day and exited the manager's office.

Finally, she stared back at the tank; the eye had gone and the multi-coloured fish once again worked their way through the tangled forests of sea plants as if nothing unusual had occurred.

Chapter 21

The gritting lorry's flashing yellow lights reflected off the shop windows, throwing crazy dance-floor patterns onto the expanse of snow-covered pavement. Rachel paused to allow the vehicle to pass by, enabling her to admire the free light show and, importantly, to regather her breath.

Earlier in the evening, due to the ferocity of the snowstorm that had submerged London beneath a thick white blanket, motorised transport had proven impossible to locate. The Vestibule's concierge had come to Rachel's aid and provided her with a sled. It had taken her just forty-five minutes to drag the provision-laden sled a little under two miles from the hotel to the corner of Chalton Street. Carrying that load on her back, along those treacherous streets would have proved a far more daunting prospect.

Leaning forward and pulling on the sled's rope, Rachel followed the lorry north along Chalton Street. At this time of the evening the wide pavement would normally be bustling with pedestrians. Tonight, Rachel was one of only a few brave souls trampling their lonely way through the thickening crisp white powder.

Growing up on the edge of the Pennines, Rachel had become used to occasional severe winters and heavy snowfalls. It was an inconvenience, but people quickly adapted and life rapidly returned to normal. By contrast, London rarely experienced such harsh weather and consequently its inhabitants were prone to treat even the lightest dusting of snow with a mixture of irrational fear and ineptitude.

The entrance to 42b, Chalton Street was a rusty red metal door nestled between a café and a 24-hour grocery store. The café was dark and unoccupied, whereas bright fluorescent lights flooded out of the grocery store. The harsh rays illuminated the lone employee tasked with keeping the entranceway and the adjoining pavement clear of snow.

Banging on the metal door, Rachel noticed that her reflection in the café's window was almost unrecognisable. She had tucked her jeans into her boots to keep them dry and borrowed a ushanka from the hotel's lost and found box. A thick jumper, a sweatshirt, a tee-shirt and a vest were squeezed under the now-bulging red leather coat. Thick socks and woolly tights filled out her normally loose-fit jeans. Yet, despite these many layers of thermal protection, she could still feel the pervasive cold.

The door eventually rattled open. Arthur Pickering appeared, wrapped up in an oversized puffer jacket. With suspicion in his voice he asked, "Can I help you, luv?"

Rachel pulled down her woollen scarf. "Hiya, it's me. I brought food and spare blankets from the Vestibule. Donations for tonight's rounds." She pointed at the sled, its cargo covered with a plastic sheet and held in place with bungee cords.

Arthur stared at her, asking incredulously, "Is that really you, Rachel?" She nodded in response. After a moment's hesitation he invited her into his yard and the two of them manhandled the heavy sled down the narrow passageway between the shop and the café.

Arthur's home consisted of a walled-off portion of the grocery store's back yard. Hidden from passers-by and, importantly, from council officials, he had made remarkable use of the compact space.

Half of the ten-foot by twelve-foot yard had been taken up by his shack. The ramshackle building was constructed from packing cases, pallets and a multitude of other rescued pieces of wood. The roof had been waterproofed with a thick layer of supermarket bags for life. Inside, the effective insulation consisted of layers of old rags glued and duct taped into place. An electrical wire, precariously dangling out from the shop's toilet window, provided the power for his single light bulb and a tiny electric heater.

The other half of the yard had been packed high with the supplies he had gathered for the homeless and, of course, his trusty soup cart.

Bundled up in a thick blue parka coat, green face scarf and orange woolly bobble hat, a man was crouched down by the cart. Surrounded by tools, he was working on attaching a pair of old skis to the cart's wheels. "Thanks so much, mate." said Arthur patting the man on the back. "Let's hope they make the going a bit easier tonight."

The cart's conversion was completed by the time Rachel had unpacked the sled's load and Arthur invited them both to join him in the shack for a cup of hot soup.

It proved a tight fit for the three of them. Rachel squeezed onto the bed next to Arthur; the stranger, being a good deal taller than the two of them, perched on the lone metal folding chair and stretched his long legs out through the doorway. Despite its tumbledown appearance, the shack was surprisingly cosy and comfortable, if a little cramped.

Three pint-sized white tin mugs filled with hot soup from the urn were handed out. Rachel removed her thick gloves as she received hers, gratefully cradling the mug in her chilled hands before taking a welcome sip of the delicious contents.

"I should really introduce you two to each other," observed Arthur. The taller man interjected, "Actually, Arthur, we've met before." Rachel glanced up from her cup, having recognised the voice. "Oh, it's you, Alex. Well, isn't this a small world?" She was surprised and, at the same time, genuinely pleased to see her fellow server room burglar. As Alex flashed a cheeky grin at Rachel, she smiled warmly back at him before enquiring how he came to know their host.

"Well, the truth is, Arthur helped me when I was sleeping on the streets." His face bore a look of pain as he recalled, "I'd run away from home as a teenager. I had serious problems there that I had to escape from. So, like many others, I ended up on the streets. If it hadn't been for Arthur, I dread to think what could have happened to me."

Fondly patting the older man on the shoulder, Alex's jovial demeanour returned. "Arthur kept me alive when things got rough and he introduced me to people who helped me turn my life around."

Arthur coyly took a drink. He was obviously a man who didn't enjoy being talked about in such glowing terms and quickly changed the subject. "That's enuf bout me, Alex. Now, what about you, Rachel? I am truly flabbergasted to see you up and about. When I found you on the street, I thought you were almost certainly a goner."

For a moment she considered spinning a yarn; a tale about how her injuries were only superficial. But both men were, to some extent, part of the strange world she had tumbled into. "Well, a woman who only went by the name of 'the Physician' looked after me. I don't know how exactly, but she got me back on my feet remarkably quickly."

Arthur and Alex stared at each other, before Arthur clarified "It was the Physician that tended to you, right? A woman, yeah?" Taken aback by the scepticism in his voice, Rachel confirmed that it was.

"Holy crap!" swore Alex. "Arthur, I reckon we're in the presence of proper noble lineage." Confused by their reaction, Rachel could only muster an inane 'What?'

Arthur explained. "Listen luv, the Physician is like an urban legend to us. It's said she looks after the needs of the special ones, the powerful geezers, the important ones. If she tended to you, well, you must have some very special connections." Rachel had no answer but to shrug pathetically.

Alex taunted her with a mischievous grin. "So, do I bow or curtsy in your presence and should I address you as your Highness or your Majesty?" Rachel gently poked him in the chest as a rebuttal. Alex mockingly held his ribs in pain and shouted out, "Come and see the violence inherent in the system! Help, help, I'm being repressed!"

"All right, all right, that's enuf from you two," interrupted Arthur. "Alex, time we got to get a move on, the soup ain't gonna deliver itself." Gathering up the empty mugs, Arthur dropped them into a faded plastic washing bowl.

As they all clambered back out into the chill of the yard, Rachel ventured, "I could I give you a hand tonight if you could use the help?" Pulling on his heavily patched, fur-lined trapper hat, Arthur replied, "If you think you're up for it, luv, I'll never say no to help on a night like this."

And so, wrapped up against the biting wind, the intrepid trio set off to face the snow- and ice-bound city.

Quickly they settled into an efficient routine. Alex pulled and pushed the hybrid ski-cart with soup, food and a large pile of blankets. Arthur provided the rough sleepers with soup and a roll. Rachel saw if they needed an extra blanket and checked on their general wellbeing.

While it felt good to be helping Arthur and the homeless, Rachel harboured a secret pang of guilt. After all, she did have an ulterior motive for joining this mission of mercy.

Earlier in the day, as the concierge had handed Rachel a large envelope containing the twenty-seven A4 pages, she had asked: "Is there somewhere I could possibly lay these out?"

Checking his computer screen Dean apologised. "I'm sorry, Ms Minos. All the meeting rooms are in use. The poor weather has caused quite a surge in demand for them." He clicked through further options on the screen before offering, "Hmmm, the ballroom is available until this afternoon; you would be more than welcome to utilise that space." Rachel had expressed her surprise that the Vestibule had a ballroom and agreed that any large, open area would suffice.

Having descended to basement level two, the concierge had flung open the two ornately decorated doors to reveal a vast, dark space. As he searched for the master light switch, Rachel had ventured out across the dance floor. The echo of her flat boots clicking on the wooden floor reverberated off the unseen walls.

Standing alone in near total darkness, Rachel had been struck by how familiar it felt.

Lurking at the edge of her memory hid a forgotten childhood recollection.

A moment she could tantalisingly almost see again.

A young Rachel had once stood facing the endless abyss and...

The emerging memory, like the darkness, was instantly washed away by the light flooding into the ballroom. Suspended high above the dance floor, two vast and elaborate crystal chandeliers threw glittering patterns of light in all directions. The ostentatiously decorated room was laden with gilt trim and baroque plaster designs. Large mirrors covered two walls, creating the illusion of an even greater space.

Apart from the chairs and tables stacked in one corner, Rachel had the ballroom to herself. "People will be coming in to set up for an evening event at around 3pm," the concierge warned. "Otherwise, it's all yours, Ms Minos."

Thanking Dean for his help, Rachel moved one of the tables into the centre of the room as the concierge closed the doors behind him. She removed the twenty-seven pages from the envelope and carefully checked they had been correctly printed. Once satisfied, she had laid them out onto the dance floor in a three by nine pattern.

Frustratingly, staring at the patchwork of paper revealed nothing. The pattern she had spotted on the previous evening now eluded her.

Was she mistaken? Had the pattern more to do with the two bottles of Australian Merlot than hidden mystical texts?

Pulling the table further forward, she sat down on its edge, removed her boots, and placed them on the floor. Bringing her legs up onto the table, Rachel folded herself into the lotus position.

Carefully controlling her breathing, she recalled Darius's previous words of encouragement: "Focus. You are of the Minos line; it is in your blood. Focus."

The tiny printed letters twitched.

Slowly, they began to shudder and move across the pages. With gathering momentum, they merged with other letters, growing ever larger in size and forming new words.

The letters appeared to indulge in a bizarre game of musical chairs, each one attempting to locate a space to settle down on. Until, at last, the final word scampered to find the remaining vacant spot, completing and unlocking this secret document.

Immediately, Rachel experienced the start of a headache. Remaining focussed, compelling the words to give up their hidden meanings, the pain steadily grew in intensity. Despite this, she continued to commit the document's contents to memory.

Completely absorbed by the task, all sense of time began to ebb away as she marvelled at the document's contents. Each sentence of the remarkable contract had been crafted with exceptional care and astonishing precision. Each concise paragraph left the reader in absolutely no doubt as to both parties' obligations.

Its elegant simplicity coupled with a devilish attention to detail left no apparent room for doubt or duplicity in its execution. It proved impossible for Rachel not to admire the subtlety of this contract's concealment within the Decem Fossas document.

Now she understood how a party to this contract could be blackmailed. Why they might choose to kill in order to protect the secrets that lay hidden within it. To Rachel, it was also frighteningly clear that an outsider meddling in such complex dealings would find themselves at considerable risk.

Despite the ever-increasing pain, Rachel reread one specific paragraph. She checked and rechecked that she clearly understood its contents, its meaning and its consequences.

Tears now streamed down her cheeks, induced by the agony she was experiencing, as it dawned on Rachel that this paragraph of one hundred and one words offered her perhaps the only chance to resolve the mess she had become embroiled in.

"So, there - against the far wall - I want a gold replica of the Trevi fountain, but, darling, make sure it cascades champagne instead of water." The two women entering the ballroom had shattered Rachel's concentration.

The contract instantly broke apart. Fracturing into smaller texts, each of the tiny letters scurried across the pages to retake their original positions.

"Rachel. I'm so sorry, darling. I didn't see you there." It was the Dowager from the previous evening, now accompanied by a younger woman. The Dowager had barely toned down her dramatic attire from their previous encounter, wearing a cleavage-revealing, flouncy silver blouse, skin-tight lurex trousers and matching silver heels.

Her companion, who Rachel assumed to be her assistant, wore a plain white linen trouser suit with dramatic black flashes down its sides.

Spotting the stream of tears trickling down Rachel's face, the Dowager exclaimed, "Oh, my goodness. Quickly! Give her a tissue." The assistant reluctantly stepped forward, handing over a large white handkerchief. Rachel thanked her and explained away the tears as a severe migraine. Wiping and dabbing her eyes, she felt grateful that the worst of the pain had already receded.

With her vision clearing, she could see that the assistant looked to be in her late twenties and of Indian descent. Her mocha complexion was framed by short jet-black hair. Stepping back to stand beside the

Dowager, her face betrayed no obvious emotion nor any recognition of Rachel's thanks.

"I'm so sorry, darling. I thought the room would be empty. You see, I'm planning a little soiree for a few hundred guests. Nothing spectacular." She flashed a devilish grin and completed two nimble twirls across the dance floor before adding: "But of course, there are always people desperately clamouring for an invite to one of my parties."

Coming to a stop with an exaggeratedly elegant pose, the Dowager had flashed a look to her assistant, whilst pointing towards Rachel. "Add my new friend and her partner to the invitation list." With a laugh, she added, "At least once during the evening, I hope to see you two naughty girls giving me a lesson in dirty dancing. Rooowwr!"

Rachel had already abandoned any hope of correcting the Dowager's views of her relationship with Hannah and thanked her for the invite as she swept up the twenty-seven sheets of paper. "Oh, my darling, forgive me. I'm such a dunderhead. I'll leave you in peace and return later." Rachel asked to her stay, explaining she had already finished her work.

Grabbing her boots, she had headed for the exit as more plans for the party were being hatched. "Au revoir, sweetie. Now, you, pay attention. Over there I want Sam and his band. Make sure to let him know that the theme will be Venetian Masquerade. You know how he loves to dress up..."

And so, back to this evening and her ulterior motive for joining the nightly errand of mercy. As they worked through the bitterly cold night, she had taken the opportunity to ask each person they helped two simple questions:

One: When were the people who had disappeared from the street last seen?

Two: Did they notice a black Mercedes lurking around the people who had vanished?

As the evening had progressed, Rachel compiled a consensus of the answers. To the first question, as she had anticipated, most disappearances happened towards or at the end of the calendar month. The second proved less conclusive with some identifying a Mercedes, whilst others had no idea what such a vehicle might even look like.

Approaching the end of their night's expedition, she asked Arthur if he knew of anyone that had gone missing so far this month. She felt relieved when he shook his head.

Turning north onto Eversholt Street, they were confronted with large heaps of snow that had been ploughed off the road and forced onto the pavement. It created a formidable snowy assault course, requiring the three of them to manhandle the cart safely.

London's traffic was again on the move: trucks, cars, taxis and buses tentatively splashed their way through the blackening slush. In Euston Station, a two-tone horn announced that the next long metal beast was about to battle its way north and carry its passengers through the hostile elements. The city's transport arteries were beginning to recover from the unexpected shock. It remained to be seen how they would cope with the continuing snowfall and the forecasted further drops in temperature.

Even though Rachel was tired and cold, she couldn't shake the scenes she had witnessed that night. Men and women, young and old; these disenfranchised Londoners were engaged in a life and death struggle, hidden in plain sight on the streets of one of the world's richest cities.

Tonight, they would all make do, huddled together under blankets, cardboard and plastic sheeting, hoping these makeshift shelters would protect them against the vicious cold.

They peered out from inside their improvised bunkers, watching the rest of the world get on with their daily lives. How many of those passing people even acknowledged the existence of these lost human beings? Did they, as she had four years ago, avert their eyes and quickly pass by out of embarrassment, fear or contempt?

Assisting old Frank, whose frozen fingers could barely hold his cup of soup, Rachel heard a drunken passer-by loudly complain, "Why has no-one taken some responsibility to clear this trash off the streets?"

Incensed by the callousness, Rachel had shouted back, "Maybe we can throw them in prison or open up some workhouses for them." Downhearted by the experience, she wondered how it could be that nearly two hundred years after Charles Dickens had written so movingly about the plight of London's poor and homeless, nothing had profoundly changed.

When at last Rachel had frustratedly asked Arthur, "How do you do this night after night? We are barely making a difference. Aren't we just slapping a plaster on a dying body?" Arthur had patted her on the back and pointed out, "Listen luv, doin' summat is better than doin nuthin'. I got to hope that someone will take notice and maybe sort it all out. In the meantime, I'll keep on doing my bit."

Approaching the familiar disused tailor's shop entrance, Rachel couldn't help but smile as she picked up the last blanket from the trolley. Arthur exited the confined space, having delivered the hot soup and roll, allowing Rachel to squeeze down next to the Manpillar.

"Well, if it isn't Rachel - or is it Alice today?" he asked with a sly grin. Spreading the thick blanket over his cardboard thorax she laughed with him. "My dear, I do have staff to attend to such things. But thank you for the thought, from the very bottom of my heart." Rachel smiled and explained to him that it was her pleasure to help him tonight.

Abso looked outwards towards the snow-covered street, ensuring that Alex and Arthur were out of earshot. In a low voice he asked, "Tell me, Alice. Have you decided? Are you a songbird or are you a tiger?" As she knelt on the faded red mosaic floor, Rachel immediately knew her answer. "You know, I think I am a bit of both of those."

Looking deeply into her eyes, he slowly nodded. "Yes. Yes, you are a Singing Tiger, aren't you? And what an opera you are going to roar, my dear lady."

Leaning closer to Rachel, his voice now barely audible over the tyres that churned through the slush, he whispered, "It's the thirty-first of January tomorrow. Make sure you know where your favourite jewellery is, Alice."

He leaned back as Rachel threw him a questioning look. Before she could interrogate him further, the Manpillar pulled the new blanket over his head and began to make exaggerated snoring noises. From the street, Alex called out to her: "Get a shift on Rach, my feet are fricken frozen."

With a heartfelt 'Thank you for everything, Abso', she gently patted his carboard thorax and re-joined her companions as the snowfall began to thicken once more.

Chapter 22

Billy stood at his post outside the Vestibule Hotel, an umbrella his only protection against the relentless snowfall. If this giant of a man felt the intense cold, his chiselled face betrayed no outward sign of it.

He stood his ground as gusts of arctic wind pulled at his top hat, ruffled his jacket's gold lapels and futilely attempted to wrestle the large umbrella from his iron grip.

To the hotel's guests, he was the familiar figure that welcomed them to the Vestibule. At the end of their visit, he was the last thing they saw as their taxi drove away. He was as familiar an icon as the Statue of Liberty was to transatlantic liner passengers arriving and leaving the city of New York.

"Hello, Billy," Rachel greeted him as she walked up to the hotel entrance. Doffing his hat, he returned the greeting: "Welcome back, Ms Minos. I trust all is as well as can be expected for the homeless?" Rachel nodded and confirmed that the blankets had proved a popular donation. "Will Alex be joining you as a guest?" the doorman enquired, while giving the younger man at her side an intimidatingly hard stare. Rachel wondered what the young man could have done to justify Billy's glare.

Earlier that morning, after cleaning and drying the soup cart, Arthur had insisted they have a final hot drink together before they headed home. It had been past 2am when they finally exited Arthur's yard. Alex had grumbled about his cheap watch losing ten minutes before insisting on walking Rachel back to her hotel. As they wrapped themselves against the cold, Alex handed her a bag of sweets. As Rachel took a small handful of the contents, she was delighted to discover that they were wine gums.

The journey had taken over an hour. Despite the resumption of heavy snow, it was the engrossing conversation that had slowed their progress. In fairness, Alex had done most of the talking. The young man had big plans for his future.

He had a dream. He was going to build a New York-style cellar bar. Alex had never been to the Big Apple - he had rarely left London - but he'd seen that type of bar in movies and magazines and had, from afar, fallen in love with them.

The young man knew deep in his gut that, in the right location with the right staff and the right ambience, he could create a vibrant place to drink, eat and be entertained. His goal was that a customer walking into his bar would not be able to tell if they were on the west or east side of the Atlantic.

Alex had a long narrow basement picked out just to the north of Leicester Square, on Romilly Street. There was bubbling excitement in his voice as he confided to her that it would soon become vacant and that he intended to bid on its lease.

The detail with which he described the layout of the proposed venue gave a hint of his deep passion for this project. Only last week he had agreed with a dealer to import genuine American furniture and fittings - essential, as he explained it, to give the place that authentic feel.

Approaching the hotel, Alex had described how he would have live music bands playing on Thursdays, Fridays and Saturdays. He painted a picture so elaborate and vivid that Rachel could almost visualise herself entering it. She would squeeze her way to the front of the heaving bar on a cheerfully rowdy Friday night to order a pint of cider and a chaser. Crowded onto the tiny stage, a new local band would be enthusiastically hammering out the obligatory classic hits before starting on fresh tunes from their debut album.

It felt good to immerse herself in Alex's world. To share in his ambitious plans to create something new, to build something amazing. It had helped distract her from her own plans.

Now, standing outside the Vestibule Hotel, Rachel looked up at Alex and hopefully asked if he wanted to come in for a drink. He appeared torn as he replied, "I'd really love to, Rachel, but it's late and I should be getting gone. I have work to do for Mr Long in the morning. Those New Jersey brass fittings need to be paid for."

Alex moved forward and embraced her with a goodbye hug.

As his long arms enveloped her, Rachel felt a sharp spike of fear jab through her chest. Closing her eyes, she forced herself not to flinch and willed her body not to pull away in irrational fear. Despite experiencing an almost overwhelming urge to wriggle free from his grasp, tentatively she returned his embrace.

If he'd detected her awkwardness, he didn't show it. Under Billy's stern gaze he wished them both a good night, pulled his scarf over his face and confidently strode off along New Cavendish Street.

Watching him recede into the murky night, Rachel desperately wanted to shout after him, "Hey, do you want to get a drink some time? Maybe call me?" Instead, she despairingly watched until the worsening snowstorm engulfed him.

Cheshire would, at this point, have delivered an acerbic comment about how pathetic she was and a tiny part of her missed that distraction. She stared silently into the swirling darkness, bitterly disappointed at her reaction to his innocent hug.

"Ms Minos." Billy directed her towards the hotel entrance and out of the foul weather. Rachel thanked the stoic doorman and passed through the rotating door.

The hotel foyer was quiet; standing behind the granite reception desk, Tina looked up from her keyboard and smiled as Rachel approached. "Good morning, Ms Minos. What can I do for you?" Removing her hat and scarf she replied, "Do you know if my guest, Ms Bates, dropped by last night. I did leave a message for her."

Sifting through a small pile of paper, the deputy manager shook her head. "No, I still have your undelivered message here. I am afraid it doesn't look like she visited us last night." After also confirming that no phone messages had been left, Rachel wished her a good night and headed to the elevators.

Entering the junior suite, Rachel immediately checked the still-charging mobile phone. She felt the onset of a darkening mood as she found no missed messages and not one unread text.

Feeling too blue to consider going to bed, she stripped off the numerous layers that had protected her from the bitter cold and slipped into a grey tee-shirt, black leggings and trainers.

Rachel considered practicing with her inner flame. Yesterday afternoon, she had tentatively called out to it, apprehensive that it may have deteriorated further. With huge relief, Rachel had watched as an intense flame had willingly burst out of the darkness. Proof enough that its strength would recover if given time.

Using its power sparingly, Rachel had, this morning, surreptitiously tested its capabilities upon the unwitting Alex and Arthur. Having returned from the evening rounds, as they sat in the cramped shack drinking hot soup and chatting, Rachel had called out to her inner flame. Carefully, she had allowed it to gently bend the flow of time around the shack's oblivious occupants. She maintained it for just one minute, whilst beyond the yard, time had marched onwards for ten. It seemed sensible to allow her inner flame to continue to rest and recharge before the coming evening.

Feeling restless, she headed out of the room and up to the Djinn Bottle bar to find company and drink before a much-needed sleep.

Exiting the lift at the ninth floor, live piano music drifted across the lobby from the bar. Curiously, Rachel hadn't noticed the baby grand piano on her previous visits. A man was sat at its keyboard and expertly played its ivories. The pianist was dressed in a tuxedo, his bowtie stylishly hanging loose around his neck and his collar button undone. A glass of whisky with ice stood beside two of its empty siblings on the piano lid. He crooned about the woman who had left him for another man and how she had shattered his heart.

Rachel slumped into a soft chair at a window table. The normally spectacular night-time skyline view of London had been, much like her mood, enveloped in dark clouds.

With a cheerful 'G'day, ma'am,' Russell, the barman, arrived and enquired, "what can I get for you?" Ordering a pint of the draught cider, she asked, "So, what sandwich would you recommend?" Without hesitation, Russell replied, "The night kitchen does a superb sausage and bacon roll. You can't go far wrong with one of them on a cold January morning." To save looking at the menu, she ordered one of those.

The pianist had moved on to a new tune describing his long journey to get home to his baby and in the chorus asked, 'buddy, could you spare me a dime for a coffee'.

Placing the stubbornly quiet mobile phone on the table, Rachel thought of the information she had gathered in the last day and how good it would have been to talk the events over with Hannah. For the second time in less than an hour she berated herself, this time for not using the phone to call her.

"Ok, I will!" she abruptly said to herself and picked the handset back up. Selecting Hannah's name from the contacts, Rachel hesitated, her resolve already draining away. She told herself that Hannah was probably asleep. Best not to disturb her. She'd probably call in the morning. Rachel swore she could hear a distantly muffled Cheshire calling her a pathetic loser.

Instead, she decided to send a text. 'Hey H. Important discovery made. Call me. R.' She debated with herself for a moment before adding an 'XXX' and pressing send. As the message sped across the digital landscape to find its way to Hannah's phone, Rachel realised it had been the first text she had sent in years.

"Here's your cider, and your sandwich will be here soon." Russell placed the pint glass on a mat and headed to the pianist, delivering him a fresh glass of whisky on the rocks.

Savouring her drink, Rachel went through her fledgling plan for later tonight. At least one, maybe two, more people would be needed. Hannah would hopefully fill one of those roles. As for the other, perhaps she could ask Alex, if he wasn't already committed to helping Arthur.

Once again, she mentally reviewed the one hundred and one words of that vital paragraph, attempting to allay her fears that she had missed something critical.

The barman placed her sandwich plate on the polished wooden table. Rachel sighed to herself; it would have been so much easier to bounce the plan off someone like Hannah. A fresh pair of eyes and a new perspective could expose those potential pitfalls.

Absentmindedly, she picked up the sandwich and took a bite. Russell had been correct: the sandwich tasted sublime. She leaned back into the chair and allowed the aroma to take her back to a fourteen-year-old Rachel and a similar sandwich shared with her friend, Alison.

It was the second week of the summer holidays. Alison's family were already packing for their drive down to the South of France. Ahead of them awaited three weeks enjoying the sun, sand and sea to the south of Capbreton.

There had been thrilling talk of Rachel joining them on the trip. It would have been her first trip out of the country. In truth, it would have been her first trip out of the northwest of England. Sadly, Rachel hadn't been at all surprised when, after her father's objections, it didn't materialise.

Spurred on by that disappointment, the two rebellious teenagers had decided, over their bacon sandwiches, to hold a girls' lunchtime drinking party in celebration of Alison's imminent departure. After agreeing on the five other friends that would be invited to the secret event, Alison had been happy to just get everyone together and go for it. Instead, Rachel had insisted on planning the event in meticulous detail.

She had scoped out an abandoned house on the edge of Foxdenton Park as a suitable venue. The dilapidated mansion had been abandoned some years previously. Lost roof tiles had allowed the elements to hasten its sad deterioration. The extensive grounds had grown wild, vegetation shrouding the site from observers. It seemed the perfect venue for the seven girls to have drunken fun.

Secret invitations had been dispatched to the select members of the drinking party. The time was set and Rachel ensured each girl knew what food and alcohol to bring with them.

What could go wrong?

Quite a lot as it turned out.

Arriving at the house, they found an angry pack of parents lying in wait for them.

She never discovered what had gone wrong. Maybe a parent had found the secret note. Perhaps one of the party members had let slip to another friend and started tongues wagging. Or perhaps it was just the spiteful act of one of the other teenagers, dished out in revenge for some previous slight.

Rachel, as the apparent ringleader, had been grounded for the remainder of the summer holidays, forced to mooch around the house and their postage stamp-sized garden waiting for the end of those sun-drenched weeks and the resumption of school.

Back in the bar, the pianist had moved on to a dirge: a slow-paced tune lamenting the tragic loss of his girl and detailing his crawl into the demon bottle. As the pianist concluded the tune with an extended musical flourish, Rachel excitedly picked up her phone as it issued a loud chime.

A text had arrived from Hannah.

After reading it, Rachel barely noticed the phone slip out of her quivering hand and tumble onto the carpeted floor.

Chapter 23

Rachel pressed the pistol barrel into his chest. "Give me an excuse to shoot you and I fucking well will." There was no wavering in her voice. No trace of doubt that she would pull the trigger. "Now get inside, or I swear to God I will end you on this doorstep."

All colour drained from his face as he slowly backed away from the front door. His hands trembled uncontrollably as he raised them over his head, keen to demonstrate willing submission to her barked orders. Rachel stepped through the doorway after him. Never losing eye contact, with a kick of her booted heel, she pushed it closed.

The spacious hallway had been sparsely furnished with only a small telephone table, a coat rack and the burglar alarm panel. Rachel waved the gun, herding him away from the panel.

"Please, I don't want any trouble," he pleaded. "I have money. Please take it, just don't hurt me." Rachel directed him into the adjacent lounge.

The expansive room had been decorated like an exclusive Pall Mall club with dark wooden furnishings, shelves of leather-bound books, bare polished floorboards and three green leather settees arranged around a fake log fire. Proudly displayed above the fireplace was an original Piranesi pencil drawing: The Round Tower.

She risked a glance at the magnificent grandfather clock; it was five minutes until 11pm - she still had time.

"Now, get your phone out and gently toss it over here." Desperately ensuring he did nothing that Rachel could misconstrue, he carefully reached into his smoking jacket pocket and, with his fingertips, he extracted the phone and threw it towards her. His voice close to hysteria, he pleaded, "See. See, I am complying, I will do what you ask. Don't... just don't do anything rash. Please."

It had been twenty hours since Rachel had received the text from Hannah's phone. She had opened it, anticipating a message to say that she would soon call. Instead, there had been a blunt threat and a picture file. 'Give me my money and your copy of the contract, or I finish her tonight. Reply to this message for delivery details.'

With mounting trepidation, she had opened the image. Her heart froze as she saw Hannah, her mouth roughly gagged with a sheet, her right eye bloody and bruised and an ornate black steel dagger pressed tightly to her throat.

Rachel could see the fear in her dark brown eyes.

As the pianist called it a night on his crooning and weaved his way out of the hotel bar, Rachel leaned down and picked up the fallen phone to once again stare at the terrible image.

It occurred to her that this was the only image she had of her dear friend. Rachel promised that she would take some better photos of Hannah if... no...when she returned. Any negative thoughts of failure and the consequences for Hannah were blanked out of her mind.

Plan A, the subtle plan, had been blown to shit. Time for a new approach. Over another pint of cider, she worked out Plan B. It was far less elegant than its predecessor and almost completely devoid of subtlety. Finishing the pint off, Rachel convinced herself that if it got messy, Bag Head Man only had himself to blame.

After returning to her bedroom, she made several telephone calls. The sleepy recipients initially moaned about being contacted at such an ungodly hour in the morning. As they were apprised of the situation, those complaints transformed into willing agreements to help.

Finally, she replied to the text message, confirming her compliance with the demands. But Rachel was under no illusion that Bag Head Man wouldn't attempt kill both Hannah and her. When the instructions finally arrived, Rachel glanced at them before deleting the text. The meeting was supposed to be tomorrow evening at ten o'clock. Rachel was certain Hannah would be dead by midnight tonight.

With wheels now in motion, there was nothing more Rachel could do until the afternoon, so she flopped onto the bed and tried to get some sleep.

It had proved to be a futile attempt as her mind wouldn't, couldn't calm down. She thought of Hannah, the knife pressing deep into the flesh of her throat. She thought of plan B, working through each precarious step. She thought of Bag Head Man and how she wanted to make him suffer.

Eventually admitting defeat, she sat back up. Cheshire stared at her with a huge grin plastered on its scrawny face. The grin quickly vanished when she slipped off the bed, picked up its jar and violently shook it like a recalcitrant ketchup bottle.

After aimlessly pacing a few laps around the room, she entered the bathroom and turned on the bath taps. With the hot and cold water cascading into the huge tub, she examined the extensive range of bathing products. Adopting the role of an alchemist, she meticulously began to blend salts, oils and bubble-bath into the water.

Content with her creation, she stripped off her tee-shirt and leggings and slowly slipped into its hot, soothing embrace. Stopping only when her nose skimmed the surface, she stared across the mountain of bubbles, watching wisps of steam twist free and launch themselves into the air.

Gradually, Rachel slid her head beneath the surface until she was isolated from the rest of the world. Submerged beneath the covering of bubbles, completely encased in hot, soothing water, her mind, at least for a little while, had let go of Hannah's haunting image.

A loud knock on the bedroom door interrupted her soak. With a grumble, she stood up and wiped off the excess suds that clung to her body. After a further urgent knock, she grabbed a towelling robe from the heated rail and splashed her way to the door.

Waiting outside was Police Sergeant Barkham. He had a grave look on his face as he apologised for disturbing her at this early hour of the morning. Rachel assured him that it wasn't a problem and that she had been having a bath. "I see," he commented.

Pulling out his notebook, he continued, "I understand, Ms Minos, you are a close friend of Ms Hannah Bates?" There was something about his voice that put Rachel on edge. A calming tone adopted for the passing on of bad news. "I am afraid to inform you, Ms Minos, that last night we recovered the body of Hannah Bates from the Thames."

Rachel felt lightheaded and short of breath as the sergeant continued, "I know this will come as a shock, but we would be grateful if you could come to the morgue to help identify her body."

Rachel slumped down onto her knees, tears streaming down her cheeks as she gasped for each breath. She was dead... Hannah was dead... Rachel may not have done the actual deed, but it was all because of her that the beautiful redhead had died.

With growing concern in his voice Sergeant Barkham asked, "Are you alright, Miss? Perhaps I could get you a glass of water or maybe a paper bag?"

Rachel ignored him. In her mind's eye, she could see Hannah's ice-cold corpse. The redhead's pallid body would be laid out on the white marble slab, ready to be identified, tagged and finally disposed of. Bag Head Man had done this, and she would have to make him pay.

"Perhaps you could do with some help, madam. I've brought an old friend along to assist you." Bent over double, her chest heaving with painful sobs, she was barely aware of someone kneeling beside her, putting their arm across her shoulder.

"Come on, Babs. I think you have made enough of a mess out here. It's time to admit you were wrong. It's time for you to come home. It's time for you to do as you're told."

With a start, abruptly sitting up, she had awoken from the nightmare. A tsunami of scented bath water cascaded over the tub's rim and onto the bathroom floor. As the waves settled down, she glumly stared over the tub's edge and muttered "I am so going to be in Housekeeping's bad books."

The snowstorm that had stubbornly sat over the south east of England finally relented. By mid-morning it had crossed the Channel, ready to inflict record snowfall upon the French coastline.

The passing of the storm ushered in clear skies and even colder weather. When evening descended, snow and slush would freeze into an iron-hard, frictionless sheet. The roads would become treacherous ice rinks. Railways would struggle as points became fused into position. Once again, London's arteries would stop flowing, throwing the city into further chaos.

After lunch, Rachel recovered Shank's automatic pistol. Hannah and she had hidden it in the appropriated black Mercedes, now parked in the hotel's basement. They had debated disposing of it but eventually agreed it might come in useful.

Returning with the firearm to her room, she placed the nickel-plated weapon on the writing table. Rachel then cautiously stood back from it. During her childhood in Chadderton, she had never seen a real gun with her own eyes. There were obviously plenty of weapons on TV. American shows seemed to be awash with a dazzling array of deadly hardware. Seeing one in the bare metal always made her uncomfortable.

Four years ago, Sheol Publicity had arranged a day at a shooting range. Purely for team building, of course. Rachel had been a reluctant participant in the event, but once she began firing at the paper cut-outs of people, she had become engrossed. There was something compelling about a tool that could take away a life with the gentle squeeze of a trigger.

From within its jar, Cheshire viewed the pistol with suspicion before vanishing back into nothingness.

There was no point in delaying. For plan B to work, she would have to look comfortable with the gun. She needed to convince him that she was willing to use it in anger. Her dilemma being that its actual use would probably result in immediate disaster.

She stepped forward and placed her hand on its cold, hard surface. "Get on with it, Minos" she told herself. Picking it up, she walked into the bathroom and stood before the mirror. For the next quarter of an hour she practiced, as her schoolyard friend Alison would have put it, 'lookin' hard'.

At 9pm she prepared to leave the Vestibule. Rachel had to decide between staying warm and preserving mobility. Given the gamble she was about to take, mobility, on this occasion, had won. She dressed simply in her red leather coat, blue jeans, white tee-shirt and trusty flat boots. The fur ushanka and woolly scarf provided both head warmth and anonymity from the relentless surveillance cameras.

Slipping the pistol into her coat pocket, she looked around her room. Opening the door and heading outside, Rachel experienced a peculiar sensation that she might be leaving it for good.

Upon exiting the lift, she paused beside one of the large potted ferns. Glancing around, she took a moment to soak up the dynamic atmosphere.

Tina on reception was dealing with a line of guests. Seven short people with identical brown suitcases were silently waiting in line to check in.

The concierge was talking with a blonde woman in a white and blue dress. Apparently, she had little time in London, so Dean attempted to sort out a comprehensive tourist itinerary for tomorrow.

The maître d' at the entrance to the dining room was engaged in animated conversation with an American couple. He was explaining that they didn't offer an all-you-can-eat buffet option.

The rotary entrance twirled in constant motion with people arriving and leaving the hotel. Rachel realised she had grown accustomed to living at the Vestibule. She had begun to feel safe within its walls. She had come to trust its employees.

The hotel had become her home.

"Is it lurking time again, Ms Minos?" enquired the manager. She laughingly nodded before adding, with melancholy, "For a little while, yes, it is." He produced a slip of paper and pressed it into her hand. "The address you asked for." Rachel took it with thanks.

Tina, now struggling with her seven guests, waved to Mr Typhon for assistance. Before he left, he paused and added, "Ms Minos, I would like to say that it has been a genuine pleasure having you stay with us at the Vestibule Hotel. I know I speak for all the staff when I say that we hope you will choose to stay for some time to come."

Rachel managed to muster a thin smile and nod in agreement with the manager's warm words. But she couldn't shake the sinking feeling that she would never lay eyes on the hotel again.

Finally passing through the rotating door, she found Billy standing outside laughing with two young children. She had wanted to say goodbye to him, to thank him for his help, but decided not to interrupt him. Instead, she waved goodbye. He, in turn, nodded to her.

The walk to Kensington should have been completed in an hour; instead, it had taken nearly twice as long. The pavement proved to be as dangerous as the roads. Rachel experienced three near misses and one backside-smashing tumble onto the slick surface.

At last, she turned into Queen's Gate Terrace. It was filled with snow-covered, eye-wateringly expensive cars parked outside their owners' luxurious and spacious apartments. An estate agent would gleefully tell you that starting prices to live in this exclusive terrace commenced at seven figures.

Given the late hour and the weather, Rachel had not been surprised to be the only person carefully working their way along the pavement. At last, she came to the address on the slip of paper. Glancing around, she clocked the multitude of watching cameras. After estimating the best angle to stand to hide her actions, she walked up the three white steps to the door.

Her pulse quickened as she confirmed the name printed beneath the illuminated doorbell: Conrad and Neil Paymon.

Slipping her right hand into her pocket, Rachel firmly grasped the butt of the pistol. Mrs Thomas's negotiation advice came to mind as she pressed the doorbell with her left hand. 'If you bluff, you must go all in. Half-hearted attempts provide lacklustre results. If you believe in the bluff yourself, they are far more likely to buy it'.

The porch light lit up and the front door swung open. Rachel immediately recognised Conrad Paymon. He wore a claret quilted smoking jacket, and black silk pyjamas. "Good evening, can I help you?"

Shifting her position to mask her actions from the watchful cameras, Rachel drew the pistol from her jacket and pressed the barrel hard into his chest.

Chapter 24

"Get down on your knees," Rachel ordered. She waved the gun towards the floor, emphasizing her intent. Conrad immediately dropped down onto the wooden boards, his arms still held high over his head. Tears welled up in his eyes as he blubbed, "I'm sorry, whatever I have done. Please, please don't shoot me."

Doubt was beginning to creep into Rachel's mind. This was certainly not how she had expected Bag Head Man to react. As a tear rolled down his cheek, she tried to work out the angle he was playing.

"Ok, where have you stashed Hannah?" she demanded. "Given it is nearly eleven o'clock, I know she has to be in this apartment somewhere." Conrad put on a convincing look of confusion as he babbled, "What are you talking about? Who are you talking about?"

Interesting, she thought, he wants to keep playing dumb. Well, I have time. Keeping the gun trained on him, she strolled over to the nearest of the green leather settees and perched herself on the cushioned arm. From here she could detect a hint of lavender and jasmine cologne.

Resting the pistol on her knee, she unwound the scarf and removed the ushanka. Disappointingly, Conrad continued to stare at her in confusion.

"Don't you recognise me, Conrad?" she asked, growing more impatient with his charade. He shrugged his shoulders and shook his head. "I'm Rachel Minos, the woman you have been mistakenly hunting for blackmailing you."

Conrad's eyes opened in recognition of the name. "Rachel? Oh my God. I'm sorry I didn't recognise you, but it's been years." His eyes were focused on the gun barrel as he confessed, "I'm confused; what blackmail are you talking about?" His act was convincing. She was beginning to believe that he might be genuinely clueless.

Rachel reminded herself of the picture he had texted. She could vividly recall Hannah's eyes, filled with terror, the knife held tight against her throat. It was enough to extinguish any thoughts of Conrad's innocence.

"You're not fooling me. How many people have you killed to maintain your part of the contract? Do you enjoy using the knife they provided to slit their throats?" Her voice grew louder and harsher as she continued. "Is that what you intended to do with Hannah, to cut her throat and bleed her dry?" Rachel had to temper the fury building within. The temptation to pull the trigger and shoot him between the eyes was almost irresistible.

The reality was, given the inadequate pistol skills she had demonstrated during her one and only visit to a shooting range, hitting Conrad at all would probably require a minor miracle.

"Hannah?" queried Conrad. "Do you mean Hannah Bates? Why would I want to kill her?" There was a look of desperation in his eyes as he implored, "Please, I think there has been a mistake. I think you have mixed me up with someone..."

"Shut the fuck up!" Rachel growled. He was far too convincing in his performance. Conrad's whole body trembled. His eyes had filled with tears. His breathing was desperate and ragged. If she didn't know better, it could have been enough to convince her that he wasn't Bag Head Man.

"How long do you intend to keep this deception up for, Conrad?" she paused; he said nothing. "I've read your secret contract. Very clever of you to hide it in plain sight within the Decem Fossas document." Rachel scrutinised his face, searching for a tell-tale crack in his performance. "I know all about the sordid deal you entered into with Decem Fossas."

Still, Conrad continued to play the fool. "Rachel, I'm sorry. I have absolutely no idea what you are talking about." His lines were delivered with the skill of a West End actor undertaking his finest ever performance. "Look, I had extraordinarily little to do with the Decem

Fossas contract. In fact, you had more dealings with it than I did." He paused, attempting to regain his breath and composure, before asking, "Why on earth do you think this all has something to do with me?"

Struggling to maintain her own cool facade, Rachel replied, "It's all in black and white, masquerading as appendix nine. After five years, when the Decem Fossas contract comes up for renewal, John Viath will suffer an unfortunate, terminal accident." She pointed the pistol at Conrad, "And you will be promoted to the role of CEO for Sheol Publicity."

She paused to let the information sink in. "For your part, you committed to sacrifice one person a month for those five intervening years." She shook her head with disgust at him. "They even provided the knife to be used, specifying the sacrifice must take place on the last day of each calendar month, between the hours of eleven pm and midnight GMT."

As if she had timed it deliberately, the grandfather clock began to whir and click, chiming eleven times to mark the top of the hour.

Conrad stared at her in horror. "No, no, no, that's insane!" Shaking his head in denial, he exclaimed, "I have never killed anyone and I certainly didn't make such a foul deal with Decem Fossas." He paused, momentarily lost in thought. "Wait, I remember, those appendices were all provided by Decem Fossas themselves. We... I had nothing to do with them."

The sound of the apartment's front door opening almost caught Rachel off guard. In making her plans she had completely forgotten about the husband, Neil. She put her finger to her lips, signalling Conrad to remain quiet, while lifting the pistol from her lap to emphasise the threat.

"Conrad darling, I'm home. What a crappy day I've had. I am thinking about getting a ba..." On entering the lounge, he stopped dead in his tracks. Neil was similar in height and build to Conrad and dressed in a sharply tailored brown suit, with a bespoke white shirt and dark blue tie.

Neil looked with concern at his husband kneeling on the floor, hands quivering in the air. Next, he looked at Rachel, her gun trained on Conrad. Finally, he sighed, "Oh great, it's you."

Rachel could smell the pungent cologne that had followed Neil through into the lounge. With a dawning realisation in her voice, she uttered, "Lavender and jasmine!"

He calmly strode to the baroque globe bar, lifted the lid, and perused its collection of liquor bottles. Rachel called out to her inner flame which, in response, flared into the darkness.

"I am going to have a glass of the Glen Grant. Rachel, can I pour you anything? Conrad, how about you? A vodka, perhaps?" His voice remained smooth and even. Rachel may as well have been an invited dinner guest, rather than a gun-wielding intruder.

Switching her aim towards Neil, Rachel instructed him not to move. Conrad remained frozen, his arms still in the air as he struggled to make sense of the situation. Neil took out a glass and coolly poured a generous measure of the fifty-year-old malt.

"Rachel, please put the gun down," Neil's voice continued unflustered. "You have read the contract; you know that as long as I fulfil the terms of the deal, there is nothing you can do to hurt me." He smiled. A predatory, triumphant smile.

"Are you sure you won't join me, Rachel? Conrad ensures we have an excellent liquor selection." Desperately struggling to hold on to her own cool visage, she shook her head.

"Your loss, my dear." He took an exaggerated swig from the crystal glass tumbler, before issuing a contented, "Ahhhh, that is damn good."

Rachel hesitated, not sure how to react. She had been convinced that it was Conrad. She had never entertained the idea that it could be his husband.

What proved to be worse, frustratingly, was that he was right. Under the provisions of the contract, he and Conrad were effectively untouchable.

She had to focus. Hannah's life hung in the balance. Her strategy remained valid, only the target had changed. She had to buy time. She had to let plan B play out. "So, you're Bag Head Man?" she queried.

Neil smiled at the moniker Rachel had given him, "What a manifest description. Yes, of course that was me." Now Neil paused and pieced parts of the puzzle together.

"Oh my, you really didn't know did you?" He laughed and took another drink. "Amazing. I thought you were playing me; I obviously gave you far too much credit, Ms Minos."

"Tell me this isn't true, Neil. This is insane; it can't be true." Conrad had finally dropped his arms by his side. With a mix of fear and horror, he stared at his husband.

"Oh, my sweet Conrad, this was going to be a surprise for your sixtieth birthday next year." After taking a further swig of whisky, Neil continued: "You see, Rachel, Conrad should be the CEO of Sheol." He sighed loudly. "But his ambition, like his hairline, receded when he turned fifty."

Conrad stood up, his hands firmly planted on his hips. "I was comfortable with what I had achieved, Neil. Our life is perfect or at least I thought it was." He hesitated as if he had seen a ghost before continuing. "I certainly didn't want the stress of the CEO job. Why in God's name would you inflict that on me?"

Neil swirled the remains of the whisky around before emptying the glass. "Conrad, when I met you, you were a beautiful shark. People feared you. I loved that they were so terrified of you. Now they see an old man happy to tread water. Waiting to retire into oblivion - or Tuscany, which I think is much the same."

"But I thought you loved the villa in Tusc..." Conrad halted as a veil of confusion lifted from his face. "Wait. I've had this conversation before. We have already argued about this, haven't we?"

With annoyance in his face, Neil turned on Rachel. "Now look what you've done. I am going to have to get someone to patch his memory again. Thank you so very much."

Rachel needed still more time. She had to keep Neil talking. "So, did you kill Shank?"

He smiled and from within his suit jacket produced an old revolver. Rachel swallowed hard, hoping she hadn't pushed him too far too quickly.

"Yes, I shot the little weasel. He was going to turn me in to the police. I actually thought about paying someone to do the deed. Then it occurred to me: why not do it myself? I deserved a bit of... fun."

"You killed them; you killed them in your art room, didn't you?" Conrad muttered accusingly. "You murdered all those people in cold blood." He was barely keeping it together as he pleaded, "Neil, you have to stop; I love you, but this is insanity."

Neil smiled lovingly at his husband.

"I killed them for you, my love. Most of them were just homeless people. They were no-one of consequence. But their sacrifice paved the way for you to have the authority and power you deserve." Chillingly, he concluded, "For the man that I love, I would willingly do so much worse."

"What about the real blackmailer?" Rachel interrupted.

With contempt spreading across his face, he refocussed on Rachel. "Anyone would think you were playing for time, Ms Minos." He glanced towards the grandfather clock "I really can't imagine what you think you have coming that could possibly trump my deal with Decem Fossas?"

Rachel put the pistol down on the settee cushion and meekly shrugged. "You're right. I can't touch you. But at least you can tell me who you think framed me and that you're going to get even with them as well."

"My, my! What a vindictive bitch. Well, I can relate to that." Neil had a hint of admiration in his voice. "Well, with you and Bates out of the picture, that really only leaves Viath's scrawny little protégé. Don't you worry, Rachel, I will ensure she is dealt with soon enough."

Neil sighed, "Right, it's ten past the hour. I don't like to leave the sacrifice too late." Placing his glass and revolver on the side of the globe, from within it he drew out an ornate black steel dagger.

"Now, my dear, if you promise not to resist, I will make this as quick and painless as I am able." Testing the edge of the blade, he nicked the skin on his finger. He let out an 'ouch' before sucking on the small pearl of blood.

"On the other hand, if you choose to be troublesome, I will ensure that your friend Bates suffers many days of torturous agony before I allow her to expire. Now, it's time for you to do as you're told."

In a well-practiced act of subservience, Rachel dropped her gaze down towards the apartment's polished floorboards. A defeated air surrounded her as she dutifully stepped towards her would-be executioner.

Neil bore a satisfied expression as his prey voluntarily approached him. With a firm grip on the knife, he readied himself for the coming thrill.

Standing on the far side of the wooden globe, Rachel awaited her demise. "There now," Neil soothingly called to her. "This will soon be over for you. Just know that you die so that my husband will shine once again."

Abruptly raising her head, Rachel revealed a huge grin, worthy of Cheshire. Confused, Neil began to ask why she was smiling, only to be silenced by Rachel loudly shushing him, and putting a finger to her lips.

In the distance, a church clock had chimed the top of the hour. The tolling bell struck One... Two... Three...

Spinning to face the grandfather clock, Neil could see it clearly showed a little before quarter past eleven.

Seven...Eight...

He fumbled out his pocket watch and stared down at the face, it too showed coming up to quarter past eleven.

Eleven...Twelve...

"Happy February the 1st. You're in breach of your contract, motherfucker," Rachel seethed.

Panic in his voice, Neil demanded to know how.

Rachel mimicked his voice, "Anyone would think you were playing for time." She laughed at Neil. "Well, it turns out I can play with time. I worked out how to slow it down just a little bit. It only works in a small area, but that suited me fine." Pointing to the grandfather clock, "For us, five minutes passed; outside our bubble, nearly a full hour. Such a crying shame your contract stipulates GMT."

Rachel's inner flame was extinguished as an icy wind howled from a darkness deep within her. Rachel imperiously stared at Neil, who desperately lunged towards the revolver and cried out in despair, "No!"

As the bitter wind spread throughout her body, she felt nothing for this pitiful excuse for a human. She no longer possessed any interest in the misdeeds it had perpetrated. There was no consideration for the suffering it had caused to innocent people. All that mattered was that it had broken the terms of the contract and that it must suffer the consequences.

Impassively, Rachel watched Neil's desperate manoeuvre slow to an imperceptible crawl. He would never reach the revolver.

The crack appeared behind him. It started as nothing more than a tiny slice through the air. Rachel waited as it expanded before finally, with a pulsing surge, growing into a man-sized hole. Inside it there was nothing: a non-reflecting matte blackness.

Thrusting out of the darkness emerged the long, thin, writhing tail. Onwards it came, gathering into coils that threatened to fill the room with its apparently endless length. Finally, the questing tip touched upon Neil's shoulder. Slowly, it began to form loops around the motionless man.

Only when his waist and upper torso had been fully encircled did it violently tighten its grip, firmly securing its victim in its rib-crushing embrace. Lifting him off the floor with slow, deliberate tugs, the coils lazily retreated, dragging Neil through the closing portal.

As Bag Head Man vanished into the darkness, Rachel felt no joy or satisfaction as her tormentor's terrified face was remorselessly dragged beneath the opaque surface.

As the icy wind enveloped her, she felt no emotion at all.

Chapter 25

Slumping onto the polished floorboards, Rachel propped herself up against the globe bar. The numbing effects of the icy wind were painfully slow to dissipate, even after it had ceased to howl within her.

Her pulse raced, a bass drum rapidly thumping within her head whilst waves of frigid shivers washed up and down through her body. Closing tired eyes, Rachel fought to regain control.

Many times, she had attempted the same feat after suffering one of Barry's tirades. Rachel could hear him loudly accusing her of wanting to be with other men. He would threaten to have her sectioned, to be locked away forever. "You're ugly and stupid; I could do so much better," he would sneer at her.

Yet, as Hyde must give way to Jekyll, the man of charm would inevitably return. Gently comforting her; putting on a well-rehearsed show of tender affection; providing a glimmer of better times ahead if she would just do better.

As she endured those relentless cycles of mental torture, her pulse would race and her body shiver. At first, they would leave her emotionally crippled and physically drained for long periods.

Yet, like the sharp blade forged by a master swordsmith, she became tempered to the fallout of his manipulations. It was that growing resilience that prevented Barry from shattering the thinly stretched veneer of Rachel Minos into a thousand confused fragments.

An adjacent creak of a floorboard focussed her attention. Wrestling to quell her inner demons, Rachel had failed to notice Conrad stand up and retrieve his late husband's discarded revolver.

He stood by the globe, turning the weapon over in his hands, his face a tortured mix of confusion and anger. Tears rolled down his cheeks as he unintelligibly mumbled to himself.

Startled by Rachel pulling herself up into a more comfortable sitting position, Conrad wildly pointed the revolver towards her.

"No, this is so wrong! I must make it better. It's so wrong!" His eyes were windows into the cauldron of pain boiling uncontrollably within him. "He did this. We did this." His voice croaked as the emotional cauldron painfully overflowed with guilt and horror. "We destroyed so many people. So many victims. So many lives."

With a sharp intake of breath, Conrad thrust the gun under his chin, a quaking finger on the trigger. "I'm so sorry for what he did to you, Rachel," he pleaded, "Forgive me; this will make it all better."

The remnants of the icy chill that had gripped her, wanted to see the trigger pulled. The morbid desire was not formed in malice, but from emotionless curiosity. That disturbingly cold part of her wanted to witness the bullet tearing through his head, wanted to see the creation of a macabre fountain of blood, wanted to watch his shocked expression as life was brutally extinguished. 'Tell him to pull the trigger,' a chilled voice whispered from within her.

Conrad closed his eyes. Not half an hour ago, he had been sitting by the fire, drinking a glass of Armagnac and planning their upcoming flights to Florence. He had been momentarily distracted by an interesting article on 'Retiring to Tuscany during uncertain financial times' when the doorbell had rung.

Now, the man Conrad had loved had been exposed as a monster. Years of lies, manipulation and murders had been rudely revealed, atrocities committed out of Neil's twisted love for his husband and his own aspirations to greatness. Conrad couldn't begin to conceive how such appalling acts could have had their roots in love.

His finger trembled on the trigger.

"Conrad, keep calm," Rachel urged, as the bitter coldness finally melted and released its emotionless grip on her. "Look, I'm hardly an authority when it comes to relationships, but it seems you're just as much a victim as me in this screwed-up mess." Keeping eye contact with him, she demanded, "Don't let Neil win. You are not the person he tried to mould you into. If you want to make amends," she held out her right hand and concluded, "you can start by helping me stand up."

Releasing his breath, relief spread across Conrad's face as he lowered the revolver and placed it on the globe bar. "Thank you," he sighed and held out his hand, pulling Rachel unsteadily to her feet.

Leaning against the bar, Rachel's first thought was to ask Conrad where Hannah would be held. "I think she will be in his arts and crafts room. He always keeps the door locked. But I suspect he took the key with him to..." The doorbell's chime caused them both to jump. "That will likely be my contingency," Rachel explained as she staggered over to the front door.

Opening it, Rachel barely felt the cold rush of air from the outside. Alex stood on the doorstep, dressed in a heavy coat, a grey scarf wrapped around his face and a flat cap, its peak pulled low across his brow. From under a blanket, the two sawn-off barrels of a shotgun discreetly peeked out.

"It's ok," Rachel exclaimed, "It's all under control." Alex peered suspiciously behind her, checking for coercion. "You sure you don't need any help?" he whispered. She shook her head. "You keep the car running; I'll be out soon."

Satisfied that all was fine, the shotgun was slipped back inside the blanket. With a simple 'ok' he headed back to the black Mercedes double-parked directly outside the apartment.

Before turning to face Conrad, Rachel took a deep breath of the night air and pushed the door closed. "Do you have something we can break the arts room door down with?"

As Conrad went in search of the toolbox, Rachel retrieved Neil's revolver and slipped it into her coat pocket before also recovering Shank's automatic pistol from the settee.

Pausing to stare at the spot where Neil had vanished, Rachel quietly wondered, "Where were you dragged off to?" and then added, "What the hell dragged you away?"

Conrad didn't utter a word as he chiselled out the door lock, his face revealing the inner torments he still struggled to suppress. If he harboured any concerns as to the power he'd seen Rachel unleash, for now he kept them to himself. As the mechanism fell away, he pushed the door open and they both leaned forward to look inside. Located at the rear of the apartment, the windows had been boarded over and only the light from the hallway spilled into the darkened chamber.

Both stood motionless at the threshold, experiencing a feeling of dread at what they were about to discover. Eventually, it was Conrad who leaned inside and flicked on the light switch.

Multiple spotlights brightly illuminated the room. It was spartanly furnished with an easel, a wooden stool and a wheeled paint chest. The floor was of a uniform grey vinyl covering. Easy to mop stains off, thought Rachel.

By contrast, the walls were completely covered by Neil's paintings. All his creations showed a unique, abstract style: a single slash of paint diagonally bisecting a variety of minimalist backgrounds.

Rachel's attention was drawn to the easel and the half-finished canvas perched on it. It consisted of a partly coloured-in pencil drawing of a mop of red hair. The twisting sensation in the pit of her stomach accompanied the recognition of the redhead's hair colour that Neil had carefully replicated.

Immediately, all these paintings took on a new, disturbing aspect. Staring at the walls, both felt revulsion at this macabre gallery that chronicled each of Neil's sacrifices. With a quiet and determined voice, Conrad promised, "I'm going to burn every one of these monstrosities."

Overcoming her irrational hesitation, Rachel stepped into the room and checked behind the door. Having found nothing lurking there, she turned to Conrad and demanded to know, "Where the hell is Hannah?"

There was no sign of her friend. Had Neil imprisoned her somewhere else? That seemed unlikely to Rachel - he had arrived home in time to undertake the sacrifice, so Hannah had to be here somewhere.

Conrad walked to an adjacent wall and began to unhook Neil's paintings and throw them into a pile at the centre of the room. Rachel quickly joined him in stripping away the canvas camouflage. Removing a large floor-to ceiling canvas revealed a walled-off section of the room. Inside the tiny space, a female figure sat slumped in a wheelchair a hessian bag pulled over her head.

As Conard pulled the wheelchair out into the light, they could see she had been secured by leather straps around her ankles, arms and waist. Hesitating in fear of what lay beneath it, Rachel gingerly lifted the hessian bag to expose Hannah's slack features.

Her hair was damp with sweat, her face smeared with makeup and dirt, her right eye swollen and bruised. A tightly bound cloth gag had pulled her mouth painfully wide open, allowing drool to drip unchecked down her chin and onto her navy-blue top.

Tentatively, Rachel touched her on the shoulder. Hannah's left eye slowly flicked open, struggling to focus. As Conrad released the restraining straps, he pointed at Hannah's right arm and the signs of several needle marks, adding, "I think Neil may have kept her sedated."

Carefully, Rachel undid the gag whilst Conrad released the remaining straps. Hannah slumped forward; struggling to control her limbs, she threw her arms over Rachel's shoulders and began to wail uncontrollably. Confused part-sentences spilled out as her doped mind tried to simultaneously thank them for the rescue and describe the terrible ordeal she had endured.

Returning the embrace, Rachel tried to console and calm her. "It's ok. It's over. He's gone. Just relax." She fought back the strong desire to pull away from Hannah. It was the prissy child within her, desperate to escape the drool-covered cheek and clothes that now pressed tightly against her.

As the pharmaceuticals overwhelmed her manic exuberance of liberation, Hannah slipped back into a stupor. Rachel eased her friend back into the wheelchair before wheeling her out of that oppressively sinister room.

In the back of the black Mercedes, Hannah slumped into Rachel's lap and quickly fell into a disturbed slumber. Gently, Rachel stroked the greasy red hair, hoping to soothe away any unpleasant dreams.

Gazing out of the window, Rachel watched the white-covered city pass by. Despite the early hour, people were still working their way through the treacherous conditions. "Nothing ever puts this city to sleep," she mumbled to herself.

In the rear-view mirror, Rachel could see that Alex wore a look of determined concentration as he focussed on driving them to the safety of the Vestibule Hotel. Before calling him yesterday, she'd harboured doubts he would be willing to help her with the hastily created plan B. Rachel had felt a sense of relief as he enthusiastically agreed to join in the mad endeavour.

For a moment, Alex glanced at her in the mirror. Their gazes lingered on each other before he returned his attention to the treacherous road.

Her thoughts moved on to Conrad and whether she had been right to leave him behind. Admittedly, he had been insistent on staying in the apartment and Rachel had been in no position to forcibly object. Despite the illusion of his comfortable life shattering in the space of a few minutes, he had quickly regathered his composure, demanding that Rachel allow him to assist in cleaning up his husband's mess. From her own bitter experience, Rachel guessed the enormity of the night's revelations could take a long time for Conrad to process.

A gritting lorry rumbled by in the opposite direction, the salt pellets noisily peppering the side of the Mercedes. The redhead shifted, murmuring quietly before settling back down. Hannah had done so much for Rachel. She had saved her from incarceration, supported her when things had been difficult and had almost been murdered because of her. All this because of her love for Rachel.

But did she love Hannah with that same intensity? It was hard for Rachel to be certain. She certainly loved her as a close friend, but could that grow into a romantic passion? She couldn't be sure. When it came to affairs of the heart, Barry had twisted and warped her perceptions. For now, she felt unable to trust her own instincts. Rachel would need more time to work out her true desires. Hopefully, Hannah would be willing to wait, even if the choice resulted in her being disappointed.

Turning onto New Cavendish Street, the Mercedes' headlights illuminated the ice-laden trees that lined the road. The bleak winter scene stirred memories of the coldness that had gripped her in the apartment.

Rachel's experiences with her inner flame reminded her of a faithful working dog. It felt independent, yet willing to work with her as they developed a mutual bond of respect.

In stark contrast, Rachel felt the icy wind had emerged from deep within her own darkness. It was a chilling part of her own psyche that, once stirred from its slumber, attempted to absorb her within its emotionless thrall. Tonight, it had seemed stronger than during than its first emergence in Montague Street. If she summoned it again, she wondered, would she be strong enough to resist its frigid grip?

"Is she asleep?" Alex asked in a hushed voice. Distracted from her dark thoughts, Rachel nodded and added, "Thanks for doing this and for being there in case it all went sideways." He smiled. "It was a pleasure. Plus, how could I turn down a mission to help a damsel in distress?" Looking at him in the mirror, she smiled back.

"So, is it over?" he asked.

Rachel shook her head. As he had agreed to help, she had explained some of her background to the younger man. "No, there is still the blackmailer, Bethany." Alex nodded, before adding, "Well, it's not like she can hurt you anymore. Maybe it's time to quit with a win?"

Rachel looked down at Hannah's battered visage. In that moment, part of her wanted to exact terrible revenge for the hurt that had been inflicted on them by Bethany. Without any evidence, she had begun to suspect that Bethany had introduced Barry into her life, a carefully choreographed play to remove an obstacle from her career path. For all the woe she had inflicted on others, Beth had to be made to pay.

"It would be nice to walk away, but Beth is in line to one day grasp the reins of a powerful corporation. I have to do something." Hannah stirred, disturbed by their conversation or perhaps in reaction to Rachel's attempt to justify her wrathful intentions.

Leaving the road, the tyres squealed on the polished concrete as they began their descent of the tightly curved ramp leading to the Vestibule's underground car park. Alex parked the Mercedes before heading upstairs to get assistance.

As soon he was out of sight, Rachel slid Hannah back over to her own seat. Exiting the car, she popped open the boot and hid the revolver and pistol under the space saver wheel. She already had plans for them.

Having closed the boot, the lift door opened and Alex returned with Mr Typhon and a porter pushing a wheelchair. The manager greeted her: "Ms Minos. Alex has explained the situation. Do you wish Ms Bates to be placed in your room?"

Rachel considered the manager's offer. Would waking up in her bed give the wrong impression to Hannah? Would people think they were a couple? Rachel felt disgusted with herself for even worrying about such trivia at this time. Yet, despite herself, she requested, "Can you put her in a room of her own, on my tab, please."

He nodded. "Of course. There is a single room next door to yours, if that would be suitable?" She agreed, feeling deeply ashamed of herself.

As Alex and the porter slid Hannah onto the wheelchair, Rachel requested, "Could you arrange for someone to check her over, please?" Mr Typhon confirmed he would make the call immediately and have someone attend to Hannah within the hour.

Safely secure in the hotel bedroom, Rachel carefully stripped Hannah of her soiled clothes and then gently cleaned the dirt and drool from her face with a damp sponge. The prissy Rachel initially balked at cleaning away the unpleasant smears of the redhead's bodily functions, but, after fortifying herself with a whisky from the mini bar, she had pressed on with the unpleasant task.

Dressing Hannah in her own pink and white cotton pyjamas, she darkly joked to herself, that seeing her friend naked for the first time had not proved to be the erotic experience it could have been.

There came a knock on the door. Rachel opened it to reveal the Physician. "I don't normally get involved with these types of people," she immediately explained, an undisguised tone of disdain in her voice, "But Mr Typhon explained that this is a close personal friend of yours." She entered the room, slipping off her beige anorak and placing it over the back of an adjacent chair. "So, I have decided to make an exception – I trust you will do the same for me one day." She abruptly halted, black bag in hand, staring at Rachel.

"Err, ok. Yes." Rachel finally responded. The Physician nodded, opened the bag and proceeded to examine Hannah.

Rachel took the opportunity to look around the room. It was smaller than her junior suite and lacked the seating area. Looking into the bathroom, she smiled. Hannah would be livid, she thought: the bath was a more modest affair than Rachel's and the shower cubicle was almost boringly conventional in its design.

After fifteen minutes, the Physician had completed her examination and treatment. Hannah's eye had been covered with a pad and secured with tape. The redhead seemed more relaxed and had begun to quietly snore.

"There is no significant damage, but I have injected a healing solution to speed her recovery. Obviously, highly diluted in deference to her limited lineage." The black bag was snapped shut. "I have tended to her eye and applied a regenerative salve. It will also speed the process of recovery. The damage to her eye is, however, superficial and I expect no ocular issues. Keep the pad in place for at least one day."

She paused before warning, "If you happen to see traces of scaly skin developing... best to give me a call. Urgently." Rachel couldn't decide if she was being serious or facetious. Given the woman's reputation, she decided to stick with the former assumption.

Slipping her anorak back on, the Physician concluded, "I have given her a further sedative. She should sleep calmly until morning."

Her demeanour mellowed slightly as she enquired, "What about you, Rachel? You seem tired. Have you been exerting yourself?" She nodded in response, adding, "You could say that, but I really had no choice."

"Hmm. Understandable, I suppose, given the circumstances." She led Rachel to the room's door, ensuring they were out of Hannah's earshot. "I would strongly advise against calling upon your father's powers until you are fully recovered." Grasping Rachel's hand, there was almost a tenderness to her voice as she concluded, "I do wish I could explain more to you, but I must adhere to my oath." Without further explanation she opened the door and left the room.

Finally returning to the bedside, Rachel stared down at her friend and whispered, "I'm so sorry for all of this," before sitting in a chair and commencing her night-long vigil.

Chapter 26

"I think I've put weight on," remarked Hannah, continuing to adjust the hang of her dress. The queue to enter the ballroom was moving at a snail's pace, as each person's invitation was thoroughly checked for its authenticity. Security was determined that only genuine guests would be allowed to enter the prestigious event.

"You look fine to me," commented Alex. He was dressed in a classic tuxedo with cummerbund, the slim cut of his smart rental outfit further exaggerating his height.

Hannah flashed him a curious look and muttered, "Hmmm, maybe so," her dismissive tone indicating that she didn't value his opinion or, perhaps, appreciate his presence.

Sneaking a look, Rachel jealously admired the redhead's outfit. Yesterday, accompanied by Hannah, Rachel had returned to the dress shop in Greenland Street. It was the first time she had visited Camden since the evening of her desperate escape from the apartment. That afternoon, she had one mission in mind: to purchase the magnificent black streak of gorgeousness she had lusted over through the shop window.

The assistant had removed the dress from the display dummy and, bubbling with childlike excitement, Rachel disappeared into the changing room. It had proved to be a soul-destroying experience. Despite trying various accessories, looking into the mirror she was eventually forced to admit that this beautiful dress just didn't look good on her.

To compound her disappointment, Hannah then tried it on. She emerged from the cramped changing room and looked - well, Rachel had to be honest - devastatingly attractive in it. On her friend, the dress sensually hugged curves, whereas on Rachel it just seemed to hang flaccidly. When Hannah wondered if she should splash out and buy it,

Rachel had grudgingly encouraged her to do so.

Acutely aware of her client's disappointment, the older shop assistant had suggested that Rachel should try on a silver-grey wrap-around dress that had recently come into the shop. It wasn't a style that Rachel had previously considered.

Emerging from the changing room and admiring herself in the full-length mirror, she admitted that the assistant clearly had a good eye. The sheer material hugged and caressed in all the right places, whilst tantalisingly revealing subtle glimpses of flesh in others.

But the single bow on the dress's left side keeping the entire wrap in place had made her feel curiously vulnerable. She was about to reject it before recalling Serge's sage words of advice. 'Every woman must have something in their wardrobe that is daring, outrageous and drags them kicking and screaming out of their comfort zone'.

So, despite remaining sceptical, she had purchased it.

On the elevator trip down to the Vestibule's ballroom, Rachel had already checked the integrity of her waist bow three times, whilst sneaking another envious glance at Hannah's black flowing masterpiece.

Finally, on reaching the head of the queue, the burly head of security requested, "May I have your invitations, please?" Rachel handed over the three gold-lettered, embossed cards. As he began the laborious procedure to confirm their validity, she recalled her earlier encounter with the Dowager.

Their meeting had been arranged the previous morning with Rachel agreeing to visit the Dowager's suite on the tenth floor. Exiting the lift, she had been met by a large, muscular man wearing a black suit and shirt. After confirming Rachel's appointment on his portable radio, he had silently escorted her into the spacious lounge area, before discreetly standing guard.

Rachel took the opportunity to marvel at the uninterrupted views south across London towards the Palace of Westminster. While the city's rooftops remained thickly layered with brilliant white snow, the roads and pavements had been cleared: the traffic and pedestrians were returning to their usual routines.

After nearly five minutes, the Dowager emerged from the adjacent bedroom. Dramatically flinging open the room's double doors, she swept into the lounge, dressed in a long, golden silk dressing gown. A phone nestled between her shoulder and ear; she was engaged in an animated telephone conversation.

"Shit happens, darling, it's the nature of the beast. Anyway, perhaps it's all for the best. I certainly think he proved to be a less than ideal candidate." She had silently mouthed an apology to Rachel before continuing:

"Restart the recruitment process and provide me with some replacements. We will have to begin it all again from scratch, but we have time on our side."

She shooed the guard away, who obediently exited the room.

"Listen I have someone waiting for another meeting, so we will pick this up during our next call. Ciao, my love." She hung up, tossing the phone across to her assistant, who nimbly caught it in her left hand.

"Rachel darling, hugs." The Dowager tightly embraced her, coincidentally confirming her lack of undergarments beneath that thin silk robe. "Now, please sit yourself down and let's have some tea. Then you can explain what I can do for you." Throwing herself down on the tan sofa, she encouragingly patted a spot directly beside her.

Emerging from the third doorway, a man, again dressed in black, had placed a silver tea set on the table before silently retreating. The Dowager poured them each a cup of tea and insisted that Rachel take a slice of Battenberg cake. "It is to die for, my dear, and I am assured it barely contains any calories." Her knowing wink confirmed the claim was false.

Finally, she lounged back into the sofa, her gown falling open across her leg, and asked, "So, what can an old tigress do for a young one?"

Rachel had remained awkwardly perched on the edge of the sofa as she sipped her tea. "Firstly, thank you for seeing me - I realise you have a busy schedule." The Dowager had waved dismissively. "My dear, think nothing of it; I do so enjoy your company."

"Well, you kindly offered us two tickets for your event tomorrow evening." Rachel had felt her cheeks begin to blush with embarrassment as she asked, "I was hoping that you may see your way to sparing perhaps... three more?"

The assistant flashed Rachel an incredulous look for making what she clearly considered to be an unreasonable request. The look transformed into astonishment as the Dowager replied, "You're up to something, aren't you? I can tell. You're a devious one and that's for sure." With a snap of her fingers, she summoned the assistant forward and held out her hand. In response, with a sour face, the assistant reluctantly handed her five invitations.

Adopting a stern face, the Dowager had proffered the cards to Rachel. "I trust that, whatever it is you are planning, you won't make a scene at the event." After closely scrutinising Rachel's face, the Dowager burst out laughing. "I'm joking, my dear. A bit of juicy scandal always makes for a memorable party."

Rachel thanked her as the cards were handed over. "Right, my dear, recent events require my undivided attention, so I am afraid I must fly." With that she had stood up, hugged Rachel again and, returning to her bedroom, called out, "I look forward to seeing you and your delicious partner tomorrow evening. Maybe we'll share a steamy dance together." The assistant followed her out, closing the bedroom doors behind her.

In the lift back down to her own room, Rachel had been relieved at how easily it had gone. The Dowager had not exaggerated when she claimed that this was one of the hottest parties of the year. Attempts to source tickets from elsewhere had proved futile. Rachel looked down at the elaborate invitation and noticed, with a start, the Dowager's official title: 'Duchess Mary Scharlach. President of Long-term Projects: Decem Fossas'.

"Thank you. Please enjoy the event." The head of security waved the three of them through and into the ballroom. It had been completely transformed since Rachel's previous visit to the cavernous space. In the centre, the dance floor heaved with a mass of bodies moving to live music provided by a band dressed in golden suits. Magicians, clowns, jugglers, fortune tellers and many other entertainers mingled with the exclusive crowd. A multitude of attractions had been provided to entertain people. In one corner, a bull-riding machine; against the back wall, a champagne-spouting replica of the Trevi fountain; ornate chocolate fountains scattered throughout the event; a tented relaxation area filled with oversized beanbags in another corner and so much more.

As the theme was masquerade the guests sported a bewildering assortment of masks. Hannah had opted for a black cat mask, Alex, a horned red devil mask and Rachel, a plain white mask.

Immediately upon entering, a waiter approached, presenting them with a tray of flutes brimming with champagne. They each took a glass and the trio moved deeper into the ballroom as they began the game of Spot the Celebrity. The powerhouses of business, the movers and shakers in politics, the artists and the infamous all rubbed shoulders, exchanged stories, drank champagne, admired the intricate ice sculptures and gorged on an endless supply of exquisite party food. "I've heard tales about these events," Hannah confessed, "but none of them do it justice."

Rachel nudged her: "Over there," and pointed towards the base of the gold replica of the Trevi fountain. Amongst the masked crowd, Rachel had spotted the distinctive peacock-feathered mask that Conrad had said he would be wearing. Hannah leaned close to Rachel and whispered, "Do you think you can do your thing in such a crowded place?"

Earlier that morning, the four of them had been sitting in her hotel room, reviewing the up-coming evening's events. "As we thought, Bethany immediately accepted my offer of the ticket," Conrad had explained. "She thinks I want her help in getting a proposal through John Viath's office and that the ticket is my way of securing that aid."

Rachel had looked on with concern as he took another swig from his tumbler of neat whisky before continuing. "I spoke to my police contact last night and, in exchange for him having the Tuscany villa for the entire summer, he eventually agreed to the plan. I suspect it is going to cause him a bit of a stink, so having substantive evidence when they arrive would be preferable. Otherwise, I'll be loaning him the villa for a decade of summers."

He finished his whisky and began to pour another generous measure. "By the way Rachel, I also asked him to remove you from the CCTV watch list - the one that Neil asked him to put you on. You are now free to walk the streets of London."

After thanking him, she had asked, "Are you sure you're ok being there tonight? We could go ahead without you; you have done so much already." Conrad forced a smile. "Yes. Don't worry about me. I am finding it to be a most cathartic experience." He raised his glass taking yet another drink. "And I certainly wouldn't like to miss Ms Hopkins getting her comeuppance."

Alex had run through his assignment: "As soon as you have found Conrad and Bethany, I'll make the call to Mr Typhon who will give the police the signal to go. After that, I'll stay on hand to help out with anything that goes wrong."

Rachel leaned forward and held his hand. "Alex, thank you so much for doing this. I know it's not your fight." He blushed as he clumsily replied, "I'm happy to be with... I mean I'm happy to help... you, Rachel... That is..." Hannah tutted loudly and rolled her eyes, barely concealing her displeasure at the young man's fumbling response.

With a grin, Rachel had released his hand and continued, "Ok, so I have primed Mr Typhon; he will usher the police into the ballroom. Hannah, Conrad and I will get as close as possible to Bethany." Conrad pointed out that John Viath would be at the event, so Bethany would almost certainly be in close orbit to him. "That makes sense," Rachel agreed. "Right, then I will do my thing and Hannah drops the package on Beth. Simple really - what could possibly go wrong?"

Hannah had folded her arms and sarcastically asked, "Do we have a plan C?"

Back in the ballroom, the band had commenced a playlist of jive music as the trio approached Conrad. He nodded at them then motioned towards a group of people gathered near a living statue of a silver-coated Adonis. At the centre of the group stood John Viath, laughing, talking and holding court with four couples who had gathered closely around him.

Bethany's unmistakable diminutive frame stood at Viath's right-hand side. She appeared poised and elegant in a green and gold off-the-shoulder cocktail dress, extremely high heels, obligatory oversized handbag, and a black swan mask. "Ideally, we need to get her away from that group," Rachel pointed out. Hannah once again adjusted her dress and, with a little too much relish in her voice, advised Rachel, "Leave this to me!"

Giving her long red hair a good shake, Hannah strode up to the distinguished group. "Beth, you treacherous cow! I thought it was you. What did you tell Rachel? I thought we were friends. How could you stab me in the back like that?"

The group immediately fell into embarrassed silence in response to Hannah's unexpected outburst. Viath's expression never wavered as he leaned down towards Beth and asked her, "Sort this out - discreetly."

With a furious look on her face, Bethany dragged Hannah away from the group, finding a secluded, empty spot in the shadow of the champagne fountain. "What the fuck are you doing here?" she demanded of the redhead. "This is an exclusive event - how the hell did you get an invite?"

Hannah leaned forward and sneered, "Fuck you, Bethy." The sudden and blunt response, coupled with the truncated name, had the desired impact on Bethany. With hate in her voice, the shorter woman blustered, "I am a close personal friend of the Duchess; one word from me and she will have you thrown out of here like the common gutter trash you are." Hannah's face began to turn scarlet with rage, so Rachel intervened, "Hey you two! No brawling in the ballroom."

Beth momentarily looked surprised before recovering her ice-cool demeanour. "Oh, it's you. I thought you would be dead by now or at least shacked up with another man, ready to throw away your life." The last comment unexpectedly pierced Rachel like a stake thrust through her heart.

In response to the unexpected, intense pain, Rachel wanted to know... She demanded to know... had Beth deliberately brought Barry to the party four years ago to get them hooked up? Had it all been part of her Machiavellian plan to remove Rachel as the competition, to ensure Bethany became Sheol's rising star?

Beth looked at her with a mixture of pity and contempt. "You're delusional, Rachel Minos. I brought Barry to Hannah's party on our third date. He seemed to be really into me. I thought there was real chemistry between us. At last, I'd found my Prince Charming. But you turned up to the party in that stupidly tight leather dress and had all the men ogling you. Barry forgot all about me and spent the evening chatting and dancing with you. I never heard from him again. So, no, Rachel Minos, you stole him from me!"

Rachel felt the walls of the ballroom begin to close in around her. There was no sinister plot, it was just unfortunate timing that had led to her meeting Barry and allowed him to worm his way into her life. She had been attracted to his easy charm and had found herself powerless within his manipulative grip. She began to feel lightheaded as this bleak truth struck home.

Hannah grabbed Rachel's shoulder, preventing her from slumping to the ground. Urgently, she whispered into her ear, "Get it together, Minos. Time's running out!"

Beth shook her head and said something disparaging about Rachel's state of mental health before adding, "Well, it's been swell to catch up with the old Posse again. Any time you want to reminisce about how you two screwed me, let me know."

Had Rachel wronged her?

Was that the reason Beth had framed her for blackmail?

Had Bethany lashed out at Rachel in her own pain?

Should she be feeling pity for Bethany?

Hannah spotted a commotion at the entrance to the ballroom. "Rachel, you need to do your thing right now!" she hissed into her ear.

Rachel wrestled with her confused conscience. What if Bethany had suffered in her love life? How could that justify standing idly by whilst innocent people were slaughtered? Beth had profited from that suffering, her hands stained red from the handling of blood-soaked money.

Bethany turned away, intent on retaking her place at Viath's side, content that she had dealt with the incident.

Hannah desperately muttered, "Time for plan C," and shoved Rachel forward into Bethany's back. The significant disparity in size and mass sent the two of them sprawling onto the floor.

Eventually disentangling themselves, Rachel rolled to one side and allowed Bethany to stand up. Bethany's face was twisted in rage as she hissed, "I won't forget this, either of you."

Scooping up Beth's spilled bag and repacking its contents, Hannah handed it back explaining, "Look at the state Rachel's in; this is all your fault, Beth. Why don't you just go?" Without a further word, Beth stormed off. Adjusting her dress, she snatched a glass of champagne from a passing tray and rejoined Viath's circle.

Hannah furiously waved to Alex and, between the two of them, they managed to spirit Rachel away and take refuge within the tented relaxation zone.

The live music abruptly halted as raised voices and screams of rage echoed across the ballroom. Alex peeked out around the edge of the tent flap to spy on the unfolding events. "I can't see anything clearly, there's too many people in the way," he commented. "It does look like a big old barny kicking off near the Trevi fountain." There were more raised voices and some distinctly Beth-like yells of outrage. The band started playing again, attempting to drown out the argument with a raucous rendition of 'Twisting by the pool'.

After another minute or so, Alex observed, "Ok, looks like the commotion is leaving by the ballroom entrance and..." he halted mid-commentary before adding a worried 'Uh oh'.

Hannah and Rachel exchanged concerned glances as the Dowager swept into the tent. Dressed in a magnificent gold ballroom gown topped with a diamond-encrusted half-skeleton mask, she came to a dramatic halt before the three of them.

"Well!" she exclaimed with mock outrage. "That proved to be fabulously scandalous." Rachel pathetically shrugged her shoulders. Now knowing who the Dowager represented, she was keen to give little away. "Oh? We've been relaxing in here. What was the commotion all about?" She winced at her rather unconvincing attempt at deception.

The Dowager gave a knowing look. "Oh really… Well, you missed a treat. We had the police here - there had been a tip-off about someone planning something untoward. It involved a diminutive young lady who works at Sheol Publicity; perhaps you know her?"

She let the question linger and summoned a waiter to fill her champagne coupe. The threesome remained conspiratorially silent. "Well, my loves, an older man - an exec for Sheol, I do believe - he then accused the little tramp of blackmail. It was such a juicy moment."

The Dowager took a long pause and drank her champagne; all the time, her eyes evaluated her audience's reaction. "Finally, he accused her of actually murdering his husband and a man called Shank. I must say, the exchanges grew very heated, but the discovery of a revolver in the woman's bag, now that proved to be extremely damning."

She paused again, continuing to scrutinise Rachel. "Who knows what nefarious plot she was about to undertake? I guess we are all lucky that someone tipped off the gallant boys in blue. Anyhow, they have taken them all away and I am sure they will sort it all out."

Once again, she emptied her coupe and, glancing around for another waiter, concluded, "As I said, I do love a bit of intrigue to give a party a dose of spice." With no waiter in sight, the Dowager headed out of the tent. "I must go, my dears. There are so many people I must gossip with. Here's to people getting their just rewards." With that, she raised her empty glass in a mock toast and exited in search of fresh people and bubbly.

All three of them slumped down onto an oversized red beanbag. "Holy crap," Hannah exclaimed, "I think we actually did it." Alex silently nodded his head as Hannah added, "But do you think it will stick?"

Rachel let her head roll back and sighed, "Maybe, maybe not. When they match the ballistics from the revolver to the bullet that killed Shank, they will have pretty compelling evidence." Hannah agreed. "You're right - plus Conrad's testimony will certainly add weight." Rachel's foot began to tap along to the band's fast-paced rhythm. "Maybe she will manage to wriggle her way out of it, but either way her reputation will be shot. I suspect Viath will cut her loose with that kind of scandal hanging around her." Hannah chuckled evilly. "The queen bee won't be welcome back into the hive. What a crying shame."

"Do you feel at all guilty about fitting her up for a crime she didn't commit?" asked Alex. There was stifling pause before Rachel finally replied, "Fuck it, no. Because of her we both got tortured and nearly died. Meanwhile, she made money whilst people suffered. I am good with what we did." Hannah slipped her hand across the beanbag and surreptitiously squeezed Rachel's hand.

She gently squeezed it back.

A waiter entered the tent carrying a tray with three large coupes of champagne. Approaching the trio, he explained, "The compliments of your hostess, for a caper well played," and handed them each a glass before retiring.

As the other two savoured the bubbles of their success, Rachel apologised, "Sorry about that back there. I kind of lost the plot big time. Plan A didn't work out as expected. I only grasped what you were doing, Hannah, when you handed Beth's bag back."

Hannah looked steadily at Rachel; she had questions for her friend: What had caused her to freeze? What had happened during those four years with Barry? What had transpired that made her so...vulnerable. There were many questions. But they would have to wait for another time and another place. Instead, she silently watched as Rachel jovially toasted, "Here's to the sexy redhead and her audacious plan C." To which all three shouted, "Cheers" and took a well-deserved drink.

Chapter 27

"Good morning, Rachel. Mr Viath is just finishing up another meeting. If you would like to take a seat in his office, he will be with you shortly."

Dawn had been John Viath's redoubtable PA long before Rachel had joined Sheol Publicity. She was his iron curtain. No one got to see the Chairman without her prior approval. Time wasters? Well, they were dealt with politely but firmly. To have her invite Rachel to sit alone in the Chairman's office, a room she had never so much as set foot inside as an employee, felt a little strange.

The office was smaller than Rachel had expected, measuring perhaps twenty feet by thirty. Adjacent to the large window was a modest office desk not dissimilar to the one she had been allocated when she started at Sheol. With only three basic company-issue chairs and a rather antiquated desktop computer, Rachel began to wonder if Dawn had brought her into the correct office.

The right-hand wall had a single painting hanging upon it. A white canvas with nine black concentric circles, the artist having signed it with three initials: 'DbA'. On the left-hand wall, a long black wooden shelf crammed with countless industry awards and framed letters from powerful and famous people.

Crossing the charcoal-black carpet, Rachel took a seat in front of the desk. Beside the single grey plastic filing tray stacked high with handwritten client files sat the only personal item within the entire office: a worn copy of Alice in Wonderland with a familiar cardboard label sticking out as a bookmark.

It was two days after the events at the ballroom when Rachel had received the invitation to meet with John Viath. She had enjoyed an evening meal with Hannah in a busy curry house near Spitalfields. Afterwards, the redhead had taken the Tube home as she had an early morning meeting to prepare for. Rachel grasped the opportunity to walk slowly back to the hotel, relishing no longer having to disguise her appearance from the city's ever-watchful cameras.

Billy's face had lit up when Rachel presented him with the foil-wrapped onion bhajis. "They will go smashing with a cup of tea later," he enthused as she passed through the rotary door.

The hotel manager had been placating a flustered young lady, reassuring her that housekeeping had thoroughly checked under the mattress and no foreign objects were found there that could have disturbed her sleep. Upon seeing Rachel, he agreed to have the bed checked again and excused himself.

"Ms Minos, this has arrived for you." Mr Typhon handed over a plain white envelope with her name penned upon it. After thanking him, she had opened the letter and read the handwritten note: 'Ms Minos, I would appreciate a meeting with you. Would eleven am tomorrow at the office be suitable? John Viath'.

In her hotel room, Rachel had debated with herself if she wanted to go to this meeting or not. Looking towards the glass jar, she asked Cheshire, "What do you think?" The scrawny face bore a doubtful look as it sullenly stared back at her. Mulling over the invitation, she finally headed into the bathroom to have a shower and declared out loud, "What harm could there be in seeing what he wants?" Cheshire shook its head disapprovingly and dissipated into nothingness.

The following morning, Rachel had spent almost no time deciding what to wear for her meeting with Sheol's Chairman. Selecting her favourite outfit of the red leather coat, white tee-shirt, black jeans and the ever-faithful boots, she reckoned if he didn't like her dress style, that was his problem.

Crossing the hotel foyer, Rachel had found her path to the rotary door abruptly blocked by the Dowager's assistant. With undisguised contempt in her face she stated, "My employer would like to meet with you. She would like to offer you a highly beneficial opportunity. When would be convenient?"

Rachel savoured the look of surprise on the assistant's face as she replied, "Not sure; I will have to check my diary and get back to you," before side-stepping her and passing through the rotary exit.

Waving to Billy, she had eschewed his offer of a taxi and set off on foot to St James's Square. The February sun was shining brightly in a sapphire blue sky and the air temperature had risen to a brisk chill. After four years of mournfully staring out of the Camden apartment at such beautiful days, Rachel was determined to enjoy it.

Arriving at Sheol's offices, the security guard at the front entrance had greeted her with suspicion. Perhaps it was the way she was dressed that caused him to doubt she was in the right place. Upon providing her name, his attitude was immediately transformed. Apologising for not recognising her, he had called for a young receptionist, whose name tag identified him as Tom, to escort her to the VIP waiting lounge.

As she had sat and sipped on her cappuccino, she couldn't help a wry smile as she spotted a vacant spot amongst the photo portraits of Sheol's senior team members. It seemed that Bethany was already being erased from the corporate memory.

Back in the Chairman's office, the glass door swung open and John Viath walked in, clothed in his customary tailored business suit. "Rachel, I am so sorry for keeping you waiting - issues at the Tokyo office. Can I get you a drink?" Rachel turned down the offer.

"Firstly, I wanted to thank you personally for what you have done." Rachel eyed him suspiciously before coolly responding, "What I have done?"

"Conrad has shown me appendix nine of the Decem Fossas contract." He sat down in the chair opposite. "I knew that something was not right in the paperwork; I'm glad my confidence that you would discover it eventually proved to be well founded."

As Rachel replayed the last sentence in her head, she glanced at the worn book. The strange events, the crowbar, the key in the car and so many more pieces of the puzzle, finally clicked into place.

"I always knew you had great potential. That's why I was so disappointed when you decided to leave our corporate family. It's a shame the path you chose to follow didn't eventually lead you to happiness." He paused as his mobile phone rang. He apologised and, to Rachel's surprise, turned it off.

"Obviously, with the scandal engulfing Ms Hopkins I have had no choice but to suspend her pending the board's deliberation as to a more permanent solution." The finality of the word 'permanent' sent a chill down Rachel's spine.

"This turn of events does leave us with a senior vacancy here in the London office." From within the pile of client records, he pulled out a slim cardboard folder enveloping several sheets of paper.

He flashed a well-rehearsed smile at Rachel. She thought it seemed to be an alien expression for him, like seeing a shark smile. "I would like you to rejoin our family, Rachel. I believe you have what it takes to, one day, take over the helm of Sheol Publicity." He leaned forward, his eyes suddenly ablaze with a passionate intensity. "I want to give you a second chance to seize that opportunity."

Pushing back his chair, he stood up and looked out of the office window at the street below. "We have big plans, Rachel; the world out there is changing fast. Sheol must adapt and you can be at the heart of those changes. I won't lie, we have significant challenges ahead of us. Decem Fossas have fired the opening shots; their hostile intentions are now clear. We also have tricky matters to negotiate with the Redemptore." He turned back to face Rachel. "But without overcoming significant challenges can one really appreciate the glorious taste of victory?"

He leaned over the table and placed the folder beside the copy of Alice in Wonderland. "I believe we have put together a comprehensive reward package in recognition of the unique talents that you would bring to the firm."

Viath listed the package's highlights to a bemused Rachel: "A fully furnished and serviced Kensington apartment, a chauffeured car at your disposal, a generous expense account and a financial rewards package that I doubt anyone else could hope to match."

Pushing the folder another inch closer towards Rachel, he concluded: "What do you say, Rachel Minos, care to put your signature to this life-changing contract?"

Chapter 28

After escorting Rachel to the elevator, Dawn re-entered the Chairman's office. She could immediately sense his disappointment and asked, "I take it Ms Minos did not want to return to our family?" He shook his head ruefully and laughed. "No. No, she didn't. She reminds me so much of her parents in that regard." Picking up his tattered copy of Alice in Wonderland, he observed, "We will need to adjust our strategy accordingly and designate Rachel Minos as a free radical."

Dawn picked up the abandoned offer folder and tucked it under her arm. As she exited his office she stated, "In which case, sir, I'll arrange the call with the New York office."

.....

Later that night, as they entered Gordon Square, Hannah rubbed her gloved hands together for warmth and pointedly said to Rachel, "I cannot believe you convinced me to do this."

Rachel looked back and smiled at her friend buried under numerous layers of clothing, her face framed by a fake fur hood. "Look, I agreed to help Arthur out when Alex can't be here," she explained, "It seems only fair, given the help Alex has given me. Plus, I actually enjoy doing this."

With the mention of Alex's name, Hannah took on a look of grim resolve, muttering through gritted teeth, "Fine, I really don't mind helping out."

Arthur stopped his cart beside a pile of plastic sheeting. Hannah had already mistaken it for a discarded set of bin bags. "Hello in there," he called out, "Would you like some hot soup and a roll?"

Eventually, the plastic sheeting rustled and parted, a young man nervously emerging; possibly less than sixteen years in age, his face was marred by a bruise under his right eye and a swollen lower lip. Like so many people before him, it was a bitter path that had led to him living on the streets. "You're new here, yes?" Arthur asked gently.

The teenager slowly nodded as he nervously eyed the three of them. Arthur proffered the Styrofoam cup and eventually a shivering hand emerged and gratefully accepted it.

Rummaging in his coat pocket, Arthur pulled out an A5 piece of paper with a list of addresses printed on it and handed it to the young man. "Here are some places where you can get help. Please, mate, give 'em a try out."

Reluctantly, he accepted the paper with his other hand and again silently nodded. "I'll be back round here tomorrow." Arthur concluded. Immediately the face and soup vanished as a veil of plastic was quickly drawn over them.

As they moved on, Hannah innocently asked, "Isn't there someone we can call? Someone who can help him?" Arthur looked at Rachel, who replied to Hannah, "If there was someone we could call, do you think we would be doing this?" Hannah fell silent, lost in thought as they walked beside the soup cart.

Turning into Byng Place, Rachel spotted a sleeping bag tucked under an air-conditioning vent. Frank was middle-aged with a thick, bushy white beard and wild, unkempt hair. With a polite and brisk 'thank you, ma'am', he gratefully accepted the soup she had brought over to him. For a couple of minutes, she kneeled beside Frank as he told her his colourful stories of time spent serving abroad in the army.

The soup cart had turned a corner and vanished out of sight into Malet Street. Not wishing to be left behind, Rachel asked Frank to continue his stories when they next met and said goodbye.

Hurrying to catch them up, she considered what she would do next with her life. Rachel had turned down Viath's offer without a second thought. Having been a playing piece in his game with Bethany and

Conrad, Rachel had no desire to shackle herself to his larger agenda.

She was equally wary of any opportunities that may be presented to her by the Dowager. The President of Decem Fossas Long-term Projects had so far gladly accommodated all of Rachel's requests, but the contract that organisation had signed with Conrad was abhorrent to her.

As for the Redemptore: given what little Darius had revealed of that shadowy group and their eagerness for her to sign on with them, Rachel would treat them with the same level of suspicion.

Viath had hinted at some form of conflict developing between those three houses. Rachel could only guess at their goals and why each of them wanted her to take a place amongst their ranks. But having recently escaped one form of servitude, she was in no mood to sign herself into another, no matter how ornately gilded the cage.

One thing she couldn't put off indefinitely was Hannah's questions about Rachel's four years with Barry. Her friend remained content to wait patiently but was obviously concerned about what had happened to Rachel and the effect it continued to have on her. She resolved to have the conversation sometime soon...ish.

Approaching the street corner, she began to think about taking Hannah with her to see the basement that Alex had submitted an offer on. He was keen to get Rachel's opinion of it as the venue for his new bar and her life would be a little simpler if she could ease the tension between her two friends.

Rachel froze.

A hauntingly familiar voice had called out to her.

"Rachel, can we talk?"

The end

Acknowledgements

I had been kicking around the idea of the Rachel Minos Saga for some time. The bones of the story arc and world had been fleshed out, but I felt there was something missing from her background. A spark to make Rachel a compelling character for me to write about.

In the summer of 2020, during a socially distanced conversation with my friend Dean Long, we talked about how the pandemic lockdown would likely lead to increased domestic abuse.

Dean was genuinely at a loss as to how people could treat each other in such a vile way. It was during that conversation that it occurred to me that giving such a background to Rachel's story could help shed light on these insidious forms of abuse. Dean agreed it was an interesting idea and asked for a signed copy as soon as it was published.

It was Deans unexpected death several weeks later that spurred me into knuckling down and writing the first instalment of Rachel Minos's story.

With Rachel's character now clearly formed in my head, that first draft was completed in just over a month.

Sarah Race once again proved to be my grand sorceress of punctuation and grammar. She also provided sections of elegant prose that I felt elevated certain scenes to a new level. Without her unending enthusiasm for proofreading each chapter and subsequent drafts of this novel, this book would likely not have progressed beyond the first draft.

Often questioning the characters and their motivations as they developed, my wife Janice encouraged me to continue this project when the insanity that is 2020 conspired to halt my progress.

A big thanks also to my friends Andy, for keeping the police elements grounded in some reality and to Heather for review feedback.

During my research into the terrible subject of domestic abuse, I found the book 'Power and Control' by Sandra Horley an excellent insight into such relationships and recommend it to anyone who would like to understand more about this subject.

I hope you enjoyed book 1 of the Rachel Minos Saga and that you are looking forward to her next story. Finally, if you are so inclined, please leave a review on Amazon.

John Lonsdale

www.johnlonsdale.co.uk

Other books by John Lonsdale

Tales from the Library – A collection of tiny tales in two parts

Printed in Great Britain
by Amazon